POISON SPRING

LAVONNE GRIFFIN-VALADE

SEVERN ⚓ RIVER
PUBLISHING

Severn River Publishing
severnriverbooks.com

ISBN: 978-1-64875-556-9 (Paperback)

ALSO BY LAVONNE GRIFFIN-VALADE

Maggie Blackthorne Novels

Dead Point

Murderers Creek

Desolation Ridge

Poison Spring

Never miss a new release! Sign up to receive exclusive updates from author LaVonne Griffin-Valade.

severnriverbooks.com/authors/lavonne-griffin-valade

For Tom

In memory of my mother

1

MORNING, APRIL 7

I'd come to believe the long winter had finally lost its grip on our part of the world, but today's weather was proving otherwise. As predicted, an arctic blast had blown in last evening, bringing with it six inches of snow overnight. Most of eastern Oregon bore the brunt of the storm, and it didn't appear to be letting up.

Seemingly, conditions had prompted our office manager, Sherry Linn Perkins, to arrive later than the rest of us. Something that had never happened, as far as I could recall. She burst through the door flustered and apologetic and uncharacteristically dressed in slacks.

I stood behind the front counter and, embarrassingly, couldn't help but stare. She hadn't worn anything but frilly dresses and skirts to the office since joining our crew about two years ago.

"Morning, sunshine," I said.

She raked a hand through her hair. "Sorry I'm late."

"Don't worry about it. I'm sure we owe you a late morning or three."

"I lost a bet with Harry, so I had to dress in pants for work today. It took me a while to even find a pair."

"You look very stylish. Just be glad you don't have to wear this outfit every day." I indicated my cop uniform.

She smiled. "You've managed to give yours some added flair, Maggie."

I tapped my pregnant tummy. "Only for a few more weeks, I'm happy to say."

"Are you nervous?"

"Dun asks me that every morning, yet he's the one who's nervous." Duncan McKay was my relatively new hubby, but we had been together a couple of years now.

Sherry Linn hung her down jacket on one of the pegs installed next to the door, and I moved from behind the front counter so she could begin her day.

I checked the time. "I should get back to my desk and let you do your thing."

"Think I'll follow you and say howdy to Hollis and Doug."

When we arrived at the pod of officer desks, the two men were prognosticating this season's outcome for the Portland Trail Blazers.

"I think they'll make the playoffs this year," Doug declared.

"I'm not so sure about that," Hollis countered.

"Is Damian Lillard still on the team?" I asked.

"Maggie, I can't believe you don't know," Sherry Linn cried.

"Sorry, I don't pay much attention to the Blazers, I guess."

"And she calls herself an Oregonian," Hollis put in.

The main line rang at the front counter, and Sherry Linn moved to answer it. Moments later, my desk phone buzzed.

"Sergeant Blackthorne speaking."

"Maggie, this is Mike Drake out near Kimberly."

"Hi, Mike. It's been a while. How are you?"

Mike and his wife, Lisa, owned Poison Spring Ranch. Their place was one of the few truly successful spreads in Grant County and took up about five hundred acres north of the Sheep Rock Unit of the John Day Fossil Beds. Wild country, and beautiful for all its austerity and strange, other-world-like formations.

"Well, I've been better. Just found one of my bulls slaughtered out in the field, and not by no wild animal. Just the human kinda animal."

"Any thoughts about who might've done something like that?"

"No, and excuse my French, but the son of a bitch who did this butchered one of my prize bulls. This guy was worth six or seven thousand dollars. So if I meet up with the asshole before the law does, I might return the favor using one of Lisa's dull kitchen knives."

"Well, I wouldn't want that to happen, so I better get out to your place ASAP."

"Be sure to drive carefully. We got lots of snow out here, and it doesn't seem to be stopping anytime soon."

"We've got lots of snow too, but I'm all set for anything but a tornado."

"See you in about an hour, then," he said in his husky voice.

I hung up and turned to Hollis. "We're taking a little trip this morning."

"Oh?"

"That was Mike Drake on the phone. Somebody killed one of his prize bulls."

"Remind me, who's Mike Drake?" he asked.

"Owner of Poison Spring Ranch out near Kimberly. He was also a county commissioner for several years."

"Why don't you just send me? I don't know what Doug had planned for the day, but if two of us need to go, he could accompany me."

Trooper Hollis Jones was my patrol partner and my closest friend, but the closer I got to my due date, his overprotective nature had flat-out gotten on my nerves.

He read the look on my face. "Maggie, I'm not trying to insult you, but what if we got stuck in snow somewhere?"

"We'd call for help, just like we'd do if we got stuck in any other kind of weather and needed assistance."

"I'd be happy to ride out there with Hollis," Doug volunteered.

I turned to face him. "You mentioned yesterday if the storm actually arrived, you planned to take time to work through that mountain of paperwork on your desk."

"It can wait a day," Doug answered.

I glanced at his overflowing inbox. "No. It can't. Let's go, Hollis."

Hollis rose from his chair and followed me to the front counter. We retrieved our coats and official fur-lined Oregon State Police hats and let Sherry Linn know where we were headed. Once we were inside my cop Tahoe and moving through town, our conversation continued, but not our little dust-up, as it had clearly been settled.

"I think I remember who Mike Drake is," Hollis said. "Big guy? Red hair going gray? Drives a black BMW convertible?"

"That's him."

"Pulled him over for speeding once. He was none too friendly."

"Mike Drake has a reputation for being excessively friendly," I said. "Always chatting everyone up. Even heard he shows up with groceries for his elderly neighbors on occasion, that kind of thing."

"Let's just say he didn't appreciate me pulling him over and telling him he needed to slow it down."

"He likely wouldn't have been happy if I'd pulled him over either."

"Ah, I get it. Friendly, but above the law."

"Entitled, probably. But I do get a kick out of his license plate: *POISON*."

"I don't remember that."

"What? That's the kind of thing you usually carry around with you forever, Holly."

"Guess I'm getting old, Mags."

Being slightly older than him, I had to crack wise in response. "Watch your language, dude."

"Whatever you say, Sarge."

"That's more like it."

We drove west on Highway 26 through town and on toward Mt. Vernon, eight miles away. Snow fell heavily on the pavement. "Why don't you find some music to listen to?" I suggested.

"You okay with jazz?"

"Sure."

"How about Meschiya Lake?"

"Is that a person or a place?"

"She's a New Orleans jazz singer. Usually backed up by the Little Big Horns."

"Sure, I'm game."

He turned on the music, and we passed by the spring green hills, pastures, and tabletop buttes now covered with a thick layer of flakes. In the coming few months, the countryside would return to its high desert shades of flax, goldenrod, and buff.

Traveling alongside the John Day River, we crossed over the bridge my mother had slammed herself off of almost thirty years ago, ending her dark thoughts forever. The memory of that time and this place had often resurrected my grief, but thankfully, not today.

~

As we arrived in the town of Dayville, snow fell in earnest. We passed a weathered and boarded-up house sitting at an angle under a couple of ancient oaks at the end of a crumbling walkway. When I was a girl, my father, Tate, would repeat the story of the two elderly women—a mother and daughter—who had lived there and hoarded plastic bottle caps, disposable trays from frozen dinners, and any other sundry items they deemed to be useful should another Great Depression descend upon the world.

Although we drove slowly, we motored the length of Dayville in barely sixty seconds and began to make our way beyond the fields of fallow alfalfa and farms and on toward Picture Gorge. Once we'd moved through its narrow chasm, we turned north on Highway 19 and sped along the far western edge of Grant County, paralleling the course of the river, which wound past Sheep Rock and Cathedral Rock. Forged during the Cenozoic Era, their layers of sage-and-ochre-tinted fossilized rock remained visible even in snowy conditions.

Hollis lowered the volume on Meschiya Lake and the Little Big Horns. "I wouldn't mind living out here."

"Me either, Holly. But you know who would really like living out here?"

"Doug Vaughn?"

"Yeah. I think he spends a lot of time out here already."

"It's interesting how his amateur geologist skills came in handy when we were working those two homicides out near Murderers Creek."

"Doug's a good addition to our team, all right," I added.

"That reminds me, any word on filling Mark's position?"

"No, but that doesn't surprise me."

Mark Taylor, a longtime Fish and Wildlife trooper in our office, was killed last November while responding to a domestic violence call. Like

Taylor, Vaughn was a game warden, and the two of them had become pretty tight pals before murder ended the friendship.

I had waited awhile after Taylor's death to request a replacement for him. We were a small crew, and I knew there would be some sensitivity around welcoming a new hire under the circumstances. Hollis even gave me kudos for holding off a bit, but it had been six weeks or so since I'd put in the formal ask. I made a mental note to contact the powers that be and nudge them along.

Two miles or so south of Kimberly, I decelerated slowly and pulled onto the paved road into the Drake property. A large sign suspended above the entrance announced we had arrived at Poison Spring Ranch. The spread was known for its herd of Black Angus cattle, as well as its paddock and livery stable where locals could exercise and board their horses.

I parked in the small gravel parking lot in front of the ranch house, a large, older home with an expansive yard in which a tall weeping willow tree and two large Lombardy poplars grew. Mike's BMW convertible was parked in the lot, and beside it was an older Ram truck with the name of the ranch lettered on the doors.

We disembarked, slipped through the gate, and strolled toward the house. Lisa Drake padded out onto the porch before we reached the steps. She had wrapped herself in an ecru-colored cashmere shawl. A thin woman, she was attractive but dour. Her hair had been pulled back in a tight bun, which served to enhance her forbidding manner.

"Margaret," she said, eyeing my round belly disapprovingly.

In the long-ago past, she had taught my sixth-grade Sunday School class. Strict and conventional, she always called us by our given names. Katie was Kathryn, Jamie was James, Elly was Eleanor, and so on. And we kids were to address her as Mrs. Drake, even though we might know her as Lisa outside of church. I never understood it, but it could have been her way of conveying the seriousness with which we should approach faith and prayer. God and the scriptures were to be taken very, very seriously.

"Mrs. Drake." To this day, I followed the requirements she had set back then.

"You're looking to speak to Mike about the bull?"

"Who is it, Mother? Who's here?" her adult son called from inside the house.

She shut the front door behind her.

"Mike's waiting for you at Poison Spring. Just continue up the road a half mile or so." She pointed to the ranch road that drifted on through the fields beyond the house and outbuildings. "There's a marker pointing out the spring. You can't miss the place or my husband. He's driving a pickup truck similar to the one parked next to the BMW."

She turned, opened the door, and stepped inside the house.

We got back in my rig and headed toward Poison Spring.

"Mrs. Drake seems kind of aloof," Hollis remarked.

"Formal, I'd say."

"And they have a son, it sounded like."

"Christopher. Their only child. Mid-thirties. Still lives with mom and dad."

"You sound like you disapprove."

"Don't have an opinion one way or another. But he's an odd duck. And that's not an opinion, that's a fact."

~

Following what I assumed were tire tracks from Drake's vehicle, I continued slowly up the ranch road until we met up with a weathered signpost alerting us we had arrived at Poison Spring. I set the brake and idled next to a small lagoon formed by the spring.

Mike Drake and his truck were nowhere to be seen, but the lifeless bull lay mere feet from the signpost. Peculiarly, there was a paucity of blood near the carcass.

"Where's Drake?" Hollis asked.

"Not here, it seems."

I spotted evidence of a snowmobile, which appeared to have recently traveled along the road shoulder by the look of the fresh imprints of the front skis and rear Kevlar tracks. It had been driven from a location further on up the road. And it was clear the operator had stopped a few yards from the slain animal, dismounted, and walked to the carcass. A different-sized set of boot prints moved from the road to the vicinity of the bull and back to the road; those belonged to Mike Drake, I reasoned.

"What are your first thoughts, Holly?"

"About the bull," he began. "There's not much blood present."

"Yeah. Pretty weird."

"Might be covered by the snow, I suppose."

"Maybe."

He continued. "And a snowmobile cruised here alongside the road from the opposite direction. Also looks like we've got two sets of boot prints."

"Drake's and the snowmobiler's, don't you think?" I asked.

"Yep. I know it's snowing, but let's get out and give the bull a closer look."

"I also need to get some shots of the boot prints and the trail left by the snowmobile. And the bull, of course."

I shut off the engine and we both stepped outside, careful to avoid disturbing the evidence present in the snow.

I began taking photographs while Hollis squatted two feet from the carcass.

"This reminds me of those strange incidents that occurred on various ranches in eastern and central Oregon over the last several years," he said, then yanked his phone out of his pocket and began to thumb away.

"What are you looking up?" I asked.

"Cattle mutilations in Oregon."

"I remember those cases. No tracks or evidence of animal predation, or who or what was butchering bulls and cows. Their sex organs and sometimes other body parts removed. It's a freaking bizarre mystery, and I don't think anyone's actually figured it out yet."

"No, but listen to the predominant theories. A ritualistic—and dare I say sick—act perpetrated by a cult. Visiting space aliens from planet whatever. Or some kind of bird."

I took another gander at Mike Drake's prize bull. "This poor animal reminds me of a deflated basketball. How is that?"

"You don't want to know, Maggie."

As had happened earlier that morning, I normally would've had a fit about him taking on this caretaker role—in this case, protecting me from uncomfortable facts while pregnant. But unless knowing all of the particulars about this sorrowful, dead creature lent any meaningful information or evidence, I was fine with not knowing more details about the bull's demise.

"I'll take your word for it. This time," I replied.

With a gloved hand, he carefully brushed away a swath of snow near the bull. "We were right. There's barely any blood. The ground should be covered in it."

"The animal, too, if you think about it. Any guesses about when it happened?"

Hollis rose from where he'd crouched. "At least twelve to eighteen hours ago."

"Are you cold?" I asked him.

"I am."

"I'm done taking photos. Let's head on up the road and see if we can find Drake."

"Sounds like a plan."

We piled back in the Tahoe, and while I drove, Hollis carried on with his search of reports detailing the maiming and extermination of cattle. I suddenly felt very tired.

"Strange," he said. "Guess I didn't think about it, but this appears to be the first time a case like this has occurred in Grant County. Several surrounding jurisdictions have seen multiple incidents—Harney, Umatilla, Crook, and Wheeler Counties. And similar incidents have been reported in other parts of the country since the sixties."

"No shit. Since the sixties?"

"That's what one article claims."

"I have a hard time believing this is caused by any space-alien beef connoisseurs."

"Me too. I'm doubting the bird angle, too."

"I'd be more impressed with that theory if other large animals had been the victims of such birds," I added.

"I agree."

"Just out of curiosity, which law enforcement agencies typically look into these cases in Oregon?"

"Usually county sheriffs, it seems."

It was slow going on the ranch road, but a little over half a mile further along, we came to a small, lone fossil formation. It was as strange as it was beautiful, but instead of sage or ochre, it appeared to be a light shade of coral—a beacon in the storm.

Parked near it was a Ram pickup belonging to Poison Spring Ranch. Presumably the vehicle Mike Drake had been driving when he made the trip back out here after contacting me.

The truck's passenger-side door was wide open. But through its rear window, we could see he was leaning to one side, his head propped against the driver-side door.

"Is that him?" Hollis asked.

"I believe so."

"Is he taking a nap or something?"

"Don't know."

"You could sound the horn."

"Nah, let's check in with him from the open door. I'd hate to honk or rap on his window and give the guy a heart attack."

Hollis nodded. "Kind of cold to keep a door open, isn't it?"

I shrugged. "Maybe he needed to cool down."

We climbed out of the Tahoe and moved toward the pickup.

When we reached the open passenger-side door, I noted the set of boot prints on the ground next to it.

I raised a hand, signaling for us to walk no further. Out of a sense there was more here than an open door and someone's boot prints in the snow, I suggested we avoid moving any closer to the door.

Peering inside the truck, it was obvious Drake wasn't napping. His eyes were wide open, and unlike the slaughtered bull, blood was everywhere. The man had been shot to death, the bullet having traveled through his upper torso.

"Holy fuck," I whispered.

"Or words to that effect."

2

MID-MORNING, APRIL 7

While I drove back toward the ranch house, Hollis contacted regional dispatch and reported the murder of Mike Drake. We had agreed I would give the news to Drake's wife and son.

Hollis was further charged with contacting Sam Damon, the county undertaker who owned and operated the Juniper Chapel Mortuary and Crematorium in John Day, to let him know we'd need his services later today.

I parked, made my way to the front porch, and knocked on the door. Christopher opened it after a minute or so.

"Oh," he said. "Mother didn't think you'd come back to the house."

"May I come in?"

"Um, I guess. Wipe your feet, though. I'll go get Mother." He walked toward a hallway to the left of the entrance.

I kicked the snow from my boots, moved into the foyer, and closed the door. Waiting for Lisa and Christopher, I scanned the largely empty room and the wide stairway leading to the second floor. Although it was toasty inside, the décor was as cold as our wintry weather.

Mother and son emerged from the hallway.

"You're back so soon, Margaret?"

"Mrs. Drake, can we all take a seat?"

She eyed me warily. "Certainly."

Mother and son sat side by side on a brown leather settee, and I took the matching chair across from them.

I hated this aspect of the job. I'd been on the receiving end of a member of law enforcement bringing me word of a loved one's death. Twice, and each time, I'd felt a tinge of bitterness toward the person delivering the news.

"I'm afraid something terrible has happened. Trooper Jones and I found Mr. Drake. He'd been shot."

Lisa glanced at Christopher before turning her attention back to me. "Did you call an ambulance?"

"I'm sorry, but he was...he had already passed by the time we arrived."

She took a deep breath, and we all sat quietly in the still room.

Finally she spoke. "Thank you for letting us know, Margaret. I suppose I should call Sam Damon."

"Trooper Jones has likely already gotten in touch with him," I said.

"Who's Trooper Jones?" Christopher asked.

"I presume he's the officer who arrived with Margaret."

I was uncertain as to what to say or do next but ended up pulling out my phone and calling Hollis. "Did you contact Sam?"

"He'll head out here once we send him word regarding the medical examiner's ETA. Shall I get in touch with Harry, ask him to be on standby?"

"Yes. And give Whitey Kern a heads-up."

"How's it going in there?"

"I'll see you shortly." I clicked off the line and regarded Lisa Drake and her son. "Sam has been notified."

"Whitey Kern owns the towing company, right?" Christopher asked.

"Yes."

"Why does he need a heads-up?"

"A forensics examiner needs to check out the truck, and after that, we'll need to impound it. Or we may have to send it to the State Police lab in Bend."

"Well, that's BS. What if we need the truck here on the ranch?"

"Christopher," his mother said brusquely. "Margaret has a job to do."

He stood abruptly. "I'm driving out there to see Father for myself."

"I can't allow you to go to the scene right now," I said.

Christopher sent his mother a grievous look and marched from the room and up the stairs, slamming a door behind him.

Lisa sat mutely for a moment and then gave me a tiny, mannered smile. "If you'll excuse me, Margaret, I have some phone calls to make."

"I do have a couple of questions." I lifted a notebook and pencil from my pocket.

"All right."

"Does your family own a snowmobile?"

"Mike had one once, but Christopher wrecked it, and we never bought another one. Why do you ask?"

"Someone had been out there on a snowmobile."

"Lots of people in the area have them, I think."

"Anyone you know?"

"Roger and Corky Edwards at the next place over had two of them at one time. But I haven't seen or talked to Roger or Corky for years."

"Do they live north or south of Poison Spring Ranch?"

Mrs. Drake tilted her head and offered a blank look, which I took to mean she wasn't very attuned to cardinal directions.

I rephrased the question. "Would I go back toward Dayville, or is it closer to Kimberly?"

"Toward Dayville. The first driveway you come to on your left."

I jotted down *Edwards*. "Did your husband have any enemies that you know of?"

"Mike's beloved by all."

She had said that last in monotone, as if repeating an oft-used line.

I put my fur hat back on and wrenched myself from the leather chair.

"Congratulations," she said.

My confusion must have been apparent.

"The child you're expecting. Soon, I believe."

"Thank you for your time. I'm sorry for your loss, Mrs. Drake."

"Please, you're welcome to call me Lisa."

But I couldn't imagine ever calling her by her first name.

I got in the driver's seat and started my vehicle.

"Are you okay?" Hollis asked.

"I don't know." I backed up and pulled onto the ranch road again. "I've given next of kin the bad news several times, but I don't think anyone has ever reacted the way the wife did just now. I might be imagining that, but I was expecting some kind of show of grief or maybe anger —or both."

"Her son reacted, though?"

"He did. Especially when I told him he couldn't go see his father's body."

"Maybe his mother just keeps her feelings bottled up," Hollis suggested.

"That's possible, I suppose. I've noticed that about her before. Anyway, apparently they don't own a snowmobile any longer, so that's something, I guess."

"We can check DMV for snowmobile ownership in Grant County and surrounding counties, or all over the state, if necessary."

"Mrs. Drake told me the folks next door owned a couple of snowmobiles in the past and may still. Let's stop by there when we're done here. In the meantime, I'd like to make sure we get casts of the boot prints near the bull. Should've done that earlier."

"You brought a spray can of snow impression wax?"

"I've carried it in my pack since last fall."

"I'm impressed."

"Har, har. Got any more little puns?"

"No, really, I'm impressed," Holly said unconvincingly.

~

We spent a short time at Poison Spring making a few casts of the two sets of boot prints. Afterward we headed back to the scene and again parked behind Drake's pickup. Out of concern for the unlikely possibility of curious passersby climbing inside the truck and possibly disturbing evidence, I'd made the decision to remove the keys and lock up the vehicle before returning to the ranch house.

The interior of the Tahoe was a bit too warm but cozy. Soon, our conversation drifted off, and both of us stared out the windshield at the falling snow. It had eased up some as the morning went along.

A blaring radio callout interrupted the quiet—Homicide Detective Alan Bach, on the road somewhere, perhaps making his way to our murder scene.

"Detective Bach, what's the word?" I asked, answering the call. The man had worked with us to solve too many homicides over the past few years. He'd been a terrific mentor and, to be honest, a friend. At least from my perspective.

"Maggie, I'm leaving Bend soon and heading your way to size up the homicide Hollis called in earlier. But I need directions to the location."

"I know you usually come this way via Highway 20, but your best bet this time is Highway 26 and then turn north at the junction with Route 19. I figure it's about a two-and-a-half-hour trip. Although the weather might slow you down a bit."

"Poison Spring Ranch, correct? Just south of someplace called Kimberly?"

"Yeah. There's a large sign at the entrance to the ranch. You'll notice the owner's home on the left, but just keep driving past it for about a half mile and you'll come to a signpost calling out the namesake spring. You might also notice a dead Black Angus bull nearby, but keep driving up the road another half mile. We're parked behind the truck where we found Mr. Drake's body."

"That sounds more complicated than it probably is, but I'll radio you when I get closer if need be. Right now, I'm on my way to pick up the medical examiner before taking off."

"Drive carefully, Al. See you when you get here."

I wasn't going to ask if the ME was Dr. Ray Gattis. Ray and I had chatted by phone recently, and she indicated the two of them had agreed to end their long-running affair. One of Bach's daughters had gotten wind of it and confronted him. Ray made it clear in our conversation that she and the detective had also agreed to avoid working together whenever possible.

Ray Gattis was a kick, and we had bonded over *having an attitude*—if that accurately described our mutual affinity for snarky commentary. It would be nice to spend a bit of downtime with her, have one of our little chats, take her out to the Blue Mountain Lounge for dinner and a chocolate peanut butter shake. But that was likely not in the cards.

"Harry just texted me to say he should be here in half an hour," Hollis said.

"That was fast."

"He was on his way to John Day when I reached him."

"Did you by any chance give Sherry Linn a heads-up about the homicide?"

"I did."

"Thanks." I stared at the murdered man's pickup. "I didn't notice when we were out here earlier and found Drake's body, but there's more evidence a snowmobile traveled on the road shoulder."

"It's hard to tell if it was coming or going."

"Both, I'd say."

"Well, if our working theory is correct, the snowmobiler came upon the dead bull, but he or she didn't drive any further beyond Poison Spring toward the ranch house."

I reached into my pack and brought up my fancy new binoculars—a birthday gift last month from Duncan.

"Yeah, the snowmobiler looks to have generally gone back over the first set of tracks. I see spots where during one of the trips, the driver had moved out of one set of tracks and crossed over the other."

"You can tell even with the additional snow that's fallen?"

"Here." I handed him my binoculars. "Take a look."

Hollis adjusted them slightly. "I see what you're saying. I can see those tracks pretty clearly. Your new binoculars have great sighting capacity."

"If I were you, Hollis, I'd start dropping hints to Lil about picking up a pair for you. Subtle at first, of course."

"Thanks, but Lil's not in the mood for that kind of hint right now."

"What's going on? I thought she was doing well and in remission."

Lillian Two Moons, Holly's wife, had been diagnosed with ovarian cancer last summer. Her treatment had seemed to be working, or at least that's how I'd read the signals from him, and from Lil.

"That doesn't mean the cancer is gone, Maggie."

"I'm so damn sorry."

"I'm trying to stay upbeat, but Lil's anxious to try for another kid, and that's just not in the cards right now."

"If you'd like, I can invite her to join me at Nade's Coffee Den one of these days. Whenever you think the time is right."

"That's a good idea, Mags. She's pretty excited about the birth of your child."

"So a visit from me wouldn't make it worse?"

"I don't really know, but my gut tells me she needs to talk to a woman, and you're about the only woman she'd be willing to have any kind of conversation with."

"All right, let's get this murder sorted out, and I'll set up a time for Lil and me to go to Nade's for herbal tea and a chat."

In an act as rare as Hollis turning moody, he reached across the seat and gave me a hug. "Thank you, Maggie."

"Anything for you and Lil. And little Hank, of course."

I leaned back on the headrest and closed my eyes.

~

Mere moments later, Hollis nudged me lightly.

"He's here."

"Al?"

"No, Harry."

Harry Bratton was a forensics examiner who'd retired in Silvies a few years back. He contracted out his services to our Oregon State Police field office in John Day as well the Burns unit, ninety miles down the road from ours.

"Maggie, you stay here and rest while I unlock Mr. Drake's truck."

I palmed the sleep from my eyes. "Nah. I'm feeling pretty spry after my catnap."

I didn't notice the man roll his eyes, but I was sure he had.

"It's stopped snowing. After we talk to Harry, I'll go take a few photos of the boot prints next to the passenger-side door. Make impressions, too," I said.

"The snow eased off about twenty minutes ago, so I went ahead and did all of that while you were snoozing. Along with more snapshots of the snowmobile trail."

I thanked him, stepped out into the chill, and whispered a blessing in honor of my wool socks and winter gloves. Hollis joined me outside, and we met up with Harry, who carried his exam kit.

I listed off the details of what we had found at the scene, which wasn't anything more than the dead man slouched against the pickup door, his blood, some boot prints, and the snowmobile tracks.

Harry offered a nod. "Was the guy's seat belt locked?"

"I think so. Or am I wrong about that, Hollis?"

"I'm pretty sure it was."

"All right," Harry said. "Let's go take a look. The last thing I want to happen is to have the body fall out of the truck when I open the door."

That explained his question about the seat belt. Which, in the end, turned out not to be a problem. Drake had followed the law and, in terms of driving conditions, had also used some common sense in doing so. Not that using common sense mattered much in the end.

We stood three abreast and inspected the ground below the driver's-side door. No footprints in the snow.

"Well, clearly he didn't get out of his vehicle here," Harry said, stating the obvious and placing his exam kit on the snowy ground. "You have the key fob, right?"

"Right here," I said and handed him the evidence bag containing the key fob.

"I just know you were gloved up when you removed it from the victim's person," Harry added.

"You can count on it."

Harry put on a pair of disposable gloves, unlocked the door, and opened it.

"You said he was shot in the upper torso?" he asked.

"We believe by someone standing outside of the passenger-side door, which was wide open when we arrived."

"So the bullet entered the right side, but there's no exit wound on the left side."

He brought Drake's body forward slightly, bracing it carefully using the seat belt, which strained from the weight.

"No exit wound out his back either. The slug will have to be removed during the autopsy."

"The ME is on the way," I assured him.

"Ray Gattis?"

"I don't know who's assigned to the case."

Harry placed the cadaver back against the seat, removed his gloves, and gathered what he needed to dust for prints. Next he put on a fresh pair of gloves to examine the body.

"I'll be here awhile, so you two should warm up in your police vehicle. I have a feeling you'll be out in the weather for much of the day."

3

MIDDAY, APRIL 7

We had left the office this morning in the belief we would be back before noon, which meant our lunches were parked in the refrigerator back at the station house. Fortunately, at some point mid-pregnancy, I started keeping a stash of emergency rations and a bottle of water in my pack for the not-so-rare occasions when I might be waylaid somewhere without sustenance—such as waiting for a homicide detective to arrive at the scene of a killing.

I retrieved two snack bags and offered one to Hollis. "Unsalted peanuts or unsalted peanuts?"

"Oh, how about some unsalted peanuts."

"Here you go." I passed Hollis one of the bags of nuts and filled a couple of paper cups with water.

I reminded myself to chew slowly, famished or not. "You know, I think we need to see where this road takes us."

"Do we have time for that?"

I inspected the clock on my fitness tracker. "It's more than an hour before Bach and the ME get here, so yeah, I think so. And maybe we can also figure out where the snowmobile rider came from and went back to."

"Sounds like a plan. We might as well make use of the time until they get here."

"My thought exactly."

He wolfed down his peanuts, while I stashed the remainder of mine, locked my seat belt, and put the Tahoe in gear.

We pulled out and began to move past Drake's truck, but Harry waved us over. Idling the Tahoe, I rolled down my window.

"How's it going?" I asked.

"It's going okay, but I'll need the truck moved out of the elements to lift any exterior prints."

"Whitey Kern will be out here later. We'll have him tow it to his shop."

"That'll work. Where are you two headed?"

"We're checking out the rest of the ranch road, see where it ends up and whatever else might turn out to be of interest."

"Got it. In case I'm gone when you get back, is there anything else you need me to examine before I leave?"

"What do you think, Hollis?"

"We've taken photos and made casts of the boot prints here and back at Poison Spring. We've also grabbed pictures of the snowmobile's trail in both places," he said. "So, I'd say you just need to do your magic inside the Ram truck here."

"Send along the photos and get the casts to me once they harden. In the meantime, I've found several sets of fingerprints and partial sets, at least as far as I can tell with the naked eye." He passed me the baggie with the key fob for Drake's pickup. "You'll need this in case I'm gone by the time you get back. And I'll lock up before heading out."

"Thanks, Harry. You know where to send the bill."

"You all take it easy. I'll get back to you about the prints or anything else I find in the victim's vehicle."

I continued on as Harry tipped his chin up, then down, signaling his adios for now.

"He's an interesting guy," Hollis said as we moved up the ranch road.

"He is. And really smart, I think."

"Yeah. He reminds me of people I've met who read those thick science fantasy novels."

"I was into one of those series for a while."

"Really?"

"Sure. When I was a senior in college and bored out of my mind. Can't even remember the name of the author or the series now."

As we moved past the fossil formation we'd spotted earlier, I sensed we were subtly climbing in elevation. Soon enough, we came to a gate in the fence running to our right. The snowmobile had left the shoulder of the ranch road at that point. Evidently the operator had opened the gate and crossed into the property south of us, then continued on across a field on the opposite side of the fence line.

The rock jack on either side of the gate reminded me of childhood visits to my grandparents' property along the John Day River. Unlike the metal fence stabilizers many farmers and ranchers use now, rock jacks were shaped like tetrahedrons—three-dimensional triangles—and built out of juniper balusters and filled with basalt boulders to add weight. Rock jacks held the barbed wire taut enough between fence posts to withstand even the most brutal wind, or so went the lore.

I filed away the momentary rock jack distraction and thought back to something Lisa Drake had mentioned. She'd said the folks from the ranch next door had once owned snowmobiles. Perhaps the gate in the fence led to their property. Had I jotted down the name of her neighbors? I thought back on the strange conversation with the woman—yes, now I recalled, I'd written down their last name.

∽

Rounding a corner, we met up with a wide swath of pavement allowing vehicles —including large livestock trucks—to turn around and head back the opposite direction. A loading chute had been constructed on the Drakes' property to allow for transport of the Black Angus cattle raised on Poison Spring Ranch.

On the other side of the ranch road was a fenced-in parking lot available for folks visiting this particular site in the John Day Fossil Beds National Monument. Marked hiking trails spread from the asphalt-covered lot. A couple of structures—a large visitor information kiosk and a building providing running water and restrooms—stood near the entrance to the parking lot just off of Route 19.

I parked near the fence standing between the ranch road and this section of the national monument. The fence wasn't a particularly intimidating barrier, and the restrooms were very inviting at the moment.

Hollis clicked off of his follow-up call to Whitey Kern letting him know we would need him at the scene by four o'clock to tow Drake's Ram to his storage facility in John Day.

"Do you think I can climb over that fence, Holly?"

"How do I say it? No."

"Oh, if that's not a challenge, I don't know what is."

"Believe it or not, I meant it would be difficult because of the snow."

"Oh, yeah. Sure you did."

"Why on earth would you want to climb over the fence?"

"Nature calls, dude. And my choices are limited."

"Ah, the restrooms. They might be locked, you know."

I shut down the engine. "Well, you better hope not."

"All right, but I'm going with you."

We zipped up our coats, put our hats and gloves back on, and stepped outside. Crossing snowy ground while navigating through frosty sagebrush to get to the fence was easier than we had anticipated. And once there, we noticed a small break in the fence line where it met up with a rocky outcropping. We decided to take a chance there was enough room to squeeze between the last fence post and the outcropping.

After we made our way to the spot, with Hollis's assistance, I was able to maneuver through the gap and enter the parking lot. I wasn't sure what I might have done had the restrooms been locked tight, but as I learned from signage, all outdoor areas, facilities, and trails were open year-round, be there rain, snow, or scorching sun.

Holly was waiting for me under the visitor information kiosk's wooden awning when I returned from the restroom. We retraced our steps and made it back to my vehicle. I fired up the engine and the heater, and we headed back toward the murder scene.

"You know what that secret passageway into the parking lot did, don't you, Mags?"

"Allowed us to use the restrooms?

"Well, if you think about it, before we made it through to the parking-lot side, we were caught between a rock and a hard spot."

I couldn't help myself—that stupid bit of funny prompted me to laugh.

～

Strangely, with the help of powerful winds transporting the snow clouds further east, the sun appeared. A midday brilliance fell across the snow-covered high desert, encasing the miniscule patch of Earth in light as bold as that of late summer.

"When we're done here today," I said, "we need to stop by the place next door and ask the owners about their snowmobiles."

"Yeah, I noticed those tracks ended up going someplace nearby."

"The neighbors Mrs. Drake mentioned, I believe." Keeping my left hand on the wheel, I lifted the notebook from my shirt pocket and flipped to the entry. "Their last name is Edwards."

"Edwards, huh?" Hollis mumbled and dove into his phone. "Roger and Corky. There was an article about the two of them a while back. They're coauthors of a couple of books about birds. She's the photographer and primary writer, and he's the ornithologist."

"Interesting."

"This is not a judgment, but from the photograph of the couple, he appears to be considerably older than her," he added.

"Okay?"

"Just saying."

"Now don't get testy just because you missed having lunch. I should've given you my bag of peanuts, too," I said.

"No, in fact, you should eat the rest of the peanuts in your bag."

"Or what, you'll eat them?"

"You know what I'm getting at."

"Thanks for the reminder, Dad."

"Well, at least you didn't call me *Mom* this time."

"Find something for us to listen to, okay? But before you do that, would you get in touch with Sam Damon again and let him know the ME will be here within the hour?"

"Sure thing," Hollis said and made the call. Afterward he turned Meschiya Lake and the Little Big Horns back on.

"Would you mind getting the bag with the rest of the peanuts out of my pack?" I asked him.

"You bet." He reached into the pack and brought up the half bag of nuts.

"Half for you, and half for me," I suggested.

"Nope, that's not how this works."

"Okay, would you get my water bottle out of there too?"

He reached into the pack a second time, brought out the half-full bottle, and handed it over to me.

"What would I do without you, Holly?"

"I think you would do fine without me. I'm not sure I'd do okay without you as my patrol partner, though."

"Where the fuck is that coming from?"

"You're gutsy, and you don't give up. You're brash and bold. Which means you have no trouble pushing the envelope when you believe it's the right thing to do. And I've never seen it turn out not to have been the right thing to do."

"I love you, but you've gotta admit, the absolute exception to all that was my marriage to J.T. Lake."

"You lost your mind for a while. Then you woke up, cleaned up your mess, and got back in the saddle."

"That's a heap of metaphors there, my good man."

"You're welcome. Now, just get us back to the crime scene before Al Bach arrives. And eat your dang peanuts."

∽

Al introduced us to Dr. Sara Lewis, the medical examiner who had accompanied him from Bend. She appeared to be close to forty, her stark blond hair pulled back in a ponytail. And she was all business.

For the purposes of conducting a preliminary examination of the body, Dr. Lewis slipped on a waterproof body-length apron and rubber gloves. "There's not much I can do at this point, other than to affirm he's deceased," she said, all of us gathered around the open driver's-side door of Mike Drake's Ram truck.

"The mortician should be here soon," Hollis said.

Without responding to Hollis, Dr. Lewis turned to me. "When did the two of you discover the body?"

"Mr. Drake contacted our OSP station in John Day at approximately eight twenty this morning to report the slaughter of one of his Black Angus bulls. We arrived at the ranch at approximately nine thirty and spoke with his wife. She explained that her husband would be waiting at Poison Spring where he'd found the animal. On your way out here, you passed a signpost marking the spring, and you may have noticed the bull's carcass nearby."

"I didn't," she said, "but the detective may have."

"When we arrived at the spring, Mr. Drake wasn't there. We spent some time examining the dead bull and the scene. After which, we drove further on up the ranch road in search of him, saw the truck parked here, and found him inside the vehicle in the condition in which you find him now, fatally shot in the right side of his upper torso."

"Interesting story, Sergeant Blackburn."

"It's Sergeant Blackthorne, Dr. Lewis," Al put in.

"But you didn't exactly answer my question, Sergeant. So let me clarify, what *time* did you find the body?"

"I'm attempting to arrive at that, ma'am, as I don't recall making note of the time at any point along the way."

She nodded tersely. "You said you arrived at the ranch around nine thirty and received directions. Let's say it took another five or six minutes to drive to Poison Spring, and then you stayed at that location for twenty minutes before driving up the road and finding Mr. Drake's body."

"Because of the snow, I would say it took a bit longer than five or six minutes to travel the half mile from the ranch house and reach the spring. Our search of the area near the animal involved taking photographs not only of the carcass but of boot prints and also evidence that a snowmobile had recently been there. So I'd say we were at the location at least twenty minutes. Afterward, when it appeared Mr. Drake had continued driving further up the ranch road, we went in search of him."

"Why didn't you consider going in search of him prior to dealing with the dead bull?"

"We were called out here because of the bull. And we didn't contemplate that Mr. Drake might've been waylaid, and we certainly didn't expect to find his body."

"How long did it take to get here and find the cadaver?"

"We're slightly over a half mile from Poison Spring. I drove slowly again, so it probably took a few minutes longer than it would normally."

She sighed. "I see. Did Mr. Drake contact you from his home, or was he still at Poison Spring and using a cell phone when he called your police station at eight twenty?"

"I don't know. And I didn't ask Mrs. Drake," I admitted. "But she told us we would find him at Poison Spring where the bull was killed, so I assumed they had spoken in person regarding the matter."

"But again, you didn't verify that, Sergeant Blackthorne?"

"What are all of these questions about, Dr. Lewis?" the detective asked. "You must have some sense of how fluid these situations can be."

"I'm attempting to get at the time of death. Was he killed shortly after the call to Sergeant Blackthorne alerting her about the bull? Or was he killed shortly before the sergeant and trooper here found him dead in his truck?"

"We didn't hear gunfire while at the ranch house. And I'm not sure we would've heard much of anything over the road and engine noise on our way out here," I said.

"As the expert, isn't that up to you to determine during your examination of the body?" Al's hackles had been raised. "Seems to me that for the purposes of establishing the time of death at this point, an approximation of between eight twenty a.m. and ten twenty a.m. when the homicide was reported to regional dispatch is fairly accurate, at least until you are able to refine it further using your expertise as the medical examiner."

"It's best to quantify the parameters as precisely as possible," she answered.

"And I believe that's been quantified. Now let's move on," Bach said. "I'd like to suggest that we all climb back in our warm vehicles and out of the elements until the undertaker arrives."

~

While waiting for Sam Damon and his four-wheel-drive hearse, Hollis and I passed some snark back and forth regarding Dr. Lewis, and by the time Sam pulled up, we had generally rid ourselves of giving a shit about her attitude.

"All I care about is that she can perform the autopsy and determine if there's something more here than meets the eye," I said finally.

"Yep, that's all that really counts."

"I wonder if anyone has explained to her that she'll probably have to examine the body at Sam's morgue?"

"You think this is her first case in the boonies?"

"I have no idea."

"Well, it could get interesting."

In the rearview mirrors, we could see Sam Damon pull in behind Al's Ford Police Interceptor.

"I know you're a little queasy about dead people, but I'd like you to help Sam load Drake's body into the hearse," I said.

"My guess is Dr. Lewis feels the need to dictate who does what, Mags. In fact, it seems like she might insist on it."

"You've gotten a lot more peckish these days, Holly."

"Peckish? Is that a word?"

"Yep, look it up. But wait until we go say howdy to Sam. We need to make sure Doc Lewis doesn't start ordering him around or anything."

I put my gloves back on and got out of the Tahoe. Hollis followed suit.

4

AFTERNOON, APRIL 7

Dr. Lewis oversaw the transport of Mike Drake's body from the Ram pickup to Sam's hearse. She also insisted on riding along to the funeral home with him in order to supervise the handling of the cadaver once they arrived.

I might've suggested to Dr. Lewis that Sam was all about the respectful caretaking of those deceased individuals in his charge. But the woman hadn't been impressed by his long prayer and short sermon in honor of Drake, or by me for that matter, so I had to assume she wouldn't be interested in anything else I might have to say.

While Al took a call in his Interceptor, Hollis and I waited in my Tahoe. The two of us watched Sam turn around and drive back toward the main highway. He'd gone about fifty yards when Whitey Kern pulled up, headed in the opposite direction. They had to maneuver slowly past one another, but both were old hands at making room for other rigs on narrow, snowy roadways.

Once Whitey had navigated his way to the appropriate spot in the road, he rather handily lifted the truck and placed it on his wrecker in order to secure it and tow it away. We'd watched him do this dozens of times as he retrieved automobiles and heavy equipment in every situation imaginable, including at the scene of a few murders.

Hollis and I got out of my Tahoe and went to greet him. For an older guy, he was damn fit. He'd already climbed up on the bed of his wrecker and was securing the Ram by the time we met up with him.

"Need any help, Whitey?" Hollis called out.

"Got it, thanks." He clambered down off the wrecker bed. "How are you folks today?"

"We're good, Whitey," I said.

"Sam's hearse carried away Mike Drake's body, I guess."

"Yep."

"Don't mean to speak ill of the dead," Whitey began. "But he weren't all he was cracked up to be, if you know what I mean."

I'd never heard such criticism from Whitey regarding anyone dead or alive.

"Oh?" I asked.

His face reddened. "Uh, in my experience, and it weren't a lot, but he could be kinda...what's the word? Uppity? No, that ain't it. Expecting folks to abide by his idea of how things oughta be."

If that wasn't uppity, I didn't know what was.

"Appreciate your time," Hollis put in. "I bet you've been pretty busy today on account of the weather."

"Yep. I should take the truck to my shop for the time being, right?"

"That's the plan for now," I said.

"Nice to see you both. And Maggie, you be careful out here in all this snow," he added, tipped his hat, and got back in his wrecker.

~

After Whitey took off, Hollis and I walked toward Al's SUV. When he saw us, he got out and waited for us to join him.

"You and I should stop in at the ranch house and make sure Mrs. Drake and her son know that Mr. Drake's body is on its way to the mortuary," I suggested to Hollis.

"Knowing Sam, I wouldn't put it past him to stop in himself."

"In all likelihood, but let's make certain."

"In the meantime, what can you tell me about the snowmobile tracks?" the detective asked.

"Well, it appears the rider stopped at Poison Spring, took a look at the bull, and eventually turned the snowmobile around, passed by here, and continued on up the way. Its trail eventually leaves the ranch road and enters a gate, possibly property belonging to someone else. We plan to stop in at the neighbors, who Mrs. Drake indicated had owned two snowmobiles at some point. She wasn't sure that was still the case, though," I said.

"You'd think, with so few neighbors out here, she'd know if they still owned snowmobiles," Bach mused.

"It didn't seem an appropriate time to pursue the matter further. I'd just let her know her husband had been murdered. Plus she told me she hadn't seen or talked to the neighbors in years," I added.

"Think I'll join you when you stop in to see Mrs. Drake and her son."

"I like that idea, Al."

"Is her son a teenager?"

"No, somewhere in his mid-thirties."

"I'm not sure why I thought he was younger."

I refrained from going into my *odd duck* assessment of Christopher Drake. "I think they'll be pleased about a homicide detective from Bend leading the investigation."

"We all know that I'm going to depend on the two of you to lead the investigation," Bach said. "I might add, I'm fortunate—and so are the residents of your county—that the two of you are good at it. And this is where I encourage you both to consider joining the OSP homicide unit someday. We could use your help. *I* could use your help."

"I'm flattered, Detective. But timing is everything."

"Same here, sir," Hollis said.

"Al, okay? We've worked together for a few years, and I'd prefer you to call me by my first name or by my rank. Save the 'sir' for when regular citizens are present."

"Got it, Al."

"All right. If we're done here, let's drop by the ranch house and speak with the dead man's wife and son."

∼

Reality appeared to have set in for Lisa Drake, as evidenced by her red and swollen eyes. I also thought I detected the scent of alcohol on her breath.

"I was on the phone with Mike's youngest sister for about an hour," the woman offered shakily. "She's pretty devastated."

We were seated in her cozy sitting room, as opposed to the foyer. The space was considerably homier. Framed family photographs were mixed in with antiques and various other mementos, and a small table in the corner held a partly completed jigsaw puzzle. Two bookshelves stood against one wall, both filled with all manner of novels, memoirs, travel guides, and books on ranch management.

"I didn't have a chance to introduce Trooper Hollis Jones earlier," I said.

"Nice to meet you, Trooper."

"And this is Detective Alan Bach. He arrived from Bend earlier."

"Good to meet you too, Detective," Lisa said. "Christopher and I saw your vehicle when you drove past the house. Sam Damon's too when he arrived at the ranch. Also someone else—I didn't recognize him—prior to the detective or Sam. And Whitey Kern, of course."

Harry Bratton was no doubt the someone else Mrs. Drake didn't recognize.

"How is Christopher doing, by the way?"

"I'm not sure. He left a short while ago to visit a friend."

I had noticed his father's BMW convertible was no longer parked in the lot out front.

"So if you saw Sam's hearse, you must know he now has custody of your husband's body," I said.

"Sam stopped by for a few minutes on his way back to John Day. We briefly discussed funeral arrangements." Lisa lifted a lacy handkerchief from the pocket of her sweater. "He's such a kind man."

"Yes, he is."

Lisa continued, "The medical examiner remained in the hearse while Sam spoke with me, though. But she got antsy after a while."

"Antsy?" the detective asked.

"She honked the horn a few times."

"I sincerely apologize for that," he said.

"I'm not trying to cause trouble for anyone."

"Of course not, Mrs. Drake," Al reassured her.

I knew him well enough to know by his expression he could barely contain his anger at Dr. Lewis.

"Mrs. Drake, I have a couple of questions about this morning."

"Okay, Margaret, but please call me Lisa. We've known each other a long time."

"Did Mike return to the house after finding the bull's carcass near Poison Spring?"

"Yes, he came back to get his gun. And he contacted you while he was here."

"A rifle or a handgun?" I asked.

"Some kind of handgun. I have no idea what it is, but Christopher might know."

If the weapon was anywhere in the Ram truck, including on Mike Drake's person, Harry had collected it. I made a mental note to call him on the way back to John Day.

"What prompted Mike to drive up the ranch road in the first place?"

"He had gotten a phone call, possibly about the bull, I guess. But he doesn't usually check in with me on ranch matters. *Didn't* usually check in with me, I should say."

"Might he have mentioned something to Christopher?"

"Our son was in bed when my husband took off this morning, and also when he came back for his gun."

"I believe those are all of my questions for now. Perhaps Detective Bach or Trooper Jones have some questions, though."

"Apologies if this has already been asked, Mrs. Drake," Al began. "Had your husband had any serious disagreements with anyone recently, or was there any kind of animosity between him and someone else?"

"Mike's beloved by all."

She repeated precisely what she had said earlier, and again in present tense.

Bach continued, "Perhaps Mr. Drake didn't realize he had made someone angry or that a neighbor was out for revenge over a perceived wrongdoing. Possibly a dispute over water rights, that kind of thing."

"Well. I would find that surprising, if not shocking."

The detective indicated he understood. "We'll want to speak with your son relatively soon. Do you know when he plans to return to the ranch?"

"He's with his girlfriend. My guess is he'll likely spend the night with her. I could call him, but I don't think he'd answer. He was very unhappy about not being able to go see his father's body where...where he died, and he partly blames me for that."

"I see. Family members are often angry when something like this occurs. We'll check in tomorrow and set up a time to talk to him."

Lisa sighed and massaged her temples.

"Would you like me to call someone to come stay with you?" I asked.

"I'll be fine, Margaret. There's no one to call, anyway."

"No friends or relatives? Someone from church, perhaps?" I wasn't sure why I was pressing the matter.

She affected a look of grief and loneliness. No, not loneliness. It was closer to aloneness.

"I haven't been to church in many years, Margaret. Now if you will excuse me, I need some rest."

"Thank you for your time, Mrs. Drake," Al said.

The three of us stood and made our way outside. I closed the door, and we heard the sound of the lock being set behind us.

We gathered next to the detective's rig. The snowstorm had seemingly paused, leaving an impenetrable bank of clouds in its wake.

Detective Bach turned up the collar of his coat. "It's dang cold."

"It truly is," Hollis said in agreement.

"Al, did you want to be there when we talk to the Edwards couple?" I asked.

"Remind me why you wanted to talk to them."

"They're the neighbors who may own a couple of snowmobiles."

"Right. I think I'll make my way to Mack's Motel, get rooms for Dr. Lewis and me, and make some phone calls. But contact me if anything significant turns up."

"Sounds good. After we stop in at the neighbors just up the road, I plan to check in with Harry about Mike Drake's gun."

~

I pulled over and idled next to the neighbors' extra-large mailbox. Painted silhouettes of birds encircled the names of the residents: Coreen "Corky" and Roger F. Edwards. I drove down the driveway and parked next to the picket fence surrounding their white house.

Tire tracks were present on the snow-covered driveway, but there were no automobiles in sight. Whoever had driven onto the property and tracked through the snow before we arrived was seemingly gone.

"Let's go knock on the door," I said.

"My feet were finally starting to warm up."

"You're welcome to wait here with the engine running while I try and roust someone in the house."

I got out, walked to the front door, knocked, and waited. Soon, I knocked a second time. Except for the porch light, it appeared no other lights were on, and no one was home.

I drew out one of my business cards and wrote, "Please contact me as soon as possible" beneath my name and title. Looking around for a spot to leave the card, I decided the gap between the door and the doorframe would have to do.

"Nobody home," I said, getting back in the driver's seat.

He pointed at the single outbuilding on the property. "How about I check out the shed?"

"Don't think anyone could get a car in there. Besides, it looks to be padlocked."

"I think it could hold a couple of snowmobiles, though. I'll take a look."

"I thought your feet were cold."

"*Were* cold is the operative term."

"Go for it, Holly."

I watched him attempt to peek inside the building through the narrow space between the front double doors. That apparently didn't work because he walked to the rear of the structure and disappeared behind it. Moments later he reappeared wearing a toothy, kid grin.

"You found something, I take it," I said as he opened the door and kicked the snow from his boots.

"There are windows at the back of the shed, filthy and hard to see through. But there are definitely two snowmobiles parked inside. Also found a trailer to transport them behind the building."

"It's hard to tell for sure, but those tire tracks near the shed might be the result of hauling a snowmobile on that trailer you found."

Hollis shrugged. "Could be, I suppose."

"We could try spraying snow impression wax on the tire tracks."

"The tracks are too messed up for impressions, and so are any footprints," Hollis argued. "They're melting, and they've been driven over, including by us when we pulled in."

"Yeah, you're right. Not to mention, without something more substantial to go on, we really have no reason to suspect the Edwards couple of anything other than possessing a couple of snowmobiles. And not being around when we wanted to talk to them."

"And being bird fanatics."

I fired up the Tahoe, turned around, and pulled up to the highway. "Still wish we could ask them if either went out for a ride in the snow this morning."

About fifty yards from the Edwards place and on the other side of the highway was another residence set back from the road. Three riders on snowmobiles were carving figure eights in the small field of snow in front of the house.

"Interesting," Hollis said.

I slowed and turned down the driveway. There were no birds depicted on their mailbox, but spelled out in self-adhesive capital letters was the name JOHNSON.

I parked, and we got out. The carving of figure eights had ended the moment we drove onto the property, and all three snowmobiles were now powered off and riderless. A woman and two teenage girls had removed their helmets and now stood together near the house.

"Good evening," I said when we reached them and held out my card for the woman to take. "I'm Sergeant Blackthorne, Oregon State Police. And this is Senior Trooper Jones."

He handed her his card as well, and she studied both.

"My name's Charlotte Johnson. These are my girls, Paula and Laney. We've been enjoying all the snow."

All three were in some state of beautiful—pink cheeks, large dark brown eyes, and strikingly tall and elegant. They also appeared wary, if not downright suspicious.

"Ms. Johnson," I began.

"Mrs. My husband, Troy, is a long-haul trucker. If this is about the girls operating these contraptions, they have their driver's licenses, and we're all state certified for snowmobiles."

"Glad to hear it, but we didn't stop in about that," I clarified.

"Oh?"

"Could we speak to you privately?"

"Girls, go back in the house for a while," Charlotte said to her daughters and watched as they shuffled back inside. "What's this about?"

"Mike Drake, your neighbor up the road. Someone shot him to death this morning."

"What the fuck? Who would kill Mike? Most people think he's one of the nicest people they ever met."

"His body was found in his pickup on the Drakes' ranch road up a ways. Approximate time of death is somewhere between eight thirty and ten thirty. The thing is, someone had also been out there on a snowmobile."

"It definitely wasn't one of us, I can assure you. The girls and I took off for Prairie City this morning around seven to visit my mother in the county's nursing home. She's not expected to live much longer. You can call and confirm it. Her name's Gloria Harrison."

"I'm sorry to hear about your mother," I said.

Charlotte glanced at my card. "Appreciate that, Sergeant. Have you informed Roger and Corky Edwards just down the road about Mike's death?"

"We stopped by, but they weren't home."

"Oh God, how could I forget? Roger had a stroke a few days ago, and he's in the hospital in Bend. I understand he's pretty bad off."

"Thank you for letting us know that, Mrs. Johnson. One more question. Did you notice anything unusual when you took off for Prairie City this morning?"

"A shit-ton of snow. In April."

I refrained from chuckling at her answer. "Thank you for your time. If you think of anything that might be helpful to our investigation, you have our cards."

"It seemed like you and your daughters were really having a great time riding around on your snowmobiles," Hollis put in.

She smiled. "It felt good to have fun for a while."

"There's still plenty of time for more," he added.

"Are you a fan of these contraptions, too?"

"Never tried riding one. Not yet, anyway."

"You two are stationed in John Day, right?" she asked.

We indicated we were.

"Drive careful."

5

EVENING, APRIL 7

We had driven about a mile from the Johnsons' property when I remembered we needed to contact Harry and ask if he'd found a handgun in Drake's truck.

"You want to get in touch with Harry about Mike Drake's handgun," Hollis reminded me.

"I was about to ask you to do that," I said. "But before you make the call, would you jot down Mrs. Johnson's name somewhere. And her daughters' names. The mother too."

"You doubt Mrs. Johnson's story?"

"One of us would've contacted the county nursing home if I doubted her story."

He brought out his phone and opened his notes app. "Charlotte Johnson and daughters Paula and Laney," he muttered as he typed, then paused to remember the name of the woman they had visited in the county nursing home. "Gloria Harrison."

"Husband's name is Troy. Long-haul truck driver," I added.

He entered the husband's name. "Don't think I'd want Lil and Hank living alone out here in the middle of nowhere, essentially, if I were a long-haul truck driver."

"I don't know. She seemed to have it under control, plus she's got neighbors living nearby."

"I guess."

"Call Harry, please."

After he dialed Harry's number, I listened to their back-and-forth.

"He found an unloaded Browning 1911-22 in the glove compartment," Hollis said after clicking off.

"For now, we'll have to assume that's the weapon Drake retrieved when he came back to the ranch house after finding the bull."

"Harry didn't think it had ever been fired. And he also found a full box of .22 cartridges next to the pistol."

"Maybe Mike thought he wouldn't actually need to use the weapon," I speculated.

"Could be. Anyway, Harry couldn't match Mike Drake's prints to any law enforcement fingerprint database he has access to. In fact, despite having gathered several sets of prints, he wasn't able to ID any of them."

"So that means anyone who's been inside of that Ram pickup lately is an upstanding citizen?"

"Hard to know, but maybe the ME will come up with something."

"And Detective Bach will have to fucking pry it out of her," I declared.

"See, there you go again."

"Turn some music on. Please."

He dialed up a satellite station featuring Chris Rea, one of my favorite singer/guitarists. Something Hollis was fully aware of.

～

East of Mt. Vernon and a few miles from John Day, sunlight broke through the remaining clouds and lit the snow-covered land. It was close to six fifteen in the evening, and it seemed the storm had done what it had come to do and moved on.

My phone rang. I saw it was Duncan and activated Bluetooth.

"Howdy," I said.

"Headed home soon, babe?"

"Hollis and I have been out near Kimberly most of the day."

"I thought maybe that was the case. Mike Drake's murder was breaking news on KJDY. I can't believe it. He was always so friendly when he came into the feed and tack. I don't get it. Who would want to kill Mike?"

"That's the question for the ages, Dun."

"So no one's been arrested, I take it?"

No one was even remotely a suspect at the moment. "Not yet."

"Have you talked to Detective Bach?"

"Yeah, he's already in John Day, and so is the medical examiner."

"Where are you now?"

"Almost back to town and headed to the office. How about you?"

"I'm home. Will I see you soon?"

"In an hour or so."

"How are you feeling?"

"Pregnant. Tired. Looking forward to going home."

"I'm making Zoey's fried chicken for dinner."

Zoey was my long-dead mother who had made the best fried chicken ever, which sadly stood in stark contrast to most of her endeavors in life.

"All right, that's all you needed to say. I'm starving, and I'll be home as soon as I can."

"I love that recipe," Hollis called out.

"You're welcome to join us, Hollis. Lil and Hank, too, of course," Duncan offered.

"Thanks anyway, but I know Lil's already made stew for dinner."

"Well, tomorrow I'll send along a couple of pieces with Maggie for your lunch."

"I'll take you up on that offer for sure."

"See you when you get here, babe. Good night, Hollis."

"Hey," Hollis began. "Let's meet for a beer soon."

"Sounds like a plan."

"Adios, Dun," I said.

"I wasn't kidding when I said I love that fried chicken recipe," Holly added after I hung up.

"Stew sounds good, though, especially on a cold evening."

"Not Lil's veggie stew. You'll have to take my word for it. But she's convinced if she avoids eating meat, her cancer will remain in remission."

"She could be absolutely right."

"Oh, I believe that's more than possible. I'd just like her to find a recipe for a better version of veggie stew. And so far none of my hints have worked."

"How about just being direct with her?"

"You're the only person I can be direct with."

"You need to try harder."

"What do you mean, Mags?"

"You're not very direct with me most of the time. But I'm on to your one-liners that are really suggestions in disguise."

He appeared to think about that for a moment before tossing me one of his one-line suggestions. "You must really be in a hurry to get home."

Holly's way of indirectly implying I was driving a little too fast.

"Would you like to walk the rest of the way to the office?"

"You mean the last block? Half block, now."

I pulled up in front of our cop shop, next to his identical police vehicle.

"I love you, Maggie."

"I love you, too. Now get out so I can go home."

∾

After dinner, Duncan and I stashed the leftovers in the refrigerator and loaded the dishwasher. We'd made a pact not to discuss Mike Drake's homicide and now lounged on the daybed in the great room. We were each reading a different novel by Percival Everett, a writer whose humor and storytelling we were both drawn to.

"You know, I think we need to trade out the daybed for a couch," Duncan said after several minutes of quiet reading.

"But why, Dun? The daybed is so comfortable."

"For you, maybe. You're all comfy at the end with a back and armrest, while I've got not much for support over here on my end."

"How about I buy you a recliner, old man?"

"How about we buy two recliners?"

"Like the matching ones your parents have?"

"Sure," he said.

"All right, let's trade the daybed in for a couch."

"And I'll fetch your mother's rocker from the attic to rock the baby to sleep."

"I like that idea. But for now, let's go upstairs and read our books in bed."

He pulled me closer and put his arm around me. "You had me at bed."

We kissed.

He stood, handed his book to me, scooped me up, and cradled me in his arms.

"What the fuck are you doing?"

"Carrying you upstairs."

"Are you trying to pull your back out?"

"You're not that much heavier than the last time I did this. Just a little bulkier."

"I'll show you bulkier."

He laughed. "Bulkier because you're carrying our books. That's all I meant."

"Like hell. Now get a move on."

~

The next morning I arrived at the station about an hour earlier than usual, anxious to write up our report on Drake's murder as well as the slaughter of the Black Angus bull he'd discovered on his ranch property nearly twenty-four hours ago. Hollis's rig was parked outside of our police station, a sign he might have wanted to get the show on the road, too.

"Morning, Holly," I called out as I entered the office and moved to my desk.

"Morning, Mags. You brought me a piece of Duncan's fried chicken, I hope."

"Yep, two pieces." I placed the baggie containing the chicken on his desk.

"Great. Did you know there's another Poison Spring in Grant County?"

I sat down and opened my computer. "How about that."

"Out in the Malheur National Forest, just northeast of Izee. And it actually shows up on a map, unlike the one at Poison Spring Ranch."

"Maybe that's the difference between public and private land?" I suggested. "And I suppose if we can have two different Bear Creeks in Grant County, we can have two Poison Springs."

"There are two Bear Creeks in the county?"

"At least two."

I could tell I'd piqued his curiosity by the sound of the rat-a-tatting on his keyboard.

"There are five different Bear Creeks in our fair county," he announced.

"I don't suppose you started writing up a report about our adventures yesterday?" I asked.

"No, but I did box and label the casts for Harry. I was also waiting for my boss to assign me something specific to write up."

"Okay, why don't you write up the piece about the bull and our attempt to talk to the Edwards couple, as well as our conversation with the Johnson woman. And I'll write up the discovery of Drake's body and what transpired afterward, along with any possible evidence connected to his murder."

"After I put my chicken in the fridge, I guess I better get to work."

"That's right. And would you mind stashing my lunch in the refrigerator, too?"

"Good morning." Sherry Linn, who was always at the office early, had arrived, and Harry Bratton was with her. Apparently she hadn't lost another bet with him, as she wore a sequined sweater set, a gathered skirt, and some low heels.

We both greeted them, then Hollis carried my lunch and his chicken to the alcove.

Sherry Linn removed her puffy coat. "I'll be glad when all this snow melts."

"We don't want it to melt too fast," I put in. "The John Day River Valley has flooded before after a big storm."

"You've said that a few times since I started working here," she reminded me.

"Maggie likes to repeat herself," Hollis teased, returning from the alcove.

"All right, you two, is that any way to treat a pregnant woman? Especially one who writes up your performance reviews every year?"

"I'm shaking in my boots," Holly said.

I ignored that comment and turned to our office manager's husband. "Do you have any more news for us, Harry?"

"No, but if you go back to Poison Spring Ranch today, I'd appreciate you taking family members' fingerprints. I'd like to be able to determine whether their prints match any of those I took from the interior of the dead man's truck."

"They probably won't like it," I began, "but if it needs to be done, we'll do it. Besides, having their prints on hand could ultimately eliminate them as suspects."

"And I'd like to pick up those casts, assuming they're ready."

"I'll get those for you," Hollis volunteered and walked toward our evidence locker.

"I have to pick up some supplies at McKay's Feed and Tack, and then I'm off to Whitey Kern's shop to see what I can find on the exterior of the victim's Ram truck."

I checked the schoolhouse clock on the wall. "I have it on good authority the feed and tack doesn't open for another twenty minutes."

"Guess I'll have to visit Nade's Coffee Den before heading to the feed and tack, then."

Hollis returned with a large box containing all the casts we made yesterday and handed it over to Harry.

He peered at the collection. "Thanks, I think." He picked up the box and gave Sherry Linn a peck on the cheek. "See you tonight, hon."

Harry slipped out of the office, and Sherry Linn moved to the front counter. Shortly afterward, Doug Vaughn and Al Bach arrived. They both chatted with Sherry Linn before making their way back to the crowded set of officer desks.

The detective eyed the one unused desk. "I'd almost forgotten. Mark Taylor's replacement hasn't yet been assigned to your unit yet. I'll reach out to Major Macintyre right away, Maggie."

Macintyre hadn't been promoted, but his position title had changed from corporal to major. I was having a hard time getting used to the change, but I'd pledged to get over myself about it.

"I know a Fish and Wildlife trooper who's been hoping for a transfer," Doug chimed in from his desk.

"What's his name?" I asked and glanced at Hollis. I wanted to be able to nip Doug's suggestion in the bud if the person he knew was someone I'd had run-ins with back in the day.

"Her name is Daniela Park."

"From the Bend unit, right?" Bach asked.

"That's right, Detective."

"Maggie, Daniela Park is top-notch. Maybe too top-notch for Major Macintyre to part with, but I'll give it a try."

"Appreciate that, Al."

Best of all, this Daniela person was someone I had never met; no baggage on either side.

"I'll give him a call today."

"Even better," I said.

"Okay, let's start our murder board," Bach suggested firmly.

The detective appeared to be ready for action; so much for getting on our reports first thing.

"Is Dr. Lewis at Sam's mortuary?"

"Yeah, I dropped her off on the way here."

"Great, things are moving along, then. Shall we gather in the alcove for our discussion?"

Al nodded. "Sounds like a plan."

"That way, Doug can finish dealing with his backlog of paperwork at his desk and without distraction."

"I'm thinking I'll be done with a lot of it by noon, Maggie. I had it in mind to check out the Logan Valley area this afternoon, depending on snow conditions."

"You think it'll be passable?"

"Given the higher elevation out there, it might not be. But if it's not passable for me, it won't be for poachers."

"I know you'll be careful out there, Doug."

6

MORNING, APRIL 8

Detective Bach, Hollis, and I gathered around the table in the alcove. This was the sixth time we had gathered in this very space and drawn up a murder board since twins Dan and Joseph Nodine were shot to death just over two years ago.

And on that happy note, I tacked up a sheet of chart paper and wrote *Mike Drake, resident of Kimberly, Oregon (owner of Poison Spring Ranch) killed by gunfire on his property Wednesday, 4/7 between 8:30 a.m. and 10:30 a.m., pending ME's autopsy.*

"So tell me what you know about Mr. Drake," Al said.

I took a chair. "When I was a kid growing up here," I began, "he was generally well thought of, and I know he often reached out to neighbors, delivering meals, offering help, things of that nature. Before I moved back to Grant County, he'd been an elected county commissioner for several years. I think that rendered him a bit more gravitas."

"So a devoted community member, generally speaking," the detective suggested.

"I'd say so. And people have talked about him being especially kind. But I have a hunch Mrs. Drake, and maybe their son, weren't necessarily the recipients of his kindness. We'll want to press them on that, I believe."

Hollis picked up a marker, stood, and jotted down *Assess wife and son's relationship w/ deceased*.

"Interestingly, Whitey Kern, the owner of the towing company, and truly the gentlest, most patient, and least gossipy local we ever work with— right, Hollis?"

"Absolutely."

"Anyway, Whitey said he found the man to be uppity, and clarified that as something like, Drake always expected everyone to go along with his way of seeing things."

I checked Hollis for confirmation of Whitey's sentiment.

"That's basically exactly what he said," Holly added. "And Maggie's point about Whitey's general nonjudgmental disposition makes that comment stand out even more."

He noted that on the murder board as well.

"Drake also gave Hollis some grief about a speeding ticket at one point, but in general, making a stink about a speeding ticket isn't deemed a character flaw."

"I agree with Maggie there. As she pointed out when I mentioned the encounter, it was likely more about entitlement than anything else."

"Is the ranch successful?" Bach asked.

"Yes," I affirmed.

"Hollis, note that the victim was a former elected local official and successful rancher," Al said.

He added that, but afterward came a bout of silence.

"Oh, and we talked to one of his neighbors yesterday evening," I chimed in. "She was shocked anyone would kill him, said everyone called Drake the nicest person they'd ever met, or words to that effect."

Bach sighed. "Not much to go on, I'm afraid. So I think we need to go back out there and talk to Mrs. Drake again as well as her son. And it needs to be done ASAP."

"I agree, Al," I said.

"Maggie, sorry to interrupt, Mrs. Drake is on the phone. She'd like to talk to you."

"Thanks, Sherry Linn." I stood and followed her back toward my desk, observing how confidently she walked while wearing heels. I'd never mastered that—low or otherwise—and gave up trying along the way. I even wore slippers on my wedding day last November; they were satin, at least.

I picked up the receiver on my desk phone. "Good morning, Mrs. Drake. How are you this morning?"

"Oh, you know."

I didn't really, but now wasn't the time to get into all that.

"What should I do about the bull, Margaret?"

The animal had succumbed to something other than being shot and had likely been dead for twelve to eighteen hours when we arrived at the ranch yesterday. For those reasons, I sincerely doubted the bull's demise had anything to do with her husband's murder. With that in mind, I decided to suggest another branch of law enforcement.

"I'd recommend that Sheriff Norton become involved in the matter, particularly since we're investigating your husband's death. Would you like me to make the call to him?"

"You're willing to do that?"

"Sure." Unlike our former sheriff turned killer, Sheriff Cal Norton was reasonable, honest, and collegial about working together with our office. "I'll call him right after we hang up, and then we plan to drive back to your ranch and speak with you again and also Christopher."

"He's here this morning, Margaret. And I've already let him know he should expect a visit today from you and Detective Bach."

"All right. We'll see you in a little over an hour."

"Thank you for calling Sheriff Norton's office for me."

We hung up, and I called the Sheriff's Office. It took a few minutes to get Cal on the line, but once he picked up, he was as cordial as the day is long.

"Maggie, I hear you're working another murder case."

"Afraid so. That's tangentially why I'm calling."

"Whatever you need, just let me know."

"Did you know Mike Drake?"

"Heard a lot about him, but I never met him. I understand people are pretty riled about his death, though."

"I guess I'd expect that."

"Yeah, there's supposed to be some kind of public meeting about it."

"That's interesting. Keep me posted if you hear more," I said.

"And you, likewise."

"I'm calling to see if I can get your assistance with another matter having to do with Drake. He called our office yesterday morning to report that one of his Black Angus bulls had been slaughtered. It might fit the pattern of similar cattle deaths in central and eastern Oregon over the past few years."

"I've been following those cases. If it matches those other bizarre incidents in any way, I'd be interested in being involved for sure. As long as I don't get in the way of your homicide investigation," Cal said.

"Nah, we believe the bull succumbed long before Drake found it."

"All right. Maybe I'll check in with Jen Wilson, see if she has time to accompany me and add some wisdom about the bull's carcass."

"Terrific idea." Jen was the local vet, and we probably should've contacted her yesterday. "I just got off the phone with Mrs. Drake. She wanted to know what to do about the bull. I suggested she contact your office, since we're involved in finding her husband's killer. I also agreed to make the initial call to you."

"I've got something else going on right now, but I'll get out there as soon as I can."

"You need directions or anything?"

"No thanks. I've driven by the ranch several times."

"I should tell you the area around the bull is contaminated with boot prints in the snow, some of which belong to Hollis Jones and me. There were two other sets present when we arrived but were clearly made after the bull was dead."

"Oh?"

"Yeah, it hasn't been verified yet, but I think one set belonged to Mike Drake. There were also snowmobile tracks present, and I believe the second set of prints belong to the snowmobiler."

"Did you happen to make snow impressions of the boot prints?"

"We did."

"Of course you did."

"Anyway, unless you want to call Mrs. Drake directly before you drive out there, I can let her know you'll be coming by to see about the bull. We're heading back to the ranch in just a bit."

"Appreciate that. Maybe I'll see you there. If not, say howdy to Hollis."

After we hung up, I called Lisa but ended up leaving a message. Listening to Mike Drake's recorded voice was eerie, and his tone was, in lieu of a better description, unfriendly.

I returned to the alcove and summarized my conversation. "Mrs. Drake was concerned about the dead bull, so I roped Sheriff Norton in on that."

"Shall we head back to the ranch, then?" Al asked.

"After a bathroom break," I said.

"Oh, of course."

"I'll get our lunches out of the refrigerator, Maggie," Holly added.

"Thanks, Dad," I said.

~

Hollis drove his Tahoe to Poison Spring Ranch with me sitting on the passenger side for a change, and Al followed in his Interceptor. As always, the detective had to be prepared to be called out to some other eastern or central Oregon outpost to preside over a different homicide case. That fact required him to invariably take a separate vehicle wherever we traveled in the county.

Along the way, Hollis kept alert for slippery spots on the highway, which was now generally clear except for those places where the snow had melted, left a pool, and frozen overnight. Just the kind of thing drivers here in God's country had to get used to mid-November through mid-February but generally not in April. At least over the last several years. It didn't help that I made a terrible passenger, which I realized I'd become whenever Duncan was behind the wheel and I sat across from him.

And as per usual, I noticeably held my breath during every turn and applied the nonexistent foot brake on my side of the front seat.

"I think it's time to come up with music for us," Hollis suggested finally.

"I like the quiet. I'm enjoying watching the scenery instead of driving."

"You don't seem to like it."

"Ignore me. That's what Duncan does."

"I want to listen to some music—or news, whatever—just so I don't have to hear you on the verge of screaming in terror every time I slow down or speed up."

I scrolled through several channels, landing on one called East Era Sound. I found it meditative and interesting. And it seemed to have a calming effect on both of us.

Even with pockets of deep snow on the hills and basalt cliffs, today's restorative sunlight brought out the Suffolk lambs, as well as the Hereford and Black Angus calves, iconic reminders of spring in the John Day River Valley. And as we got closer to Kimberly, the early blooming apple, pear, peach, and plum orchards had not lost their flowering splendor to snowfall.

All of which served to distract me from our homicide case and Holly's driving for a short while.

"Have you and Duncan picked out names for your baby yet?"

His question surprised me. Sure, he was my best friend, but this was the kind of inquiry I might get from his wife, Lillian Two Moons. And I had already been asked a number of times by Dorie, my beloved surrogate mother.

"You know, I'm not sure. He likes Belle for a girl and Adam for a boy. Those are fine names, but I'd kind of like something a bit...I don't know, wilder?"

"Wilder, huh?"

"Of nature, is maybe what I mean. And gender-neutral, something like River or Sage."

"Those names sound kind of masculine to me," Hollis opined.

"Really? There's a gender-neutral list somewhere that includes them."

"Huh."

"On the other hand, I wouldn't mind Duncan's middle name, James, if we have a boy. So there you go."

"Yep, gender-neutral just flew the coop."

Hollis eased off the gas and turned into Poison Spring Ranch, the detective following close behind. Passing by the paddock near the entrance to the property, just on my right, I noted an older Toyota pickup parked next to the livery stable. A guy led a blanketed horse—his, I presumed—on a walk around the paddock grounds. He watched us drive by and tipped his cap, and that's when I realized it was Lowell Gregg, one of Duncan's regular customers at the feed and tack.

I'd barely ever spoken to Lowell, partly because he lived somewhere in this part of the county, and partly because he was a shy bachelor-farmer who I'd heard didn't get out much. But he might be someone who could further illuminate the general character of Mike Drake. And seeing him also prompted me to remember to ask for the names and contact information for everyone boarding horses on the Drake family ranch.

We parked in front of the ranch house and were met at the front door by Lisa. "Hello, officers. Please come in."

We followed her inside, and she invited us to take a seat in the sitting room.

"I'll let Christopher know you're here."

Her son soon joined us and sat as far away from the three of us as he possibly could and still be in the same room.

"Christopher, this is Homicide Detective Bach," I said.

Al exchanged a nod with Christopher.

"And this is Senior Trooper Jones."

Hollis acknowledged Christopher but received not even a glance from the guy in return. That struck a nerve with me, but it wouldn't do to admonish the shithead. Not yet, anyway.

"Christopher," Al began. "May I call you by your first name?"

"It's not my first name, which is Michael. But I've always used my middle name. And yes, you can call me by that name."

"We want you to know we're sorry for your loss."

The man shrugged. "It's not the loss you might think it is."

"I guess I misunderstood," I said, probably jumping the gun. So to speak.

Christopher smirked just a smidge. "Misunderstood what?"

"Yesterday, you were upset when I wouldn't allow you to visit the scene of your father's killing."

"I just wanted to see him...dead. But I got over that."

"You'll have an opportunity to see him at the mortuary."

His response to that was no response.

"Christopher," Al inserted. "What did you mean when you said your father's death was not the loss I might think it is?"

"Father was a complete asshole. Pardon my language. Mother will back me up on that."

"Your mother told me he was beloved," Al said.

"By all," I added.

"Well, I think if you dig into it, he was not beloved by all. A fact more apparent now."

"Was he so terribly disliked by someone who might've shot and killed him?" I asked.

"Well, if Roger Edwards hadn't been in the Bend hospital yesterday after barely surviving a stroke, I might've put him at the top of the list."

"What's that about?" I pressed.

"If what I suspect is true, you'll need to ask Corky Edwards."

"And just what do you expect to be true?"

"Well, Sergeant Blackthorne, what do you think?"

"Are you insinuating that your father was involved in a relationship with Mrs. Edwards?"

"*Was* involved in a relationship with Corky. It was years ago, but I'd bet my life he had many relationships with other women during the affair and after they broke it off."

"That's enough, Christopher." Lisa Drake had entered the room, but perhaps I was the only one besides her son who hadn't noticed.

He winced. "Mother. Someone has to be honest about the man supposedly beloved by all."

"Christopher, it was already apparent your father wasn't beloved by all. It's highly unlikely a homicidal maniac wandered onto your ranch during a snowstorm out in the middle of nowhere and randomly picked out your father as his or her next victim."

"Well said, Margaret," Lisa commented and turned back to Christopher. "Sam Damon has contacted me, asking that we select one of your father's suits and bring it to his mortuary later today."

"Why didn't he just pick up the stupid suit yesterday?"

"Perhaps he thought the time wasn't right to bring that up. Or it could be because the medical examiner riding back to John Day in his hearse kept tapping the horn. But it's neither here nor there. You're going to assist me in picking out a suit, and then you're going to deliver it to Sam."

Al broke in. "I'm sorry, Mrs. Drake, but before the two of you attend to picking out a suit, I don't believe we've asked all of our questions."

"I have one for both Mrs. Drake and her son, Detective," Hollis said.

"Would you please join us, Mrs. Drake?" Bach asked.

She eyed her watch and took a seat. "What is your question, Trooper Jones?"

"We were supposed to meet Mr. Drake at Poison Spring, but he had driven a few miles further up the ranch road and parked near a fossil formation. That's where we found him, still inside his truck. Why might he have driven there instead of waiting for us at Poison Spring?"

"It's possible he was checking on our other bulls, which are kept in the lower pasture and away from the cows and calves until breeding season," Lisa said.

Christopher scoffed and shook his head at that response.

"But he was probably meeting someone. Likely a woman," she volunteered.

"You should talk to Corky Edwards," Christopher added.

"We will," I assured him.

I'd never met Corky Edwards, but I thought it unlikely the woman drove back here from Bend yesterday, murdered Mike Drake, and returned to be at her husband's bedside at the hospital. Even knowing she had access to a snowmobile, what would have motivated her to kill her neighbor now?

I sighed. "I'm sorry to ask this next question, but is there anyone else we should interview who might've gone to meet him there?"

"Sandy Connor. She boards a horse here," Lisa said.

"All right," I continued. "And for good measure, I'd like a list of everyone who boards horses here."

"Would you fetch the list, please, Christopher?"

"Yes, Mother." He stood and left the room.

Once her son had removed himself, she turned back to me. "You might talk to Charlotte Johnson, just up the road past the Edwardses' place. Her husband is gone a lot, and Mike was doing his usual drill of frequently mentioning her name."

"His usual drill?" Al asked.

"I don't know how to put this any other way, but I think he was grooming himself in preparation for grooming her."

"You mean he was giving himself permission over time to approach her about having sexual relations with him?" I asked.

"Yes. He was a man obsessed with lechery. It's why we stopped going to church."

"Were you still attending the First Christian Church in John Day?"

"Yes, Margaret. I so regret leaving that congregation. And there was no question we could ever join another."

"Mrs. Drake?"

"Yes, Trooper Jones."

"Your son said Mrs. Edwards's relationship with your husband ended years ago. Why would Christopher tell us that Roger Edwards would be at the top of his list of suspects if he hadn't had a stroke and been in the hospital when the murder occurred?"

"I can answer that." Christopher had returned with the list of those boarding their horses on the property. "This past Sunday, he asked me if Corky and Father had an affair several years ago, and I answered him honestly."

"Why on earth would you ever do that, Christopher?" his mother chided.

"It was in the context of a larger conversation about the rift between our two families. I guess Corky told him she couldn't stand being in the same room with you after you had insulted her unforgivably."

"I never would've done that," Lisa exclaimed. "She was one of my favorite people in all the world, and I was devastated when she stopped speaking to me."

There was something about these last revelations that now made me less sure that Corky Edwards was unlikely to have driven back from Bend just to kill the bastard who may have unwittingly triggered her husband's stroke.

"Mrs. Drake, Christopher," Bach began. "I know there's the matter of delivering a suit to Sam Damon, but given what has emerged in our conversation to this point, it's become clear to me that we need to interview you separately and officially."

Christopher laughed. "You mean like on cop shows?"

"Except we won't be handcuffing you and entertaining you with the good-cop- bad-cop routine," Al assured him.

The detective's response didn't inspire me to laugh out loud, but I did wonder what happened to that staid, no-nonsense, straight-arrow police officer I met a couple of years ago.

7

MIDDAY, APRIL 8

We hadn't discussed the possibility of conducting formal interviews, but the detective had now made the call. And even though my gut still told me neither had actually killed the paterfamilias, I wasn't about to counter Al's decision.

The three of us gathered just outside of the sitting room and closed the door behind us.

"Who should we interview first?" Bach asked in a voice hardly above a whisper.

"Lisa Drake is not a flight risk in my estimation, if we decide to begin with Christopher. And I honestly think he's only slightly more of a flight risk," I reasoned.

"I'd agree with that," Hollis said. "I like the idea of beginning with Christopher. He's a little looser, and he might tell us something more useful than his mother would."

"All right, sounds reasonable. We'll start with the son."

We rejoined our witnesses, who stood several feet apart and appeared to be anxious or lost, I couldn't tell which.

"Mrs. Drake, would you please wait in the foyer?"

"I would prefer the kitchen, Margaret, if that's okay. I missed breakfast this morning and would like a bite to eat. I promise, I won't abscond. Anyway, I have nowhere to go."

"Sure, just remain on the first floor."

"That means I can't pick out a suit for Mike once I finish eating. His room is upstairs."

Not that it would surprise me at this juncture, but that last comment made it seem as though her husband had slept in a separate room.

"I believe we can allow that, Mrs. Drake."

I glanced at Bach in case he had an objection, but sensing none, I moved on.

"And I meant to offer this earlier, but we can also deliver the suit to Sam Damon for you."

"That would be so helpful."

And no trouble, really. More importantly, it would give us an opportunity to collect his boots from the mortuary and compare them to the casts we'd taken in the vicinity of the dead bull.

"Go ahead and fix yourself something to eat," I said. "We should be done with Christopher's interview shortly."

She turned to her son. "Are you hungry?"

"No, Mother. I'm fine."

She flashed a wan smile and departed, leaving the rest of us standing uncomfortably in the sitting room.

I seated myself on the chocolate-colored leather settee and removed the recorder and a waiver form from my pack. Al sat next to me, and Hollis seated himself in one of the matching chairs across from the settee.

Right on cue, Christopher took the other matching chair and addressed Detective Bach. "How does this go, then?"

"Sergeant Blackthorne will begin the questioning."

"Our forensics guy also asked for family members' fingerprints," I added.

Hollis quickly took care of getting Christopher's prints. I turned on the recorder, read him his rights, and passed him a waiver form to sign, which he did with a flourish.

"Tell us about your morning yesterday after your father discovered the slaughtered bull and came back to the house to collect his handgun," I began. "That's also when he contacted me at our police station in John Day."

"I didn't know he'd taken his gun along with him yesterday."

"According to your mother, he came back to the house for it. It was also found in the glove compartment of the truck where we discovered his body."

"What time did Father call your office, Sergeant?"

"Around eight fifteen."

"I was up shortly after that and downstairs eating my breakfast. Then I called my girlfriend, and we met up at the store in Kimberly just down the road, around nine. We were planning to grab a coffee there, but they were closed. The snow, I guess. Anyway, I went back home after that."

"What time did you arrive back at Poison Spring Ranch?"

"I was probably gone no more than twenty minutes. We sat in my truck —the older Ram parked out front—and talked for a bit."

"And you were here when we arrived just after nine thirty."

"Yeah, that's right. I'd just gotten back from Kimberly."

"And your girlfriend's name?"

"Lydia Reed. She helps her dad run the small spread they own west of Kimberly."

"What's the address?"

"Have no idea. I just know which small spread she lives at."

"But the name Reed is on the mailbox?"

"Probably, I guess. Are you going to talk to her?"

"We'll need to, yes. Her phone number, please?"

He reeled off the cell number, and Hollis pulled one of his business cards out of his pocket and wrote it down on the back.

"You seemed very upset yesterday when you learned your father had been killed. Today, not so much," I said, switching gears.

"Is that a question?"

"Tell me about your relationship with your father."

"I used to look up to him as a kid, and then I got older and realized what an ass he was. And not just to Mother and me. Cheated his friends and made light of it."

"Which friends?" Al asked.

"Well, Roger Edwards, for one. And not just because he slept with the man's wife. He also often infringed on Roger's priority water rights, which were established long before Father bought the ranch."

"I've learned water rights are a major deal out here," Hollis put in.

"They are, but Father couldn't have cared less."

"Because?" Hollis asked.

"He saw himself as a big-shot rancher. Someone nobody could touch. Thought he could do whatever he wanted and get away with it. And mostly he did get away with it."

Hollis continued down the water rights path. "Did he steal water from any other neighbors?"

"I'm sure he did."

Hollis kept digging. "Anything else that might've affected neighbors?"

I liked his line of questioning here. Obviously, someone was pissed at the guy.

"I can't think of anything else right now, but there's probably a lot I don't know about."

"Why did you stick around?" I asked. "I mean, it sounds like he might've been pretty thoughtless about you and your mother, as well as some of your neighbors."

"I stayed for Mother. I didn't care what he said or did to me, but his constant berating of her killed a bit of her soul. And the more he dished out, the more she faded away."

"Was he physically abusive?" Bach asked.

"Maybe one time when I was a boy. It was Christmastime, and something happened. There were no visible signs of it, but I could tell he'd hurt her in a different way. He even stayed away from the ranch for a week or so. After that, they slept in different rooms."

"Did anything in particular happen between them in the days leading up to yesterday morning?" Hollis asked.

"I don't know if anything happened before he drove out and found the bull, but they did have a fight a few nights ago. Not physical, but lots of loud back-and-forth."

"You didn't intervene?" Hollis asked.

"They were locked in her room and ignored my banging on the door and shouts to stop."

"Sounds to me like your mother may be stronger than you believe, Christopher."

"Well, Sergeant Blackthorne, she did outlive him, I guess."

I didn't know what to think of that response, but I decided to push this line of questioning a little further. "Is it possible your mother drove out there and shot him to death?"

"Shot him with what? You said he took the .22 with him."

"Your family doesn't own other guns?"

"Nope."

"That surprises me, I guess," I said, continuing on that track. "How about hunting rifles?"

"Well, we've never hunted, so again the answer is no. Guns have not been of much interest in this household. And Father only bought the .22 after receiving threatening letters from a dissatisfied constituent when he was a county commissioner."

Harry had mentioned he didn't think the .22 had ever been fired.

"Did you ever learn who sent the threatening letters?" Hollis asked.

"No."

Hollis continued, "Was he still getting these letters?"

"Those stopped after he was no longer a commissioner."

"Are they available for us to read through?"

"I have no idea, but Mother may know."

The guy was in the habit of scratching his arms and the back of his neck. A nervous tic I'd noticed before, and one he was occupying himself with quite a bit during our questioning. He was also avoiding looking directly at his interviewers. Of course, this wasn't a normal conversation we were having. A police interrogation often brought out the nervous tics and downcast eyes in people.

"Christopher," Al said. "Why did you have the conversation with Mr. Edwards about your father's affair with his wife?"

"Roger and I had become close friends, but we rarely talked about family matters. I didn't see the harm in answering him honestly when he asked the question. I realize now it might've been a mistake."

Bach was puzzled. "What do you mean by that?"

The younger man put his head in his hands. "Did it cause his stroke? That would be hard to live with."

I'd had the same thought about his revelation having triggered Mr. Edwards's stroke, but lots of things can trip that switch.

"Do we have any more questions for Christopher?" the detective asked.

Hollis replied first. "I don't. Not at this time, anyway."

"Just one," I said and looked directly at Christopher. "Did you kill your father?"

"I had no idea where he even was yesterday morning, so while it's not unimaginable, I suppose, I didn't shoot my father to death."

"All right, Mr. Drake. In the meantime, you're not to leave the county until we give you the all clear, and we may need to question you again as we go along," Bach said and shut off the recorder.

"But my girlfriend, Lydia, lives just across the county line. Does this mean I can't go to her place?"

He sounded awfully young just then.

Al blushed and turned to me.

"He's right, the county line is just spitting distance from Kimberly."

"I'll make an exception and say you're not to leave the county or travel beyond your girlfriend's home."

"Thank you."

~

After her prints were taken and she had been Mirandized and signed a waiver, Lisa sighed heavily. "I can't believe this is happening to us."

"Mrs. Drake," Al said calmly. "We'll try to make this as brief as we possibly can."

She nodded. "I understand this is your job, Detective Bach."

The detective gave me the sign to begin the interview.

I clicked the recorder back on. "Mrs. Drake, please describe the events of yesterday morning up until Trooper Jones and I arrived."

"When we finished breakfast, Mike took a quick shower. Soon after that, I heard his phone ringing up in his room, and then he bounded down the stairs, got his jacket from the coat closet, and left the house. He drove away as fast as the snow would allow."

"How long was he gone before coming back to get his gun and call our office?" I asked.

She sipped the tea she had brought to the sitting room with her. "Twenty or twenty-five minutes, I think."

"And he planned to go back to Poison Spring and wait until we got there?"

Lisa thought about that question. "I assumed that was his plan, but now that I think back on it, he didn't really say that. But it is where I told you he was waiting for you. I mean, why would he be waiting for you anywhere else?"

A good question.

"Mrs. Drake?" Hollis began, his voice deep and calm.

"Yes, Trooper Jones"

"How soon did he leave the house again after making the call to our office?"

"Right away."

He continued. "That's a long time to stay out there and wait for us to arrive."

"As I mentioned before, my husband didn't keep me apprised of his plans or his comings and goings."

"Were you surprised when you learned he wasn't waiting at Poison Spring for the police to arrive?"

She paused. "Not particularly, I guess, Trooper Jones."

"Were you surprised when you learned he had been shot to death?" I couldn't help but ask.

"Now that surprised me. Mike Drake was invincible, or so I thought."

Silence filled the sitting room, except for the pendulum's steady rhythm counting time from the tall grandfather clock in the corner.

I cleared my throat. "Christopher mentioned a couple of things I'd like to ask you about. He said guns had never been of interest in your household, not even hunting rifles. Is that correct?"

"Mike's father was killed in a hunting accident many years ago. Shot by one of his father's brothers who mistook him for a buck mule deer. So, no, there wasn't a gun in the house for most of our married life."

"According to Christopher, Mike purchased the gun after he started receiving threatening letters," I said.

"Yes, when he was an elected official. It was so strange. He had been adamant about having no guns on our property. Even the folks boarding horses here have had to agree to that."

"What about the letters?"

"I'd forgotten about those. He received them while he was a county commissioner."

"Did he ever figure out who sent them?" I asked.

"If he did, he didn't tell me. But it's at least possible he learned the sender's identity. And if that's the case, I can't imagine Mike letting it go."

"Meaning?" Bach asked.

Lisa almost smiled. "He would've found some way to get his revenge."

The detective continued. "Do you know if he kept the letters?"

"I suspect they'd be somewhere in his room if he did."

"Do we have your permission to search his room, Mrs. Drake?" Al asked.

"You have my permission to search the entire house if you'd like. The barn, stable, and other outbuildings too. Christopher and I have nothing to hide," she said.

I had my doubts about that in general. Everyone had something they wanted to keep hidden.

I took a sip from the glass of water I'd poured myself earlier and moved on. "Did you notice Christopher leaving the house yesterday morning after his breakfast?"

Momentarily confused, Lisa cocked her head slightly. "Uh, yes. He went to meet up with Lydia in Kimberly for coffee. She's his girlfriend."

"You saw him drive toward the highway?"

"What do you mean?"

"I'm attempting to verify that he drove toward the highway, which would take him to Kimberly, and not on the ranch road toward Poison Spring."

"Well, I was in the kitchen when he left, and I would've seen him take the ranch road toward Poison Spring, but that's not the direction he drove, Margaret."

"I just needed to make sure," I said, rather too coyly.

"I don't think he even knew Mike had driven that direction."

I'd somehow hit a nerve, so I took it a bit farther. "When did Christopher learn about the dead bull?"

"What does that have to do with...?"

"When did he learn the bull had been slaughtered?" I pressed.

She calmed herself and thought the question through. "As I mentioned yesterday, my son was still in bed when his father first took off in the morning and when he came back for his gun. I neglected to mention the bull's demise before Christopher left to meet up with Lydia. In fact, I didn't tell him about that until you arrived looking to speak with Mike about it."

"Would you also like a glass of water, Mrs. Drake?" I inquired.

"No, I'm fine, Margaret. Thank you."

I noticed her trembling slightly, and I reminded myself we were doing what was needed to get to the bottom of a homicide case.

Hollis took a turn at clearing his throat. "Mrs. Drake, Christopher mentioned you and Mr. Drake had had an argument a few nights ago. Is there anything you'd like to tell us about that?"

"Mike wanted to start charging Christopher rent. My husband paid him a stipend to help out on the ranch. Our son's primary chores are to run our horse-boarding business and oversee predator management. He also helps out when workload increases during haying season and spring calving. I was adamantly opposed to charging him rent."

"May I ask why?" Hollis asked.

"Christopher works hard and earns barely anything. And I've been hoping—praying, really—that his relationship with Lydia becomes serious, becomes a marriage. That he comes to realize he can live his own life. Here on the ranch or in his own home."

I had a sudden desire to cut to the chase. "Mrs. Drake, did you drive out there yesterday, find your husband, and shoot him to death?"

"That's ludicrous, really. I'd hardly wait until we had a freak snowstorm to drive the ranch road and confront the husband with whom I've shared a complicated life, particularly since I would have no idea how to load, let alone shoot, a gun."

I paused. "Detective, I believe that's a wrap."

"I agree," he said. "Thank you, Mrs. Drake. We may have more questions for you in the future. And that means you need to remain in the county until we let you know otherwise."

8

AFTERNOON, APRIL 8

After ending the formal interviews of mother and son, something about Mike Drake's ban on guns at Poison Spring Ranch—with the exception of the likely never-used .22—still seemed counter to what I'd come to believe about ranch operations. Which, admittedly, wasn't based on actual knowledge or experience.

"Your mother tells us you're in charge of running the horse-boarding operation here at the ranch, and also something called predator management," I mentioned to Christopher, who had rejoined the rest of us in the sitting room.

"That's correct, I am."

"I'm pretty sure I have a general understanding of what's involved in the first, but what does predator management entail?"

"I wondered about that too," Hollis put in.

"No guns, if that's what you're getting at. And if we have to stop any repeat offenders capable of thwarting our deterrents and killing livestock, we hire somebody to trap and remove them to national forest land. Usually, the culprit would be a cougar or a wolf."

"Not coyotes?" I asked.

"Oh, they're definitely a problem, especially during calving season. But we've installed high-tensile electric fencing and made sure they can't dig under it. Plus we use hazing—you know, loud noises broadcast over speakers—if we have to. And we utilize guard dogs."

That explained the large kennel next to the barn.

"And the fencing, noise, and dogs prevent predation by wild animals?"

"Most of it. Listen, every rancher has to deal with this issue." The guy was on a roll now. "And we all can legally destroy most predators that kill or maim our stock, but here on our spread, we use other means to minimize the problem."

For the first time, it struck me that Christopher might not be the odd duck I had always found him to be. All said and done, I suspected most of us appeared odd from time to time.

"And as you know, Fish and Wildlife folks aren't fans of the killing of wild animals," he added. "We're not either. And that included Father."

"Would anyone like tea?" Lisa asked tiredly. "I'm making another pot for myself, and I'd be happy to share."

"I'd love a cup, thank you," the detective said.

"Mrs. Drake, before you leave," I said, "you had offered to let us go through the house and outbuildings. Unless Detective Bach has an objection, I would like to search your husband's room for those anonymous letters."

"I was going to make the same request," Bach said. "I also think you and Trooper Jones can handle that. In the meantime, if you'll excuse me, I have a couple of calls to make out in my vehicle."

"Mike's room is upstairs, Margaret. Take the hallway on the left, and his is the first room also on the left. But first let me jot down the password to open his small safe."

Lisa rose and moved to the desk near the sitting room window, returning shortly with a page of stationery. *Poison Spring Ranch* embossed in gold served as the letterhead.

"That safe has been around a long time," she said, handing me the piece of matte paper.

"I'm curious, how is it that you know the password?" I asked after noting the combination.

"Mike wouldn't have seen a reason for me not to know it. Even these last many years."

"Is it in reference to someone you know?"

"The first part is my middle name and also the name we had planned to give our stillborn daughter."

That caught me off guard, and Lisa appeared to view my silence as a signal to take her leave. "If you have everything you need, I'd like to make that tea now."

I continued. "Have you ever opened the safe and checked out the contents?"

She glanced at her son. "Once, many years ago."

"One other question," I said. "Might he have changed the password?"

"No."

Lisa left the room without waiting for another possible follow-up question, but I didn't have one for her anyway. I signaled for Hollis to join me, and we left Christopher to fend for himself and climbed the stairs.

I didn't know if my partner had any preconceived notions about what Mike Drake's bedroom might look like, but I was astonished when we opened the door. It was clean and organized the way one might expect Buddhist monks to keep their cells—spotless, undecorated, and sparsely furnished.

After gloving up, I went after the safe stashed in the corner of his color-coordinated clothes closet, punching in the password, KATE_89. I pulled out several heavy ledgers from days of yore, a stack of bound mail, and a few stories clipped out of the *Blue Mountain Eagle*, our local newspaper. The articles recounted some of the positions he'd taken or decisions he'd made as a Grant County Commissioner.

In the meantime, Hollis carefully rummaged through the dead man's dresser drawers.

"Not much here," he soon noted. "Unless you count his collection of silk socks."

"No wool socks?"

"There are socks of every flavor."

"I might have the threatening letters," I responded.

"Let's hope so."

"Let's hope they tell us something."

"We'll need to get Mrs. Drake's permission to check out the laptop over there on the desk," he pointed out. "And hopefully she or her son knows the password."

"I wouldn't be surprised if it's some version of the password that opens the safe. I'm betting he was a guy who stuck to his quirks and habits, not to mention his passwords. But we still need to get her permission to check it out."

"I could go ask her," Holly suggested.

"Good idea. I think she's kind of tired of me today."

"How would that ever happen?"

"Go."

I set the ledgers and newspaper articles on the desk and began going through the bundle of mail. There were thirteen altogether; they all arrived sporadically thirteen years before and during the summer. Drake's name and address were typed on the front of the envelopes, and the postmarks indicated they had been mailed from John Day. Each and every note contained the same unsigned message spelled out in capital letters clipped out of magazines: *YOU FUCKED OVER THE WRONG PERSON.*

"You were right." Hollis had returned from speaking with Lisa about the laptop. "It's the same password. Also, Mrs. Drake gave no sign of hesitation when I asked for permission to look through his computer. Christopher had joined her in the kitchen, and he seemed a bit reluctant, but then he didn't raise any concerns."

"Look at this, Holly."

I had laid out the anonymous letters across the bed, and he scanned the display. "How long ago did he receive these?"

"Thirteen years ago."

He added up the number of letters. "And thirteen pieces of correspondence with the exact same angry message."

"After you fire up the computer, look up the county's website, see if they keep a list of the years that past commissioners served."

Hollis sat at the desk and opened the laptop. In no time, he'd brought up the county government's website. "I'm afraid they don't list the names of previous county commissioners."

"Don't worry, we'll ask Lisa when he retired or decided not to run again."

"Why are you interested in that?"

"I'd like to know if it was thirteen years ago when he left office. See if we might be looking at some kind of a pattern here."

"Don't tell me you believe that old superstition about the number thirteen being an omen of bad luck."

"I'm not susceptible to that, but maybe Drake was. One thing's for sure, he was killed thirteen years after he received those thirteen letters."

"Can't say I disagree with that," he said, scanning the letters again. "They were all mailed from John Day."

"Yep. Which probably means nothing definitive. Could've been someone who worked or lived in John Day. Or could've been someone who came from a nearby town to mail copycat letters addressed to a county commissioner in the belief it would be less noticeable."

"Would anyone even pay attention?"

"Any postal worker out in one of our dinky burgs definitely might've noticed."

"I suppose."

"Anyway, I'm going to go ask mother and son for more details about Mike's reaction to the letters when they first started arriving. I'm also going to see if they remember these articles from the *Blue Mountain Eagle* and if they were of concern to him. Meanwhile, you do your magic checking out his laptop."

"Will do, Sarge."

～

I had remembered to ask Hollis for the keys to his Tahoe before heading back downstairs. I was starving, and I planned to fetch our lunches out of his cooler after speaking with Lisa Drake and her son. I found them sitting at the small kitchen table, sipping tea and chatting.

"Sorry to interrupt," I said.

"That's fine, Margaret. We were just talking about which suit to send along with you to the mortuary."

"We should be done upstairs soon, I believe."

"Thank you for letting us know."

I sat in an empty chair across from them. "I do have a couple of questions for you. When did Mike decide not to run for county commissioner?"

"He stepped down in the middle of his last term, which would've been over a dozen years ago."

"Father had pretty much had it with being an elected official. And then those anonymous letters began arriving," Christopher added.

"The letters were the last straw?"

They simultaneously affirmed that to be the case.

"We'll need to take the letters with us as possible evidence. If it turns out there's no connection, we'll return them as soon as we can."

Lisa turned to her son. "I don't believe we have any need for those old letters. What do you think?"

"I agree," he said.

I showed them the newspaper articles. "Anything in these that you remember in particular? As in, some people got riled about what appeared in any of these stories?"

They pored over the articles for a short time until Lisa said she didn't remember there being any blowback from anything in the newspaper. Her son expressed his tacit agreement. After which, something having nothing to do with the letters unexpectedly occurred to me.

"Oh, and should we have questions about business operations on the ranch, who is your accountant?"

Christopher laughed. "That would be me. I'm a CPA and everything."

"I should've guessed that. Anyway, I can't really think of what information we might want to review at this point, but I'll let you know as the case goes forward."

"I can tell you the ranch is quite solvent. Father and I were as one on that point."

"Margaret, were you able to reach out to Sheriff Norton about the bull?"

I'd forgotten to mention that to her. "I apologize, I intended to say something earlier. He plans to travel out here sometime today, and he hoped Jen Wilson, the veterinarian, would be able to accompany him."

"Thank you for that."

"And I'm afraid I thought of yet another question. We have access to Mike's phone, but would either of you be able to give us the password?"

"Correct me if I'm wrong, Christopher, but your father used his phone strictly for making calls, right?"

"That's correct, Mother."

"I don't even think he sent texts, and I'm relatively sure he would never have used it to check email remotely or follow any news channel. He might've looked up something on the internet by phone, but I doubt it."

"So are you saying there's nothing available in the phone for us to look at?"

"I doubt there is anything of significance to see, really, but what I was trying to tell you is that he used the same password for his phone that he used on his safe and computer upstairs."

Just as I had thought.

"Mother's right again. Father was very much the troglodyte when it came to technology."

~

I stepped outside and listened to the melting snow falling from the Lombardy poplars. The sky was as clear as I'd ever seen, the sun's bright rays banking off the rolling hills and lighting up the layers of fossil sediment and olivine basalt. I loved this part of the world for the very fact of its wide-ranging terrain, strange beauty, and endless solitude.

I left off my momentary reverie and retrieved the cooler from Hollis's rig. Detective Bach had stepped out of his Interceptor and was also walking back toward the ranch house, carrying his thermos.

"Are you just about done in there?" he asked.

"I think so, Al."

"I'm going to be heading back to Bend shortly."

"Another homicide?"

"No, my wife is ill. She may need to be hospitalized."

"I'm so sorry."

"I don't think it's serious, but I need to be there."

"I understand, really I do."

"Be sure to call me if you need anything. And I'll keep you apprised."

"You know we will. What about Dr. Lewis?"

"That was one of the calls I made. She's booked a flight back to Bend later this afternoon. And she doesn't yet have much to tell us regarding the victim's chest wound."

He held up his thermos. "I'm hoping Mrs. Drake still has some hot tea left over."

"Let's go see."

I reached to open the front door, but Lisa did so before I could.

"I saw you two coming up the walk," she said. "I just made another pot of tea, Detective."

He blushed. "You shouldn't have gone to the trouble."

"Yeah, we're not used to folks being so accommodating after they've been interrogated," I added.

She shrugged. "Is that a cooler, Margaret?"

"It is. Trooper Jones and I stashed our lunches inside before we left the office."

"You're welcome to eat in the kitchen or the dining room. Or, if you prefer, you can have lunch in the sunroom upstairs, where there's a wonderful view."

"I don't want to be a bother."

"It's no bother. We haven't had this much company in an age."

Her definition of *company* was rather expansive.

"Besides, Christopher is in the office working, and I plan to do some reading in the sitting room. At least until you're done upstairs."

"I appreciate the offer of the sunroom," I said.

"It's just through the door directly at the top of the stairs," she began. "And Detective Bach, help yourself to tea. You'll find the teapot on the stove."

She slipped out of the foyer and into the sitting room.

"Maggie, I'll call you later today to check in."

"Drive carefully, Al."

And then he did something he had never done before. He paused and gave me a hug prior to moving toward the kitchen. Afterward, I turned and made my way back upstairs, where I found Hollis still perusing Mike Drake's laptop.

"You've been gone for a while," he said. "I thought maybe you found a nice soft bed to take a nap on."

"I wish. What's the word?"

"The guy was kind of boring. There's nothing of interest on his computer, and when I say nothing, I mean not a thing."

"No incriminating emails or web searches?"

"Nada. Although he must have been planning to write a book. He'd written the beginnings of an outline and what I guess is the opening paragraph."

"Really? Fiction or nonfiction?"

"Well, it starts off with the murder of a powerful billionaire, so I'm guessing it's fiction."

"Whoa. That doesn't sound all that boring, and you're sure it's fictional?"

"Well, the working title is, or was, I guess, *The Revenge of Billionaire Bob*. But if you had any doubt about it being fictional, read the opening paragraph."

I scanned it. "Oh. I see what you mean. Let me see the outline."

"Sure." He pulled it up.

"Um...Well, I guess most of us dream of doing something we're not really cut out for."

"Yeah, I always wanted to be a singer."

"Really? Me too."

We laughed, and I was glad I'd remembered to close the door.

"But we should print all of that out in case there's more to it than meets the eye," I said.

He removed the pages from the printer next to the laptop. "Already done."

"All right, I think we're finished here. Let's close up and go eat our lunches."

"In the kitchen or the dining room?"

"We were invited to eat in the sunroom up here on the second floor."

∼

Lisa had been right about the view. The space was wall-to-wall windows that overlooked a small orchard. Any remaining patches of snow were melting quickly, and the one-day snowstorm didn't appear to have damaged the trees or blossoming fruit.

We collected our lunch litter and stashed it in the cooler. Having finished our search of Drake's bedroom, we traipsed back downstairs and entered the sitting room. Lisa was still there but ending a phone call with someone. She signaled for us to take a seat.

"Thank you for letting me know, Maeve. I'll talk to Christopher about attending and get back to you." She hung up. "Oh dear, apparently several neighbors are upset about Mike's death. A community meeting is planned for tomorrow night at the school cafeteria in Monument."

Monument was about fourteen miles northwest of Kimberly up Highway 402.

"What's the purpose of the meeting?" I asked.

"Something about discussing the murders that've occurred in the area over the last few years."

Hollis and I knew all about those.

"We've investigated all seven other homicides in Grant County in the last two years, along with Detective Bach, and we brought the killers to justice in every case."

"Then you should be there. It starts at seven," she said. "That was Maeve Robertson on the phone. She and her husband, Clell, board their horses here. Anyway, Clell is spearheading the gathering."

I looked at Hollis, and he indicated his agreement.

"We wouldn't miss it, Lisa."

9

LATE AFTERNOON, APRIL 8

Sheriff Cal Norton and Jen Wilson, the county's one veterinarian, arrived shortly before four o'clock. Thanks to the switch to daylight savings time a few weeks back, they had at least three more hours to assess the state of the dead bull.

Hollis, Christopher Drake, and I had led them out to Poison Spring, and the five of us now flanked the carcass.

"We estimated the animal had been dead for about twelve hours when we arrived just before ten yesterday morning," Hollis explained.

Christopher shook his head. "This wasn't the work of any predator I know about."

"No, and the state of the remains are exactly like the bull I examined in Harney County a few years ago," Jen began. "It wasn't killed by a predator either, as far as I could tell. And as is the case here, it wasn't shot, but definitely drained of its blood, and the tongue and testicles had been removed."

"How could this happen?" the sheriff asked.

"In all the cases I know about, Cal, no one has come up with anything but a theory," Jen replied.

"What were those again, Hollis?" I said.

"A cult or space aliens that leave no tracks or some kind of bird."

"A weird bird if that's the case," Christopher put in.

"I don't know if I'd prefer a deranged cult or space aliens over a weird bird," I added.

Jen sighed. "The cuts look surgical to me. Not sure any bird could do that."

"I'm going to call County Animal Services and ask them to come out and remove the bull," Cal said.

"I would appreciate that," Christopher answered. "I've heard about other ranchers finding their animals mutilated this way. But I do have a question for anyone who may have an answer. Are these...I don't know what to call them. Attacks on livestock, I guess. Are they limited to cattle?"

"As far as I know," Jen began, "these events have only occurred in cattle herds, but they're not strictly focused on bulls. The animals are always left bloodless, and their sex organs are removed. Sometimes other body parts too."

"How often has this happened?" Christopher asked.

"Recently, several cows were similarly killed over a one-week period next door in Crook County. That was unusual, I think. But these events have been going on sporadically in the western US for decades," Sheriff Norton summed up.

"So it sounds like this is a mystery none of us here will be able to solve," Hollis reasoned.

"Seems like it," Cal answered. "But I'll make a call to the sheriffs of neighboring counties and ask about their experience with these cases."

"And I'll forward you the photos I took yesterday when Hollis and I arrived, Cal. Not sure those will be helpful in any way, but you never know."

"Thanks, Maggie. Appreciate that."

"Would you send those to me as well, Maggie?" Jen asked.

"Sure."

"And I'd like to take a tissue sample," she added.

"I, for one, would appreciate that, Jen," Christopher said. "And I'd like to know what you find, if anything."

"Sure. I have everyone's email, I believe. So I'll send all of you the results."

～

It had been a while since I'd had a conversation with Jen, someone I'd known for most of my life. After I moved back to John Day with Louie, my aging kitty, she had nursed him back to health several times before he wandered off to feline heaven. But I hadn't yet introduced her to Raleigh Cat, Louie's alter ego.

"You have a new pet?" she said when I mentioned our adoption of Raleigh Cat.

"We do," I replied, standing next to the passenger-side window of the sheriff's vehicle. Jen was waiting for him to finish with the dude from County Animal Services.

"And very soon a new baby, from the looks of things."

"Due in a couple of weeks."

"What are you doing out here, then?"

"I'm pregnant, not on my deathbed."

"What does Duncan have to say about you continuing to work?"

"Did you try telling Vicky when and where she could go two weeks before your baby girl was due?"

"She would never have put up with that."

"Uh-huh, that's right."

"Please say you're being careful, Maggie."

"I'm being careful." About as careful as I ever was. "And how are Vicky and little Victoria?"

"Great. We've started calling Victoria *Tori* 'cause she's a terror. But damn cute."

Sheriff Norton had finished up with the Animal Services guy and climbed back in his Ford truck.

"It was good to see you, Cal," I said. "And I wanted to let you know there's a community meeting tomorrow night at seven at the school cafeteria in Monument. Friends of Mike Drake, upset about his death, organized the event to talk about all of the recent homicides in the county."

"Monument, huh?"

"Yeah. Hollis and I will be at the meeting. We investigated the other seven murders in Grant County over the last couple of years, and I think those cases, along with murder number eight here, will be the topic of conversation at this event. Your presence would be an indication of support and much appreciated by us."

"Because I'm the elected Grant County Sheriff, I get it. Chosen by the people and all that."

"It's totally up to you and your schedule, but three law enforcement types is one more than two."

"I see your point, Maggie. It's just that's a long way out there at the end of the day."

I bit my tongue.

He started his rig. "All right, you talked me into it. See you there."

"See you there, Cal. And Jen, I'll bring Raleigh Cat in to get checked out soon."

They both said their goodbyes and headed off, followed by the Animal Services truck, which now carried the remains of the dead bull.

After they left, I met back up with Hollis and Christopher. "We should mosey after we drop Christopher back off at the ranch house."

"I think I'll walk back," he said.

"You sure?" I asked.

"Yeah, I do that a lot out here."

"We'll be in touch," I said and got in on the passenger side of Holly's Tahoe.

As we moved back down the ranch road, I looked back at Christopher. He had stopped to pick a few flowers from a bush of purple prairie clover.

∼

Hollis and I retrieved the suit and other accoutrements Lisa had collected for us to take to Sam Damon. Afterward, we decided to pay a visit to Lydia Reed, Christopher's girlfriend. We needed to confirm he had visited her the previous day around the time his father was likely murdered. Neither of us seriously considered him a suspect. But despite Lisa saying she would've noticed Christopher driving toward Poison Spring yesterday morning after her husband returned to the ranch house to retrieve his gun, there was no certainty of that.

Before pulling out onto the highway, Hollis dug his wallet out of his back pocket and removed the business card on which he'd jotted down the girlfriend's phone number. He passed it to me and drove on toward Kimberly.

I brought out my phone and dialed the number. She answered on the fourth ring.

"Lydia Reed here," she said, her voice brimming with confidence.

"Ms. Reed, I'm Oregon State Police Sergeant Blackthorne."

"How can I help you?"

"We're investigating the murder of Mike Drake. We'd like to speak to you briefly and in person. At the moment, we're on our way from Poison Spring Ranch and driving toward Kimberly."

"So remain on Highway 19, drive about three miles past the Kimberly store and the junction with Highway 402. Our place is on the left. We have a green metal gate that's currently open. See you when you get here."

Within a few minutes we pulled onto the property. I assumed the woman wearing a black down jacket and sitting on the porch steps of the house was Lydia Reed. We parked and moved out of the Tahoe to the porch.

"Ms. Reed?" I asked.

"Yep."

"I'm Sergeant Blackthorne, and this is Senior Trooper Jones."

"Is she your boss?" the woman asked Hollis.

"She is indeed."

Ms. Reed cocked her head and made some kind of assessment of me. "What is it you wanted to speak to me about, Sergeant?"

"You're aware that Mike Drake, owner of Poison Spring Ranch, was murdered yesterday?"

"Of course. Chris stayed with me last night."

"We have a couple of questions for you."

"What do you want to know?"

"Did you meet him at the store in Kimberly yesterday morning?"

"Yes, we had hoped to grab a cup of coffee, but the store was closed."

"What time did he meet you there?"

"A little after nine. We chatted for a few minutes. And then we both drove back to our respective ranches."

"All right," I said. "We appreciate your time."

"No problem. Chris is a good friend. And I can tell you, he wouldn't hurt a flea. Or carry a gun, let alone shoot his old man."

"Did you know his father?"

"The man was an asshole who considered himself a big shot. Robbed water from my pop's small ranch for years."

"What did Christopher have to say about that?" Hollis asked.

"It was before either of us were born, but I'm pretty sure Chris despised his father for many other reasons."

I stepped slightly closer to her. "Despised him enough to shoot him to death?"

"Like I said, no. Chris is a pacifist. Fucking hates guns, any kind of violence."

"Are the two of you in a relationship?" I asked.

"I'm not sure that's any of your business. But are you asking if we have sex?"

"Whatever you think a relationship entails?"

"What the hell is it called? Oh yeah, we're friends with benefits."

I adjusted my cap. "Thank you for your time."

"I have a question," Hollis put in. "Is your father available to talk to us about the water issue he once had with Mr. Drake?"

"My father is a paraplegic who has lost his ability to comprehend or speak. So, no. He's not available."

"I'm sorry, Ms. Reed."

"It's okay, Trooper. You didn't know. Now, if you both will excuse me, I need to go feed Pops his supper."

~

We got back on the road and headed for John Day. I could tell Hollis was wrestling some with the interaction we'd just had with Lydia Reed. No doubt because of the father and the likelihood the woman ran the ranch and took care of him all on her own. Those kinds of situations often affected Hollis.

I broke the silence. "Lydia Reed is a pretty tough customer."

"I feel bad for her."

"I know, Holly. But she seems like a very strong woman who loves her dad and wants to take care of him."

"Yeah, you're right," he said, moving on. "How about some music?"

My phone rang. I didn't recognize the number, but I answered anyway. "Oregon State Police, Sergeant Blackthorne here."

"Hello, Sergeant. I found your business card when I arrived home and opened the door. My name is Coreen Edwards, but most people call me Corky."

"Yes, Mrs. Edwards. Thank you for getting in touch." I signaled for Hollis to pull to curb. "I'm nearby, and I'd appreciate a few minutes of your time."

"Now?"

"If that's possible, it would be very helpful."

"All right, since you're nearby."

We were a few minutes out and luckily hadn't quite made it all the way back to Poison Spring Ranch or to the Edwardses' place right next door. Passing by the entrance to the ranch, I noted that Lowell Gregg had again come by and was riding his horse at a trot around the paddock. I reminded myself we still needed to have a chat with him and the other horse boarders.

Turning into the Edwardses' property, Hollis pulled up next to a small SUV and parked. We got out, and as was common out here, Mrs. Edwards opened the front door before we had knocked and welcomed us. Inside, their home was tidy but small. Birds were featured everywhere in paintings and photos, on a couple of couch pillows, and on the front of the magazines placed on a coffee table.

The three of us sat in the living room. After we were all seated, she got right to the point.

"How can I help you, officers?"

"First, we'd like to know if you had heard about Mike Drake's murder?" I said.

"Yes. Charlotte Johnson, my neighbor across the way, let me know. It's a terrible thing. And scary."

"That's why we're here and hoping to get to the bottom of it as soon as possible."

"I'm not sure I have anything to offer in the way of information. I've been with my husband, who's in intensive care at the hospital in Bend."

"Yes, we were told," I assured her.

"I came home today to check on our property, and I'm driving back to Bend tomorrow morning."

"Is this the first time you've come back to check on your property?"

"Yes."

"I ask because during the snowstorm on Wednesday, we observed automobile tracks in your driveway and the parking area."

"Someone must've pulled into our place and turned around, I'd guess, because I haven't been back since I drove Roger to the emergency room in Bend."

"We wanted to also ask you about your relationship with Mike Drake. We learned from Christopher that you had an affair with his father at one point in the past, and that he shared that information with your husband."

"What?" Corky Edwards suddenly looked ill. "Why would Christopher tell Roger such a thing?"

"Is it untrue? Because Mrs. Drake told us she was aware of the affair as well."

"Oh my God. She knew?"

So that was a yes, then. Corky Edwards had screwed Mike Drake and screwed over his wife.

"It was one of many such relationships, according to Mrs. Drake," I pointed out.

The woman appeared stunned and suddenly began to weep. Hollis stood and retrieved a box of tissues from the nearby credenza and placed it in her lap.

"Thank you," she managed.

We waited for her to gather herself, and once she did, she had apparently assumed we saw her as a possible suspect. Or at least someone worth taking for a spin.

"I didn't kill Mike Drake. I didn't know about his murder until Charlotte called me."

"When was that?" I asked.

"Wednesday evening."

I made a mental note to ask Charlotte Johnson if and when she had called Corky Edwards and let her know Drake had been dispatched from this Earth.

"Thank you, Mrs. Edwards. I apologize if I upset you," I said.

"I overreacted, I think. I'll call on Lisa and Christopher before I leave in the morning. Offer my condolences."

I stood to leave. "May I also ask where you're staying while your husband is in the Bend hospital?"

She weighed that question for a moment. "Mountain High Motel. It's close to the hospital."

~

After we were back on the road and both quietly mulling over our conversation with Corky Edwards, I decided to call Sherry Linn at the office. I dialed her number at the front counter, and she answered right away.

"Hi, Maggie."

"How was your day?"

"Slow. That is, up until Doug got his rig stuck in the snow out in Logan Valley. Whitey Kern was busy, and since Harry was home and relatively nearby, he met up with Doug and pulled his truck out of the snowdrift he was caught in."

"Glad Harry was available. Tell him to turn in his time," I said.

"Not to worry. That's already happened."

"Good. I just wanted to call and check in with you."

"Harry's here now, and he'd like to know if you got fingerprints of the family members?"

"All taken care of," I said. "Also, we have a set of thirteen threatening letters sent to Mike Drake we'd like Harry to check for prints."

"We're going to the Blue Mountain Lounge for supper, so if you could leave the prints and letters in my inbox, that would be helpful. Then Harry and I can pick them up after supper and drive on to Silvies."

"Sounds like a plan."

"Oh, and before I forget, someone named Clell Robertson called with an invitation for you to attend a community meeting in Monument tomorrow night."

"Yeah, we heard about that and plan to be there."

"I don't know if he's just an angry guy or what, but he almost made it sound like he was demanding your attendance," she added.

"Oh, you know how I love to mess with angry people," I said. "So if he calls back, just tell him you passed the message along to me. If he gives you any crap..."

"And you know how I like to mess with people who give me crap."

"Uh-huh, and that's one of the many things I've come to love about you."

She giggled. "Good night, Maggie."

"We received a formal invitation to the community meeting in Monument," I said after hanging up.

"I couldn't quite tell, was it an invitation or a demand?"

"Sounded like it might've been closer to a demand."

"Will people ever learn that you don't summon Maggie Blackthorne that way?"

"Doubtful, doubtful. Speaking of demands, do you still want me to find some music?"

"Nah, I'm good."

"What did you think of Mrs. Edwards?"

"I'm not sure."

"Yeah, me either. But I'm ready to call it a day, I do know that."

10

MORNING, APRIL 9

I had dreamed I'd given birth to a baby. And since the child was born with a full head of red hair, we decided the name would be Apple. But neither of us had bothered to check the gender, nor had I experienced any pain throughout labor.

Waking and recalling the illusion—or delusion where the painless labor was concerned—I laughed. And managed to wake Duncan, of course.

"What is it? Are you having contractions?"

"No, but I dreamed I gave birth to a kid we named Apple."

"Apple?"

"Yeah, because of all the red hair. Plus, it was a pain-free delivery."

"Boy or girl?"

"In the dream, neither of us inspected the little critter."

"Well, that's no fun."

"I read that a lot of pregnant women have dreams about giving birth," I said.

"I've had dreams about you giving birth."

"Really?"

"Yep," he said and yawned.

"Come here, you. I'm cold."

He scooted closer and wrapped his arms around me. "Why don't you call in sick today?"

"Because I'm not sick."

"I know. That's even better. Tell you what, I'll put Jenna in charge of the feed and tack and stay home with you."

"Is she ready for that?"

"She's the best worker I've ever hired. Even better than my nephew Rain was."

"Nice to hear that about Jenna, but I can't stay home today, Dun."

"I know, babe."

"But I can lay here with you awhile." I wiggled out of my nightgown and pressed my naked body to his. "I see I have your attention."

"Something like that."

～

The remnants of our freak snowstorm two days ago had all but disappeared along the valley floor, just not at the higher elevations. It was even warm outside, and Strawberry Mountain, with its new layer of white, was stunning against the cloudless sky.

Driving into John Day, I passed the mortuary and noticed Sam Damon pull up. I slowed my Tahoe, turned around, and parked behind his old sedan. I had remembered to remove Mike Drake's funeral attire from the back seat of Hollis's Tahoe last night. I collected it now from the back seat of my vehicle and carried everything inside the building.

Sam relieved me of the clothing bag containing Drake's suit, shirt, and tie. He carried them off to a side room I decided not to follow him into, and I stood in the high-ceilinged entryway holding the dead man's shoes. They had been shined and buffed and smelled like the wax shoe polish Duncan used.

Sam returned with Drake's boots and his wallet, cell phone, and a belt, which had been placed in separate evidence bags. "Dr. Lewis asked me to turn these over to Detective Bach, but I assume I can give them to you."

He handed me the bags. "Yes, and I'll let the detective know we have them."

"Thanks, Maggie."

"Here are the shoes Mrs. Drake sent along. The socks are inside one of the shoes, I believe."

He took the paper bag from me. "All right, I should get to work."

"Before I leave, could you tell me how it was working with Dr. Lewis?"

"She's not Dr. Gattis, that's for sure. But I've worked with surlier MEs before."

I smiled. "I forgot to ask Mrs. Drake when the funeral's taking place."

"Next Monday. Closed casket at the gravesite in Canyon City at two o'clock."

I was surprised they had chosen the graveyard in Canyon City instead of someplace closer to the ranch, but the choice didn't point to anything nefarious, so I deemed the matter to be none of my business.

"All right, Sam. I'll let you get to work."

～

I realized we had a visitor when I pulled up in front of our office. An all-white Ram 2500 with *Oregon State Police* stenciled on the doors was parked between Sherry Linn's brand-new Mazda 6 and the two cop vehicles assigned to Hollis and Doug.

I opened the station house door and spotted a female trooper with short blond hair sitting in one of our folding chairs across from the front counter. She was apparently waiting to speak to me because she stood, shot her arm out, and shook my hand.

"Trooper Daniela Park. I traveled from Bend this morning to meet you, Sergeant."

Ah, right. She was the Fish and Wildlife trooper Doug had mentioned was looking to transfer.

"Nice to meet you too. Can we offer you coffee or tea?"

"No, thanks. But I'd like a few minutes of your time."

"Sure, after I speak with our office manager a minute."

Trooper Park retook the folding chair and waited.

"Good morning," I said to Sherry Linn. "I just picked up a pair of boots from Sam Damon. Would you mind taking them to Harry when you go home tonight? They belonged to Mike Drake and likely match some of those footprint casts."

"And good morning to you, Maggie. Do you need me to take them to Harry sooner?"

"No, but thanks for the offer." I turned to the woman waiting. "Well, Trooper Park, let's move to the alcove, where we generally have meetings or eat lunch. But I need to warn you, the beginning of a murder board is posted there."

"Thanks for the warning, Sergeant. But if I can't tolerate sharing space with a murder board, then I guess I shouldn't be a police officer."

I led the way back to our set of officer desks and placed Mike Drake's wallet, cell phone, and belt on top of mine.

"I believe you know Doug Vaughn, and I assume you met Hollis Jones."

"Yeah, Doug was my mentor for a while a few years back, and your office manager introduced me to Trooper Jones."

"So that means we haven't scared you off yet."

"Not yet," she said, following me into the alcove.

At least she knew how to roll with the punches and take a joke.

"Is Major Macintyre aware you're here?"

"He is. I've been ordered not to interfere with your homicide investigation and to keep my visit short. I also think he believes you *will* scare me off, but I don't scare so easily."

We chatted for roughly fifteen minutes, and even though I was anxious to finish up the conversation, Dani—as she asked to be called—and I hit it off. I was reminded of the first time I met Sherry Linn. Although I couldn't imagine Trooper Park flouncing around the office in fluttery clothing, there was something real and refreshing about both women.

"All right," I said. "Here's what I'd like you to do. Think about it at least until Monday, and then if you're still interested, send your application and references to Sherry Linn Perkins, our office manager."

"I brought all of that with me."

"So leave it up front with Sherry Linn. But I still would like you to think about it. This is a small office with very little personal or professional space to work in."

"I'm fine with that, Sergeant."

"Maggie, remember?"

"Maggie, I love this part of the state with every bone in my body. This is where I want to live and work, and I love the idea of working for a woman, a tough woman, as I understand it. Oh, and I'm a damn good cop."

"I've heard that last part from others. But honestly, I don't have the brain space to think about hiring another trooper right now. There's the murder investigation, and my baby is due in less than two weeks."

She stood. "Fair enough. I'll leave my application and references with Sherry Linn, and I'll think about it over the weekend. I'll let you know via email if I still want the job after that, if it's okay."

"Email's fine, and I'll expect to hear from you on Monday."

We shook hands, and I watched her walk toward the front counter before heading to my desk.

Doug and Hollis worked quietly, seemingly in an effort to avoid asking me what I'd thought of Dani. I took my seat and opened my computer.

"What?" I said. "Hollis, did you write up all those reports on the Drake murder and follow-up conversations?"

"I worked from home awhile last night and came in early to finish up. It wasn't that hard, Maggie. Especially since we recorded the official statements of Mrs. Drake and her son."

"But we have a really long day ahead of us, plus that community meeting tonight," I countered.

"I know. And I also know you're sick of me looking after you because you're about to give birth, but you really can't do *everything*."

"I don't expect to do everything, but I need to do my share. Plus have some time in there to boss everyone around."

Hollis laughed. "You could stop doing that last."

"No, I couldn't."

"If there's anything you need me to do," Doug put in, "I'll have most of my paperwork caught up soon."

"I'll keep that in mind, Doug. Sounded like you had quite a time out in Logan Valley yesterday."

"Yeah. Wasted hours."

"Here's a thought. When is the last time you patrolled out near the fossil beds?"

"It's been some time. I could hit up Rudio Mountain and the area around the town of Monument, then head toward Kimberly and the fossil beds."

"How would you feel about joining Hollis and me at a community meeting out in Monument tonight?" I asked.

"A community meeting about police work?"

"Kind of," I said. "Some of the folks who live in the area are concerned about all of the murders over the last few years. I think they want to know what we're doing about all that."

"Besides solving them," Hollis added.

"Boy, I think if we could come up with a way to prevent homicides, we would've done it by now."

"You've got that right, Doug. So how about joining us there at the school cafeteria tonight? Sheriff Norton is coming, and the more police presence, the better."

"Oh, uh...," he said, blushing. "Maggie, I have a, um...I have a date tonight."

With whom, I wanted to ask. But even I wasn't going to be that rude.

"Who do you have a date with, man?" Hollis said.

"Hollis, I'm pretty sure I could write you up for asking Doug that question."

"I don't mind," Doug said sheepishly. "Her name's Kathy Ellis. She's, um, from Prairie City and in my bowling league. And it's just a date."

"Well, they're probably not going to get a huge crowd there tonight, so Cal Norton, Hollis, and I will likely be enough of a law enforcement presence anyway."

"And I'll also be relatively close to Kimberly today if you two need anything."

"We'll bear that in mind."

"I do have another question, though. What did you think of my pal Dani?"

"I liked her a lot," I said. "She left her application and references with Sherry Linn. But I told her I wanted her to take the weekend and think about whether she wants to leave Bend. She's young, and there's a big difference between there and John Day."

"You mean like ninety-two thousand more people?" Hollis offered.

"Yeah, like that."

Doug smiled. "She grew up in Vale, Oregon."

"Oh. Vale has slightly fewer people than John Day, I believe."

Hollis weighed in, "Doug, I thought Dani seemed great, too."

"She was the best mentee I ever took under my wing," Doug clarified.

"And so we only have to hear from Sherry Linn to cinch it. Well, that and not learn something weird from any of her references."

"And if she doesn't have second thoughts this weekend," Holly reminded me.

"That too."

Doug logged out of his computer and stood. "I better get to gettin' if I'm going to make Rudio Mountain, the area around Monument, and the fossil beds," he said.

"Take it easy out there today, and watch out for snowdrifts," Hollis said.

"I'll be calling you for assistance if I slide into another one."

"Are you ready to go talk to all of those folks who board their horses at Poison Spring Ranch?" I asked after Doug moved to get his coat and take off on patrol.

"I am if you are. Do we plan on calling them before we drive out there?"

"Nah, I think that would be a mistake. And I'd like to start with Lowell Gregg."

"You know him?"

"Sort of. I met him at Duncan's store. He's a shy bachelor type. I've found that sometimes those kinds of folks have learned a lot about their neighbors and have a pent-up desire to share what they know."

"I've noticed that too."

"Where does Mr. Gregg live?"

"Monument. Twenty miles or so from Poison Spring Ranch."

"Ah, been out there on patrol many times. A few people usually wave hello, like I'm an old friend passing through town." He closed down his computer and got up from his desk chair. "Let me get my lunch from the refrigerator first."

"I'll drive today, and I'd like you to check out Drake's phone while we travel."

"On my way to the refrigerator, I'll stash the belt and wallet in the evidence locker," he said and headed toward the back of the building.

~

The shortest way to the town of Monument was by way of Highway 395, so we drove to Mt. Vernon and turned north, a route we had come to know well when we were working on a couple of homicide cases last November.

We had hardly made it past Mt. Vernon when Hollis, exasperated, stashed the cell phone back in the evidence bag. "There is nothing interesting in Drake's device."

"Nothing?"

"No business emails or texts, and barely any with Mrs. Drake or Christopher. It's weird."

"Maybe he just deletes most of them," I suggested.

"I suppose. But who does that?"

"Probably lots of people. Anyway, how about contacts, besides his wife and son?"

"A few, including Duncan's feed and tack store and a couple of other businesses."

"You know, I haven't asked Dun about his dealings with Drake. In fact, I didn't even think about it until just now."

"I get that. I avoid talking to Lil about these cases, too. Would you like me to ask him for his impression of the guy?"

"I think that's probably how we need to handle this. Appreciate it, Holly."

"Not a problem."

The highway now took us through a canyon of black basalt formed along the wild and scenic Beech Creek, then rose until we reached the wide plateau of Fox Valley. After which, we wound down the mountain until we came to State Route 402—better known by locals as the Kimberly-Long Creek Highway—and took a left. The road meandered by the spring green hills and jagged rimrocks to our destination.

Monument, a village of about 130 individuals, lay along the north fork of the John Day River. The town sat in a broad valley and was surrounded by farms and ranches. The small grid of streets made it easy to find Lowell Gregg's little house.

It appeared Lowell wasn't much interested in keeping a yard, which was nothing more than a patch of soupy mud waiting to dry. We exited the Tahoe, took the wooden walkway to his front door, and knocked.

He opened the door. "Oh, hey. Um, Mrs. McKay, right?"

"Sergeant Blackthorne, Oregon State Police. I'm married to Duncan McKay, but I've kept my last name for work purposes."

He cast his eyes to my feet. "Okay, sorry."

"No worries. And this is my patrol partner, Senior Trooper Jones."

Lowell nodded at that.

"We have a few questions about Mr. Drake."

"Christopher?" he asked.

"No, Christopher's father."

"I don't know him."

"We'd appreciate speaking with you inside, if you don't mind," I said. "It's a little cold out here."

He opened the door, and we passed into the interior. After closing the door behind us, he invited us to take a seat.

"Christopher's father was killed at the ranch two days ago," I explained.

"Oh, I guess that's why I seen you both there a couple of times."

"You hadn't heard about Mr. Drake's murder?" Hollis asked.

"No, sir. Don't got no TV or radio. And I don't get no paper."

"Lowell. Is it okay if I call you by your first name?"

He signaled it was okay.

"Lowell, had you ever met Christopher's father?" I asked.

"Seen him around PSR a few times."

"PSR?"

"It's what some people call the ranch. But I only ever talk to Christopher. He's nice people. Lets me board my horse for free. All's I have to do is buy the feed, and I get that at your husband's feed and tack. And even on unemployment, I can afford it."

"How do you feel about the no-gun rule anywhere on the Poison?"

"Well, ma'am, I don't own a gun. Had a hunting rifle when I was a kid, but I sold it a long time ago."

I took Lowell as being a few years older than me. And lonely. "What do you call your horse?"

"Name's Sparky. Don't take much to get 'im going. Takes off like a spark."

I nudged him a bit. "You said Christopher was nice. How about his father?"

"Like I said, I seen him around. But I never talked to him."

"A lot of people are pretty upset about his death." Not that I knew that for certain.

Lowell shrugged.

"Do you know folks who didn't find him particularly nice?" Hollis inquired.

"Well, maybe Christopher. But I wouldn't think he'd kill his own daddy."

"Anyone else?"

"Well, Mister Trooper. You might talk to one of the other boarders, a guy named Burt. Don't know his last name."

I brought out the list of boarders. "Burt Greely?"

"Might be it, but I ain't sure."

"Could I ask you some personal questions?"

"I s'pose, ma'am, you being a cop and all."

"Do you own your house?"

"Yes, ma'am. Handed down to me from my ma."

"You said you were on unemployment. Where did you work?"

"I'm a timber faller."

"So you work seasonally, right?"

"I'd take a job in between, but there ain't no other jobs to be had out here. And the boss of my falling crew ain't started back up yet. The dang snow this week didn't help, neither."

I pulled out one of my business cards and handed it to Lowell. "If you think of anything else, please give me a call."

Hollis handed him one of his cards as well. "If you can't get ahold of Sergeant Blackthorne, here's my number."

"Thank you for your time, Lowell."

"You're welcome, ma'am."

11

MIDDAY, APRIL 9

We chose to call on Burt Greely next, in part because Lowell had indicated Greely, one of the other horse boarders at Poison Spring Ranch, had expressed his displeasure with Mike Drake.

But first, we decided to check out the small café in Monument even though our lunches were stashed in a cooler. We were the sole customers, so after we ordered burgers, we sat in the tiny, quiet space and waited for our meals to arrive. In the meantime, I could hear the music the cook/server/proprietor was playing in the background.

"Who are you listening to?" I asked when he arrived with our burgers.

"That's Valerie June. She's something, huh?"

"Yeah, I really like her."

"Enjoy your lunch, officers." After returning to the kitchen, he turned up the volume a bit on Valerie June.

"Holly, what's your take on Lowell?" I asked after eating a few bites of my delicious meal.

"Poverty sucks."

"True, but what do you think of Lowell Gregg?"

"I think he doesn't have much to bring him pleasure except Sparky. And it's a good thing Christopher has been kind to him. And I believed him when he said he'd never spoken to Drake senior."

"Yeah, I agree," I said.

Speaking of Christopher's kindness, that must have come from his church-lady mother, because apparently his father wasn't capable of actual kindness. And some people, perhaps including his killer, had definitely figured that out.

After we finished lunch, I paid the tab and left a tip.

"Don't tell Angie, but that meal rivals Prairie Maid's burgers," Hollis said after we got back in my rig.

"Oh, yeah. But we'll make that our little secret," I said, pulling back onto Highway 402.

Burt Greely lived in a small mobile home between Monument and Kimberly, and we arrived at his place in no time. The man was probably about my age, I guessed, but he appeared to be older. Or so I told myself.

"How can I help you?" he asked after inviting us to take a seat in his tidy living room.

"We're talking to folks who might've recently had dealings with Mike Drake," I explained.

"I didn't have dealings with him," Greely answered. "I board my horse there but only deal with his son. Met his wife once, though."

"You didn't ever spot him around the stable or paddock?"

"Honestly, Sergeant. I avoided the guy."

"So it sounds like you weren't a fan of Drake senior."

"I wasn't. He was a shit to his son, pardon my French."

I continued to press. "How so?"

"Talked down to him, like he was some stupid kid. Which he's not."

"Why would you care?"

"'Cause I don't care for rich assholes who treat people like shit, pardon my French."

"Excuse me, Mr. Greely," Hollis broke in. "Was that how he treated you?"

"Like I said, I didn't have dealings with the guy."

"But you observed him treating his son unkindly?" Hollis asked.

"You could say that," Greely said.

I sighed. "Well, did you or didn't you witness Mike Drake mistreating his son?"

"Not exactly. But Christopher complained about it a few times."

"Give me an example."

"Well, a couple of months ago, he said something about how his father demanded he stop dating his girlfriend."

"Parents do that sometimes," I suggested.

"Even when their kids are in their thirties?"

"I take your point."

"And not too long after that, he gave Christopher a black eye."

"What's the story behind that?"

"I don't really know, Sergeant. But I assumed the black eye came about as a result of his asshole father."

"Excuse your French, right?" I added. "Did Christopher tell you that's where the black eye came from?"

"No, but he didn't have to tell me."

"We'll ask him about it. In the meantime, do you think he might've murdered his father?"

"Christopher wouldn't hurt a fly. He's the sweetest damn person alive."

I wanted to ask Burt if he was in love with Christopher, but that wasn't the subject of my investigation.

"Did you kill Mike Drake on Christopher's behalf?" I asked.

The man stared at me strangely. "No."

"Mr. Greely," Hollis said. "Do you have a sense of who might've murdered Mr. Drake?"

"Well, have you interviewed Christopher's mom? 'Cause she probably had even more reasons to pull the trigger."

"We've taken her statement," Hollis said. "And her son's."

"I'm not sure what that means, but I've got no idea who might've killed the bastard."

"What do you think of the requirement that guns are off-limits on the ranch?"

"I think it's asinine, but I want to board my horse there, so I follow the rules."

"Are you attending the community meeting tonight?" Hollis asked.

"Nah. To my way of thinking, some of those people who were murdered in the past few years probably deserved it."

I passed him a skeptical glance. "What makes you say that?"

"I don't mean old Guy Trudeau killed at his ranch out near Seneca a couple of years ago. Or the woman who took care of the Aldrich Mountain Fire Lookout, or that cop from your office. But the rest of 'em, I'm not so sure they didn't have it coming."

"Apparently, you've been following all the recent murders in Grant County."

"Well, there's not much else going on out here, you got to admit."

"Still," I said. "I think you'd have to agree that you don't want other citizens wantonly killing people who bug them, don't agree with their politics, or for any reason that can't be regarded as justifiable."

Greely indicated his tacit agreement and turned to Hollis. "Did you know some people in the county don't like having a Black cop around?"

"That's an abrupt change of subject, but do you think I don't already know that? And why *are* you bringing it up?"

"Well, just wanted you to know that you and your family need to be careful."

"What have you heard, Mr. Greely?" I asked him.

"Nothing really, but I grew up in this part of the world, and I can read the tea leaves."

That seemed an odd way to express an observation. "And if you heard about anything explicit, what would you do?"

He looked down at his mud-caked boots. "Call your office or Sheriff Norton."

"How about both," I said. "I also grew up around here. That's no excuse for being racist."

"I'm not, I promise you." Greely again turned to Hollis. "Sorry if I offended you, sir."

"You don't need to apologize or call me sir. Just don't be a bigot or put up with that nonsense from anybody else. That's all I want for my family."

"Yes, officer. I don't know what come over me or why I brought it up in the first place."

～

Hollis brooded quietly as we made our way toward Sandy Connor's place, who also boarded her horse at Poison Spring Ranch. Lisa Drake had suggested her deceased husband may have been interested in the woman, sexually speaking.

"I've never had anyone be so direct about the racism around here," Hollis said after a while.

"Meaning most bigots are indirect?"

"Yeah, and I'm not sure I believe Mr. Greely's statement about not being one himself."

"I don't exactly believe it either. But maybe he was trying the idea on for size."

"Do you remember the guy who ran the store and gas station in Dale?" he asked.

"Two guys ran it. Um, are you thinking of Daddy?"

"No, that was his stepfather, who mostly worked in the office, wasn't it?"

"Oh, you're talking about 'Hi, I'm Hi.'"

"That's right. Hiram something."

"Appleby."

"That's it. Hiram Appleby. When he met me, he was surprised to see a Black cop. Which makes sense, given where he lives. But I didn't feel like I was being judged, looked down on, or sent a warning."

"No. Hi and Daddy were a hoot, actually. *And* they helped us make signs to put up about the dead guy's missing vehicle," I said.

"Right, I remember that now. Anyway, my point being, they weren't compelled to signal there were racists in Grant County."

"Probably because they assumed you knew."

"Yep. And I got the sense they didn't care about the color of my skin."

We had arrived at Sandy Connor's double-wide mobile home about a mile north of Kimberly on Highway 402. She had a small yard with a couple of fruit trees and a flower garden. There was no car parked out front, an indication she might not be home.

"I'll go knock on the door," Hollis offered. "But it doesn't seem like anyone's here."

He got out and knocked on the door. After no one answered, he rejoined me in the Tahoe.

"Let's go talk to Charlotte Johnson," I suggested. "Lisa Drake also mentioned her as one of her husband's possible conquests. It's not far away, and afterward we can come back here and see if the Connor woman is home."

"Sounds like a plan, Mags."

"Oh, I'm a planner, all right, Holly. Not. Thus the condition you now see me in."

"You mean happy?"

"Yeah, that too."

I turned my police vehicle around and headed back toward Kimberly. White clouds now moved gently across the cerulean sky. The temperature had warmed considerably since Wednesday's snowfall. And as we drove, the sun's now brilliant light transformed the rust-red and olive-green volcanic formations into hues of a deeper vibrance.

"I love this part of the county," Hollis whispered.

"It's something else, all right."

We passed by Poison Spring Ranch, as well as the home of Roger and Corky Edwards, and pulled into the Johnsons' driveway, parked, and got out. We could hear music playing inside the house as we made our way up the sidewalk. Classical, which surprised me for some judgmental reason.

I knocked, and Charlotte Johnson opened the door.

She smiled slightly. "Sergeant Blackthorne. Trooper Jones. You're back."

"Glad we caught you. You could have been at work or picking up your daughters from school."

"Not much industry looking to hire hereabouts, but I do make a pittance as a seamstress. I have a little sewing room set up, but other than that, I'm a stay-at-home mom. And the girls ride the bus to and from school."

"We're sorry to bother you, but we do have a couple more questions," I said.

Charlotte opened the door wider, invited us inside, and turned off the music. "Have a seat wherever you'd like. Coffee? Tea? Water?"

"I'm good," I answered and sat in a stuffed chair in the front room.

"I'm doing fine, too," Hollis said and found a place to sit.

She plopped down across from us. I couldn't help noticing her gorgeous brown eyes and full lips. Charlotte was an extremely pretty woman, and I recalled that her daughters looked very much like her.

"How can I help you?" she asked.

I brought out the small notebook I always kept in my pocket. "Well, first, would you mind giving us your phone number so we can alert you the next time we drop by with more questions."

"The next time?" she asked.

"In case there is a next time."

She listed off her number. I wrote it down, and for good measure, I repeated it back to her.

"We'd like to confirm something Mrs. Edwards mentioned yesterday," I said. "She indicated you called her while she was in Bend at the hospital where Mr. Edwards is being cared for. Said you had phoned to let her know about Mike Drake's death."

"That's true. I touched base with her the evening after you stopped by the first time. The day of the murder."

"How did she seem when you told her?"

Charlotte paused. "Well, I'm not sure this is helpful, but Corky seemed like she always does. A little confused and not particularly expressive of her emotions, I guess I'd say."

I had observed that about Corky Edwards myself. Well, except for the tears.

"My next question is a bit more personal," I said.

"Oh?"

"Mrs. Drake thought her husband might've been interested in you romantically. Did he ever communicate that to you?"

"What on earth are you asking me?"

"Was he ever flirty, or did he ever make a pass at you?"

"No," she stated emphatically.

"Mrs. Drake wasn't accusing you of being involved with him. She said he seemed rather interested in you."

"What are you saying?"

Hollis rescued me. "Mrs. Drake explained it this way. She said he talked about you quite a bit, something he apparently did when he was interested in, um, pursuing other women."

"If that's true, I never picked up on those vibes," she said rather flatly.

Her daughters suddenly and noisily opened the front door, carrying backpacks and arguing about something.

"Hi, girls," Charlotte spoke more energetically. "This is Sergeant Blackthorne and Trooper Jones."

The daughters, as I'd noticed before, had inherited their mother's beauty. And they were both rather uninterested in Hollis and me.

Charlotte went into parenting mode. "Go in the kitchen and make yourselves a snack, then get right on your homework, please."

"God, Mom. It's Friday," one of the teenagers said.

"I know," Charlotte answered. "But we have to go shopping in John Day in the morning. And if I recall, you both plan to go to the high school dance tomorrow night."

"So, we'll do our homework on Sunday," the other daughter whined.

"No, I know how this all goes. You'll sleep in late and laze around on Sunday. Plus your dad is coming home that afternoon."

"Give it up, Laney," the first daughter said. "Mom's set on this, and the police are here."

"You give it up, Paula. They're not here to enforce Mom's rules, I wouldn't think."

Charlotte laughed. "That could be arranged, I bet. Now go fix a snack for yourselves and do your damn homework."

After her girls took themselves to the kitchen, Hollis and I stood to leave.

"Thank you for your time, Mrs. Johnson, but I think Trooper Jones and I got what we came for. And by the way, your daughters are pretty fun."

"They are at that. When's your baby due?"

"Twelve days from now."

"Whoa, you look great for being this far along. Is this your first?"

"And probably last," I remarked.

"That's what I told myself after Paula was born. But I changed my mind, and Laney came a year later."

I shook my head.

"Do you have any children, Trooper Jones?"

"A boy named Hank. He's two."

"It'll get better, I promise," she told him.

"He's already pretty fun too. And Sergeant Blackthorne is his godmother."

She eyed me. "Ah, so you've had some practice, at least."

"Thankfully, yes. Again, we appreciate you taking the time to talk to us."

∾

I drove back toward Sandy Connor's place, but my thoughts circled around the conversation we'd just had with Charlotte Johnson. Something about it nagged at me; not the friendly stuff, but her response to my question about Mike Drake's possible interest in her. There was something there I couldn't quite put my finger on.

"You're awfully quiet," Hollis said. "What's up?"

"Seemed like I touched a nerve back there."

"Yeah, I noticed that too."

"I had the sense she was hiding something," I posited.

"Like what?"

"An affair, maybe. Just not with Mike Drake."

"Out here in the middle of nowhere?"

"She isn't employed outside of the home, and I bet her seamstress gig doesn't bring her in contact with many folks. Add to that, her husband the truck driver appears to be gone much of the time. She seems smart, but I bet she's bored out of her mind and lonely."

"You might be right about her being bored, but as you've pointed out before, the pickings are slim around here, boyfriend-wise."

"Hmm. Maybe Christopher Drake has two girlfriends. Or should I say, two friends with benefits."

12

Sandy Connor was at home when we arrived back at her place. She invited us inside her double-wide, a much fancier mobile home than I'd ever been in before. The woman immediately reminded me of someone, but I couldn't quite put my finger on who. She was perky, had short blond hair, and spoke with confidence.

"What can I do for you, officers?" she asked once we took a seat in her prefab living room that didn't appear to be prefab at all. The artwork—including the amateur paintings—and large fabric wall-hanging contributed to the soothing ambience.

"We're investigating the homicide of Mike Drake," I told her.

"I guessed that was why you were here, given I board my horse at his ranch."

"Did you have a lot of interactions with him, Ms. Connor?"

"Well, none, up until a couple of months ago. I've mostly interacted with his son, Christopher, who I find to be a great guy. Don't know if you know this, but he charges boarders using a sliding fee scale. I mean, that's unheard of."

That explained Lowell being able to afford boarding Sparky.

"Ms. Connor," Hollis said. "Were you surprised when you heard Mr. Drake had been killed?"

"Very," she said. "I've personally never known anyone who was murdered."

"Are you going to the community meeting in Monument tonight?" he asked.

"Well, I'm a middle school teacher in Monument. I love my kids and I give them my all, but come quittin' time on Friday, I need to leave that town behind for a few days."

Young and presumably single, what had lured this seemingly smart woman to Oregon's outback?

"Did you grow up around here, Ms. Connor?" I asked.

"Um, you guys can call me Sandy. And no, I'm from Portland. But I followed my boyfriend out here about eight years ago. Ex-boyfriend. He's now married to someone else and the father of three little boys."

"Did you notice any animosity between the elder Drake and his son?"

"The father was really tough on his son, I thought. Treated him like he was a silly teenager, but Christopher seemed to take it all in stride."

"You noticed that in the last couple of months?" I asked.

Sandy hesitated. "Well, a time or two. Mostly I got that impression from Burt."

"Mr. Greely?"

"Yeah."

"Before we head out and let you get your weekend started, we have a sensitive question to ask. It was suggested to us that Mr. Drake—Mike—might have been interested in you sexually. Did you ever think he was flirting or trying to push your relationship with him in that direction?"

"Well, of course. I'm not stupid."

"Did he ever make advances or..."

"I told him to leave me alone. Specifically, I told him to get his fucking hands off of my ass."

"Where did this happen?"

"Outside in broad daylight. This county is full of touchy-feely older men."

"Here's where I have to ask if you own a gun."

"Yes, an old .30-60 rifle I inherited from my grandfather. I'm not even sure it works any longer."

"Are you a good shot?" Hollis asked.

"I've never shot a gun in my life, and I don't plan to begin anytime soon."

"A lot of folks who live out in the country have guns for protection," he added.

"That's what I have Prince for."

"Prince?"

"My Doberman Pinscher. I stashed him in the bedroom when I saw you drive up."

"Well, I think that does it," I said. "Thanks for your time, Sandy."

"Are you two attending the meeting in Monument tonight?"

"I think we're the special guests, and we're looking for some answers, so yes."

"I have another question," Hollis said. "Did you ever observe anyone or know of anyone who might have had a serious altercation with Mike Drake?"

"No, and I thought the animosity between him and his son was more of a family thing. But I assume you've asked Mrs. Drake and Christopher about all of that."

"And Mrs. Drake?" he asked. "Did she ever have a serious argument with her husband?"

"Gosh, I have no idea. I only met her a couple of times."

There was a pause. "I think we're done here, Trooper, don't you?"

"I believe so."

"Do you guys happen to have business cards, in case I think of something later?"

That surprised me. "Not many people ask for our business cards, but yes, we're happy to leave them with you."

～

During our discussion with Sandy Connor, a voicemail had come in from Al Bach. While still parked in front of her double-wide, Hollis and I listened to the detective's message.

"My wife is out of the hospital, and I plan to return to John Day on

Sunday afternoon. I'd appreciate an in-person update on the case first thing Monday morning. I spoke by phone with Sherry Linn, and she explained you two planned to interview all those boarding their horses at Poison Spring Ranch and attend a community meeting this evening. Take care. See you after the weekend."

"I don't know if I'm right about this, but Detective Bach sounds like he might be tired of overseeing rural homicide investigations," Hollis remarked.

"I know I would be. *I'm* tired of investigating rural homicides."

"Me too. So I guess neither of us will be pulling up stakes anytime soon and joining the homicide unit in Bend."

"I don't see that happening."

Heading away from Sandy Connor's mobile home, I reflected back on our conversation with her.

"I found Sandy to be a straight shooter. Refreshingly so," I said.

"Definitely."

"She reminds me of someone, but I can't place who."

"She reminded me of the trooper we met this morning."

"Dani Park, that's it! They're pretty similar."

"I hope Dani's transfer works out."

"I'm betting it will. I think Al has some sway with Major Macintyre."

Holly's phone rang. "Hey," he said and listened to the caller. "I know, honey. We'll do it this Sunday, I promise."

He continued listening and then laughed. "Tell him he gets to plant the tatoes in a few days...I will. Bye now."

"Tatoes. That must be Hank's word for potatoes."

"Yep. We're working in the garden on Sunday."

"It's supposed to be sunny and a little warmer tomorrow, and then it gets cooler on Sunday. Why aren't you working in your garden tomorrow?"

"Because you and I will have several reports to write up after we're done today."

"I'm going to do those from home over the weekend. Duncan might have a shit fit if I go into the office."

"I've never known you to worry about anyone having a fit about something you decide to do."

"I know. But I'm tired, and I feel like I need to chill over the weekend. And also, I don't want to get Dun worked up about my job right now."

"I think staying home over the weekend is a good move, Mags. Lil said to say hi and to take care of yourself."

"Holly, I want you to be gardening at home tomorrow while the weather's more conducive. And because Hank needs to get his tatoes in the ground. Tell him hi from Aunt Maybe, and send my love to Lil."

"Will do, but I have some sad news to report."

"Oh?"

"Hank has figured out that you're Aunt Maggie, not Aunt Maybe."

"Ah, the end of an era. Before you know it, he'll be learning to drive."

~

Earlier, we had decided to visit with horse boarders Maeve and Clell Robertson last. Our reasoning escaped me now, but it probably had something to do with the fact that Mr. Robertson had called for tonight's community meeting regarding the rash of murders over the last couple of years. A surprise visit from the officers investigating the most recent homicide might convince him we were capable cops and prevent any accusations of ineptitude at tonight's meeting. The problem was our visit might just do the opposite.

The Robertsons' home was a short distance south of Kimberly down Holmes Creek Road. Their small house was next to an orchard, pear trees, I thought. The couple apparently wasn't used to receiving unexpected visitors, because they both emerged from the house and stood on the porch as I parked the Tahoe. And they didn't seem to be particularly friendly either.

Mr. Robertson was tall, beefy, and red-faced, while Mrs. Robertson was petite, thin, and somewhat dazed by our presence.

We got out and strode up the walkway until we reached the porch.

"Mr. and Mrs. Robertson?"

"Yes," Mr. Robertson said. "Who are you?"

"Sergeant Blackthorne, Oregon State Police. And this is Senior Trooper Jones."

"You're early. And in the wrong place. The meeting begins at seven in the school cafeteria in Monument," he barked.

"Yes, we know. We made plans to attend yesterday when Lisa Drake told us about it."

"Is that so?"

"It is. But I appreciated you calling our office with an invitation. However, right now we're here to have a conversation with both of you regarding Mike Drake."

"He was an old friend," Clell Robertson clarified.

"And you board horses at his ranch?"

"We do. So what?"

"You may have information germane to our investigation."

"Have you spoken with other boarders?"

"Yes. As a matter of fact, all of the other boarders."

The wind had picked up, and I was hoping we wouldn't have to have this conversation standing out in the elements.

"Clell," Mrs. Robertson said. "Let's ask them to come inside to chat. The sergeant is obviously pregnant, and it's cold out here."

He was clearly unhappy with his wife's suggestion, but he capitulated and opened the door. The rest of us followed him inside. I found the interior of the place dark, dingy, and depressing. And replete with the odor of rotten fruit. Despite all of that, the heat from the wood stove was completely worth Mrs. Robertson's invitation.

Once everyone was seated, the Robertsons stared at us, like a couple of impatient teenagers.

"So it sounds like you had a good relationship with Mr. Drake. How about with his wife and son?" I inquired.

"We're close with the entire family," Maeve Robertson said.

"So you know about Mr. and Mrs. Drake's long-time marital problems?"

"Who doesn't have those?" Clell remarked.

I was beginning to feel sorry for his wife, but for all I knew, she might have been equally cantankerous.

I nudged some more. "Were you aware of any violence in the relationship?"

"No," the husband replied without hesitation.

"I knew nothing about any violence between Mike and Lisa. But there might have been those kinds of issues between Christopher and him," the wife offered.

"Shut it, Maeve."

She ignored him. "They groused at one another quite a bit, and Christopher had a black eye a while back."

"Do you think Christopher was fed up enough to kill his father?" I asked.

"No way," Mr. Robertson claimed. "They were really close, but Mike often got frustrated with his son. And we don't even really know where the black eye came from."

"Mrs. Robertson," Hollis began. "Do you think Christopher could possibly have killed his father?"

"Absolutely not. He's very kind, maybe even too kind sometimes."

"And Mrs. Drake?" he asked.

"She's a devout Christian, so no, there's no way."

"Any sense of who might've shot Mike Drake to death?" I said.

"Maybe whoever sent all of those nasty letters back when Mike was a county commissioner," Clell speculated.

"You know about those letters?"

"Of course, Sergeant. We were best friends, me and Mike. Known him my whole life."

"Any thoughts about who might've sent the letters?" Hollis asked.

"Trooper Jones, is it?"

"That's right."

"I always thought it might've been the other county commissioner on the board. They argued about shit all the time."

"Do you remember his name?" I said.

For the first time, Clell smiled. "*Her* name is Geraldine Hankins. She's no longer a commissioner. But as far as I know, she still lives in John Day. One of the last liberal, smart-ass do-gooders in Grant County."

It was good to know there was—at the very least—another one of those in our neck of the woods. As long as she wasn't a murdering fool, that is.

"Mr. Robertson," I began. "What did you think of the gun ban at Poison Spring Ranch?"

"You know that his father was accidentally shot to death by his uncle when Mike was a kid, right?"

"Yes, we were informed."

"Well, I was on that hunting trip, and I saw what it did to Mike and his brother, Johnny. They were scarred for life. Now that don't mean I haven't gone hunting or done a little target practicing since then, but I respect Mike's decision to ban guns on his own damn property, and I've always abided by it."

~

Hollis and I came to the conclusion Clell Robertson had mellowed out a bit over the course of our conversation. And Maeve had invited us to attend the potluck supper being held at the Grange hall at six o'clock. Food was an enticement to draw more community members to the seven o'clock discussion, she had explained. She'd also encouraged us to stop at the store in Monument and pick up snacks to share at the potluck, and further suggested folks might be impressed by that.

"I think if we go to the potluck, we *have* to bring doughnuts," Hollis said when we were back in my rig and on the road.

Now that made me laugh.

But before we could take the cop-and-doughnuts stereotype any further, I received a call from Lisa Drake.

"Margaret, Christopher found an unloaded handgun hidden in the stable."

"Any thoughts about who it might belong to?"

"We have no idea, and I'm stunned there was a second one on our property. Mike and Christopher have been very strict with boarders about not bringing guns along when they tend to their horses."

I checked the time: five ten. Poison Spring Ranch was a couple of miles up the road, so I decided there was room in our schedule to pay another visit.

"We're in the area, so we'll see you in a few minutes, Mrs. Drake."

"Thank you, Margaret."

"Christopher Drake found a handgun in the stable," I relayed to Hollis after ending the call. "We'll need Harry to check it out. It might belong to whoever shot Mike Drake."

"How about one of the boarders?"

"Honestly, that would be my guess, but a guess is worth crap without proof. Or it could be some neighbor needing to hide a gun away for some other reason."

"Like what?

I thought about that for a moment. "Do you remember that incident a month or two back where someone shot and killed a dog? It happened not very far from here. But the mutt's owner was pissed as hell and wanted the shooter identified and arrested."

"I remember. Wasn't Sheriff Norton investigating that incident?"

"The Sheriff's Office got the initial call, yeah."

Hollis pulled up his phone to check the story online. "You're right, the dog's owner lives nearby."

"When I was a girl, it was pretty common for free-roaming dogs to kill newborn lambs and for sheep growers to shoot any dogs they saw going after their livestock. I bet that still happens. Country justice at work."

"Are you trying to make a connection to the gun found hidden in Drake's horse stable and the dog shooting?"

"At a ranch where guns are prohibited on the property, the stable might be a good place to stash your weapon for a while if one needed to for whatever nefarious reason and wait for the whole thing to blow over."

Hollis passed me a blank look. "Does any of that help us find Drake's killer?"

"Well, so far nothing has really helped us, unless I'm missing something you know about."

"No, unfortunately."

"And maybe the gun hidden in the stable belongs to our murderer," I added, parking next to Mike Drake's BMW.

Lisa welcomed us inside the ranch house and invited us into the kitchen for tea. Christopher sat at the table, the gun he'd found in the stable in front of him, or so I assumed. He had placed it in a baggie and sealed it shut.

"That's the weapon you discovered in the stable?" I asked.

"Yep." He handed the baggie to me. "I'm afraid my fingerprints are on the weapon, but I'm assuming you'll be able to tell mine apart from any others."

We declined Lisa's offer of tea and suggested Christopher give us a tour of the stable, which was a short walk from the house. Before leaving, I asked them both if they planned to attend the community meeting.

Lisa offered a pained expression. "I decided that Monday's funeral will be hard enough. And I'm really not interested in hearing other people's speculative discourse on the matter when they have no knowledge about what really transpired."

She was referring to her husband's murder, but her words invoked the consummate description of a problem humans shared in the main. To wit, people often didn't know shit from Shinola, but that didn't prevent them from pontificating nonstop on a given subject.

"I'm not attending either," Christopher said. "But Lydia is. By the way, you made quite the impression on her."

Good or bad, I wanted to ask.

He rose from his seat at the table, and we followed him outside.

Strangely, considering the thick layer of clouds, cold temperatures, and snow we had experienced early on Wednesday, the marine blue sky in the days that followed were a welcome sign we were back on track for a glorious spring.

The horses were outdoors circling the paddock at a slow pace or drinking from the trough of water and nibbling hay from a manger. I recognized Sparky and thought of Lowell Gregg sitting alone in his sad little house, waiting for his crew boss to call.

Once inside the stable, I commented that it was the cleanest one I'd ever been in.

"Old Clyde does a great job," Christopher said. "He comes two days a week. A steady worker, that guy."

"I didn't realize you had an employee."

"Well, we also hire a few guys every autumn to help us haul most of the herd to open range on Forest Service land. And then in late winter or early spring when we haul them back to the ranch."

"Yeah, we noticed the cattle chute on Wednesday."

"Oh, you went out there after you found Father's body?"

"As part of the investigation," I said. But I skipped mentioning that I also took advantage of the public restroom at one of the nearby Fossil Beds Monument trailheads.

"Did you ever have a cattle drive with drovers and such?" Hollis asked.

"Yeah, when I was a kid and up until I went off to college. Father and I always went along, back when we also owned horses. It was quite an experience."

"I'll bet," Hollis said enthusiastically.

My patrol partner sounded a bit like an excited kid. Which I found to be sweet.

"When was the last time Clyde cleaned the stable?" I asked.

"Well, he was here this morning and last Tuesday."

"So, he wasn't around the day your father was killed?"

"No."

"Even so, we probably need to talk to him," I suggested. "He might've noticed something, overheard one of the horse boarders say something significant."

"Clyde's last name is Lawton. He lives in the red house just as you turn down Holmes Creek Road. He's pretty shy, and he's a heck of a fella."

I signaled I understood. "Where did you find the gun?"

"Over here, behind that tack trunk."

We followed him to the trunk, which was placed against the corner wall.

"So, seemingly it was stashed there on purpose, is that what you're saying?"

"Looked like it to me."

"Might it belong to Mr. Lawton?"

"I have no idea, Sergeant."

"Let's call and ask him. Meaning you, Christopher, if you don't mind. And put your speaker on. Please."

He rolled through his contacts, found Clyde Lawton, turned his device's speaker on, and dialed.

"Howdy, Christopher."

"Hi, Clyde. Sorry to bother you."

"No bother. What's up?"

"Well, I found something behind the tack trunk in the corner," Christopher told him.

"Okay."

"I don't suppose you noticed anything there this morning."

"Last time I fiddled with that trunk was Tuesday," Clyde offered.

"Did you notice anything that seemed out of place?"

"Whatcha mean by outta place?"

"Something that you wouldn't ordinarily see at the ranch, let alone in the stable."

"No sirree, just the regular. Somebody had piled all their gear—saddle, blankets, bridle, everything—next to one of the stalls."

"Well, I know you, Clyde, you didn't leave all that stuff just sitting there."

"No sirree. Assumed the stuff belonged in the empty trunk, so I moved the trunk over to the pile and filled it up. Then I pushed the tack trunk back into the corner."

"Did you notice anything lying on the floor in the corner?"

"No sirree, I did not. I woulda told you if I'd saw somethin' weird."

"I was sure you would have, but I had to ask. Now, you have a good weekend, Clyde."

"You too. See you at the funeral on Monday."

13

EVENING, APRIL 9

Once Christopher ended his call to the stable's part-time caretaker, I asked him how it was that he came to discover the gun behind the tack trunk in the first place.

"I just happened to notice that the corner trunk didn't align with the other trunks. So I tried to nudge it back against the wall. But as it turned out, the gun was in the way."

Hollis and I hadn't been inside the stable before, but it was kept nearly as neat and tidy as the ranch house, save the animal odors.

"Out of curiosity, why are there five trunks?"

"Each of the boarders stores their tack in one of them."

"Of course. Are they assigned?"

"Basically, yeah."

"And the corner trunk belongs to which boarder?"

"Burt."

"Mr. Greely, right?"

"Yeah, he's left his tack near his horse's stall before, instead of putting it away. I've talked to him about it, but he still does it on occasion."

"Mr. Greely thinks your father was too hard on you," I added.

"He's right. It was Father's way of toughening me up. I happen to believe tough is overrated."

"I like that line. Mind if I borrow it?" Hollis put in.

Christopher smiled. "Spread the word, I say."

"How easy is it to get into the stable?" I asked.

"The lock is on a timer. Opens at six a.m. and closes at ten p.m. Plus it's next to the highway, so theoretically, passersby could get inside during that time period."

"I have another question for you."

"Ask away, Sergeant."

"A couple of folks have said you had a black eye a while back. Was that one of your father's efforts to toughen you up?"

"No, that was me being clumsy while loading hay into an old bale feeder."

I didn't know if I believed him, but I let it go.

"Any guesses why someone would stash a gun here?" I asked.

"I don't get it. Unless it was one of the boarders who forgot about the ranch's gun ban. Or Clyde, I suppose. Should I have asked him about it over the phone just now?"

"Well, he indicated the last time he had handled the trunk in the corner was last Tuesday, and unless you have some reason to doubt that, I say we take him at his word."

"Clyde is a stand-up guy in my experience," Christopher assured us.

"Trooper Jones, do you have any questions before we take off?"

"An observation more than anything. It's interesting that you use a sliding fee scale for the folks boarding their horses on the ranch."

"Oh, it's only fair, I think. There are a lot of people who are down on their luck these days, and they can't really afford a horse, or much of anything else. Lowell, for instance. And old Burt isn't very far from that. It would be a shame for them to have to sell their animals when it's not their fault the job market's hit bottom around here."

Hollis continued. "Was that your father's way of running the stable?"

"Hardly. In fact, he didn't really pay much attention to this part of the family business, so I never told him about the pricing system. And up until a few months ago, he rarely set foot in the stable. Now he had a reason to be there."

"What was that?" I asked.

"Hound-dogging after Sandy Connor."

"So we heard," I said.

"Sandy's smart," Christopher added. "Knows how to take care of herself."

~

We decided to skip the potluck being held before the community meeting and go find a spot to pull over and eat the lunches we'd packed for the road this morning. I drove to a quiet boat landing along the John Day River and parked next to the rushing waterway.

Mesas, rife with sagebrush, rose to the west of the river. Willows, showy in light vermillion, deep green junipers, and budding cottonwoods surrounded our picnic spot. We were the only humans around, and it was warm enough to roll down the windows and let the mix of scents drift over us.

A radio call from Doug Vaughn came in, disturbing our quiet little dinner.

"Hey, Doug."

"Evening, Maggie. I'm not far from Monument, so I'm checking in to see if you need me to cancel my dinner date and attend the community meeting."

"We're good. I would've reached out by now if I'd decided we needed another body, but thanks for checking in."

After signing off and finishing up the last of our meals, it was time to get on the road. We headed back toward Monument, where we had essentially begun this long day. Our picnic spot had been lovely, but as we drove toward the meeting, the sun's intense rays poured through the scattering of clouds, lit up the spring green fields, the wide rushing river of snowmelt, and the ancient basalt bluffs scarred with roseate magma.

Having only one life to live, I was tempted to pull over and watch the entire spectacular moment in time play out in front of us, but the meeting was set to begin in short order.

We stopped in at the little market and gas station in town, and while I had the attendant top off the tank, Hollis zipped inside and bought two boxes of doughnuts. From there, we headed to the small school district's campus. Several vehicles were lined up in the parking lot in front of one of the buildings, so we made the assumption the cafeteria was located just through the double doors.

As we reached the entrance, the sound of folks laughing and chatting drifted outside. But like all party poopers, once we stepped inside, we had the effect of silencing the gathering. On the other hand, we weren't there to make new friends; we'd come to hear their concerns and answer their questions about some gruesome crimes, and with any luck, learn something beneficial to our investigation.

"Good evening, everybody. I'm Sergeant Margaret Blackthorne, and the guy holding the boxes of doughnuts is Senior Trooper Hollis Jones."

The group had assembled at a few of the tables. I also noticed someone had brought a stand and chart paper and laid out a few markers for jotting down notes.

Clell Robertson, who'd been sitting at one of the front tables, now stood. "Thank you for joining us, officers."

Clell's wife, Maeve, also rose from her seat. "Trooper Jones, we plan on having dessert after the meeting adjourns. In the meantime, you're welcome to drop off the doughnuts at the dessert table."

"Thank you, Mrs. Robertson," he called out, his deep, warm voice echoing from the walls.

Hollis made his way to the dessert table, placed the two boxes next to someone's homemade pie, and took a seat next to the Robertsons.

"We have room for one more up here, Sergeant Blackthorne," Clell said.

Warily, and wearily, I made my way through the small crowd and settled in.

∾

Sheriff Norton arrived about twenty minutes after the event began, and by then Hollis and I had pretty much won over the crowd. We had started by explaining we were under the supervision of an experienced homicide detective during our investigations, after which we briefly laid out all of the recent cases and described how each crime had ultimately been solved.

Clell Robertson rose from his chair. "Thank you for taking the time to speak with us and helping us to understand these incidents better. I appreciate how you were able to find the killers in fairly short order, but I guess I want to know what's happening out here on our little patch of Earth. Why have we had so many murders in the last few years?"

"I can only speculate about that, Mr. Robertson," I answered. "Scary times, a bad economy locally speaking, possibly drugs, all of that along with some people's pent-up anger or untreated mental illness."

I almost added the proliferation of guns to my list, but of the seven other homicides in the preceding fourteen months, three died by other means. Even so, Mike Drake was the fifth person shot to death in recent years.

And all of those killings had occurred on my watch. Thinking of it that way was unsettling.

The sheriff had ended up at a table on the other side of the room. He now stood to add his two cents. "Evening. I just want to say as your sheriff, I think we're fortunate to have Sergeant Blackthorne and Trooper Jones working on this investigation—in part because of their experience, but largely because they both have good heads on their shoulders and they're under the leadership of Detective Al Bach, who has a heck of a reputation in Oregon police circles."

"Thank you, Sheriff," I said as he sat back down, and focused on the audience. "I would ask one thing of all of you. If you have any information, or if you believe you saw or heard something, let us know."

Hollis moved to the chart paper, picked up one of the markers, and wrote down our names and the main phone number at the office.

"We'll also leave some of our business cards," he told the crowd. "Back to you, Sergeant."

"To begin with, how many of you knew Mike Drake or knew of him?"

Almost every hand shot up.

"Because this is such a small community, we're interested in talking to anyone who may have heard anything related to Mr. Drake's homicide. For example, is there anyone we should speak with who held a serious grudge against Mr. Drake or made threatening comments about him?"

The audience chewed that over, and I looked around the room to see if there were any takers. I happened to spot Lydia Reed sitting at a back table and recalled her dislike of Mike Drake. She had called him an asshole who thought of himself as a big shot. Said he had robbed water from her father for years. Thinking about her remarks, it seemed possible others in the room might have had similar views and experiences.

I decided to throw out a couple of yes-or-no questions. "How many of you have dealt with Mr. Drake on a non-personal level, such as a business exchange or community-minded project?"

A few raised their hands.

"How many of you were his acquaintance or friend?"

The Robertsons and several others raised their hands.

"Again, my point in asking you these questions is that you may have unwittingly seen or overheard something that ties into the case."

The response: crickets.

Then a woman raised her hand. "I'm asking this generally, Sergeant Blackthorne, but if any one of us has a suspicion about something, can we share it with the police confidentially?"

"There are parameters around confidentiality. So it would depend on what we're told."

Based on the glance she passed me, I hadn't provided her with the answer she'd hoped for. But I didn't really have any other answer to give her. And with that, I decided to stop rattling on.

"Detective Bach, who was unable to attend, and Trooper Jones and I want to assure all of you that we're working hard to collect evidence, pinpoint persons of interest, and solve this case, and hopefully very soon," I said.

An older guy stood. "I want to thank all of the law enforcement folks for being here. I think those of us living in the John Day Valley are in purdy good hands here, and I'm ready for dessert."

~

"That went pretty well, I think," Hollis said, without sounding like he was actually sure our presence at the meeting went well. "Maybe we should've stayed for dessert."

We were back in the Tahoe and still parked outside of the cafeteria.

"I'm exhausted. And I think I talked too much," I croaked.

"Sorry you're tired, Mags. You might've talked a little too much, especially there at the end. But I also think they heard what they needed to hear. And you were right about us paying a visit to the Robertsons prior to the meeting. It was like we were their old friends or something."

"Yeah, that did work out. But here's the thing. We've got to solve this fucking case. And I honestly think we're flailing a bit. We need to just pause and look at what all we know and don't know."

"We need some time to do that, and so far, we haven't had much of that," he said.

My phone rang. "Sergeant Blackthorne speaking."

"Sergeant, my name is Hannah Barnhart," the caller stated breathily. "I was at the meeting. I'm the person who asked about confidentiality. I would appreciate a few minutes of your time, as soon as possible, and while I have the courage to tell you what I know."

"Where can we meet?"

"At my house, if that's okay. I live closer to Kimberly, but right now I'm in my car and parked on the road shoulder just up the street from the school campus. I drive a green Honda Civic. As you head back out of town, I'll see you coming and pull out onto the main highway in front of you. That way you can follow me to my house."

"That will work, Ms. Barnhart."

"I believe what I have to share with you could be important, but it was told to me by a high school student. I'm the school counselor."

"I'm leaving the parking lot right now," I said.

We got back on North Street and drove toward Highway 402, and I spotted her green Honda as she moved from the shoulder and onto the road.

I followed her out of town and along the winding north fork of the John Day River through fecund countryside, with cows foraging in the emerald fields alongside the highway. After a twenty-minute drive, Ms. Barnhart turned down a short driveway a few miles north of Kimberly. She continued on to the top of a small hill and parked in front of her garage.

I pulled up beside the front yard of her cheery-looking little house, and

Hollis and I got out of our office-away-from-the-office. Ms. Barnhart unlocked the front door and invited us inside, where we sat all around her dining room table.

She reminded me of every counselor I'd ever known, all of whom I could count on one hand. But she had the armor of self-preservation I'd discerned during conversations with a few counselor types I'd met along the way and in the sporadic formal sessions I'd forced myself to attend.

"Would anyone like a glass of water?" she asked us. "I know I'd like one."

"I'll take a glass, thank you," I said.

"I'd appreciate one, too," Hollis put in.

She served the water and sat back down. I almost asked if I could take notes, but I knew she was already reluctant to have this discussion.

"A female student has come to me about some concerning incidents. I've reported the matter to Child Welfare...but let me just explain everything to you. The girl's name is Paula Johnson. Her parents are Charlotte and Troy Johnson. The family lives out in the country near Mr. Drake's ranch. One day several weeks ago, Paula was at a friend's house about two miles down the road from where she and her family live."

Ms. Barnhart paused and took a deep breath. "On her way back home, Paula was walking alongside the highway when Mr. Drake recognized her, stopped, and offered to give her a lift. It was cold, so she got in his truck. But, she told me, he didn't take her to her house. Instead, he apparently drove up some mountain road Paula didn't recognize. She said she asked over and over where he was taking her, but he didn't answer. Finally he turned onto an isolated dirt road and parked in a thicket of trees."

The woman inhaled again. "As Paula explained it, that's when he held her down and began to grope her. She said she was screaming, crying, and attempting to get out of the truck, but he was able to subdue her. By this time, Paula told me she was sobbing uncontrollably and begging to go home. He finally capitulated and drove her there. On the way to her house, he threatened to go after her younger sister if she told anyone."

"You're talking about the elder Mr. Drake, correct?"

"Yes, the man who was murdered."

"And you think this has something to do with his death?"

"I have no idea, but I just knew I had to share the information with you. And I'm assuming this will not become public if it has nothing to do with Mr. Drake's demise."

"Of course not."

"There's more," Ms. Barnhart continued. "Paula was walking back home from the same friend's house last Sunday, and Mr. Drake drove by her very slowly. She felt scared, threatened, and then another car appeared on the highway behind him. Mr. Drake drove away, and she says that was the last time she ever saw him."

Jesus fucking Christ, which I came close to saying to this seemingly distressed woman. No wonder counselors chose self-preservation mode.

"After that, Paula decided to tell me what had transpired. We discussed it, and she agreed to call her mother right away. She asked me to be there while she talked to her mother. I agreed, and she made the call and explained what had happened."

"When was that?" I asked.

"This past Monday, during our most recent session together."

Two days before Drake was murdered.

"Paula called from the speaker phone in my office, and I listened to the conversation," Ms. Barnhart confirmed.

"And you recognized Charlotte Johnson's voice on the other end?"

"I've spoken with her informally several times. So, yes. I recognized her voice. Not only that, but Paula is also not the kind of person who would fake a phone call to her mother or falsely accuse someone of sexual assault."

"I've met her briefly, and I'm inclined to agree with your assessment," I said.

"I'm afraid there's still more, Sergeant Blackthorne. A few months ago, Paula discovered her mother's journals. Mrs. Johnson is an extremely lonely woman, and she had an affair with Christopher Drake. When he broke it off, she apparently began having suicidal thoughts and somehow was given or bought, or stole, possibly, I guess...a gun."

The room was quiet but for the slow drip of water from the kitchen faucet.

I had to ask one question for the record. "In your professional opinion, is Paula emotionally or psychologically troubled?"

"Quite the opposite. She's a very intelligent and well-adjusted young adult who has been quite worried about her mother's state of mind."

"Has Paula actually seen the gun?"

She hesitated. "Paula found it hidden in a drawer in her mother's dresser. Her parents are opposed to guns generally, and handguns in particular, so she was shocked to find it at all."

"The girl was going through her mother's things?"

"Paula said she was worried her mother might be considering suicide...I don't think the girl knew exactly what she was looking for but wasn't expecting to find the gun."

"Ms. Barnhart," Hollis began. "The girl told her mother all of this—the assault, finding her diary and the gun?"

"Yes, all of it."

"Where's the weapon now?" I asked.

That caught Ms. Barnhart off guard.

"I don't know. And stupidly, I didn't ask Paula that question."

∾

I drove to Poison Spring Ranch a couple of notches above the speed limit. We hoped to catch up with Christopher Drake and ask about his possible affair with Charlotte Johnson. I was pretty certain it had happened, and I didn't think he'd deny it.

When we arrived, the black BMW convertible was gone, an indication he wasn't home. I started to turn my rig around to leave, but the porch and foyer lights came on. Lisa Drake, wrapped in her cashmere shawl, opened the front door and stepped out.

"Why don't you let me deliver the message to Mrs. Drake that we'd like Christopher to contact us?" Hollis offered.

"Thanks, pal. And let her know I'd like him to call me sometime this weekend."

"Are you sure about that, Maggie?"

"Absolutely. This case has to be solved before I'm rushed to the damn maternity ward."

14

NIGHT, APRIL 9

The two of us were dead tired and relieved the lights were out at Charlotte Johnson's place. Her car was gone as well, so we assumed she and the girls were out for the evening.

"We need to think through how we're going to approach Charlotte about the gun, the affair with Christopher, and her daughter's assault," I began. "Alleged gun, affair, and assault, I suppose."

"I'm surprised about the affair, I guess," Hollis said.

"It's been a long day, but I did make an offhand comment earlier alluding to the possibility."

"I thought you were kidding when you said that, Mags."

"I thought I was too, Holly. Anyway, learning that Mike Drake may have sexually assaulted Paula Johnson was a shock. But maybe it shouldn't have been."

"At this point, that disturbing claim seems likely to me. And we already know he wasn't the upstanding citizen a lot of folks thought he was."

"No, he definitely wasn't," I added. "Which makes pinning down his killer even more problematic."

"The girl—Paula—was surprised to find a gun among her mother's things, Ms. Barnhart said."

"In general, the banning of guns in anyone's household or property is so unusual in Grant County, and here we have a couple of neighbors who had such a ban."

"Except they really didn't, Mags."

"Yeah, you're right. Mike Drake was supposedly spooked by the threatening letters he received. But I wonder what spooked Charlotte? Assuming we accept what Paula told Hannah Barnhart about finding a gun among her mother's things, that is."

"I think it's odd Christopher would be carrying out a romance with Charlotte Johnson and Lydia Reed at the same time," Hollis said, taking the conversation in a new direction.

"Um, did you just fall off the turnip truck?" I laughed. "God, I love that expression."

"Are you teasing me about being blind to other people's proclivities? Because where being involved with two or more people is concerned, I just don't get it."

"Maybe it was just about the physical attraction. We both know it happens all the time."

"Yes, but for some reason, it still surprises me that Christopher would be seeing, dating, whatever..."

"Being the fuck buddy of two different women? Oops, I meant having a sexual relationship with two different women," I teased.

"You really can't help yourself, can you?"

"Honestly, where my best pal is concerned—that's you, by the way—I actually *can't* help myself. Anyway, we don't know how long his alleged relationship with Charlotte Johnson lasted. But, since you brought up Lydia Reed, she left tonight's meeting kind of abruptly."

"I noticed that too, but I assumed she might've needed to get home and check on her father," he added.

"Or Christopher, perhaps. Although, if you remember, she characterized her relationship with him as *friends with benefits*, which doesn't make it sound very romantic."

Hollis shrugged. "I just thought she was being dodgy."

"Dodgy. I like that."

For the next several miles, the mingling of engine and road noise substituting for music, we each were absorbed in our own thoughts. Charlotte Johnson was still on my mind. During our visit today, she reminded her daughters the three of them were going shopping in John Day tomorrow.

"Charlotte will be in town tomorrow. I'm going to call her in the morning and invite her to drop by the office," I announced.

"Don't you think she'll wonder what the deal is?"

"Of course she will. But I doubt very seriously she'll say no."

"I thought you were staying home and writing reports tomorrow?"

"I still plan to do that and also give Harry a heads-up about the gun found in the stable."

"I'll call Harry about the gun. And let's divvy up the report writing, but I promise, I'll work on the garden tomorrow and help Hank plant his tatoes."

I started to argue, but he interrupted me.

"You're my boss, but you're also my patrol partner. Hear that word *partner*? It means two people working together to get the job done."

"All right, partner. You win," I capitulated.

"This time, anyway."

"Goes without saying."

〜

As I drove on, the baby became more active, nudging my left side with an elbow, or maybe it was a foot. I tried to find a more comfortable arrangement for both of us but wasn't successful.

"Ouch," I whined. "Damn it."

"Are you okay?"

"I'm fine, but my back hurts. Plus little tot can't seem to get comfortable and appears to be taking it out on me."

"I recommend a full body massage when you get home," Hollis said.

My phone rang, and I turned on Bluetooth.

"Hi, Dun. Hollis just recommended you give me a full body massage when I get home."

"And when is that?"

"Just drove through Mt. Vernon, and we're on our way to John Day as we speak."

"You guys have had a long day," Duncan said. "I was getting kind of worried."

"Lots of backcountry driving, talking to folks, and then the community meeting."

"How'd the meeting go?"

"We killed it," Hollis put in. "Maggie had the bright idea of visiting with the organizer ahead of time."

"Hey, sometime this weekend, let's go grab that beer we keep talking about," Duncan suggested.

"Good idea," Holly said. "How about after you shut down the feed and tack tomorrow?"

"Sounds like a deal. I'll meet you at 1188 Brewing around four thirty and leave it to Jenna to close up shop for the day."

"Sounds good."

"I'll see you at home, babe," Duncan added.

"I'm looking forward to my massage," I managed to sneak in before he clicked off.

We drove on, listening to a Springsteen oldie, and by the time the ending riff played its way through, we had arrived at our police station. I dropped Hollis off and moved on up the road. We had agreed to touch base at some point tomorrow, leaving it open to accommodate whatever the four winds might blow in.

Duncan met me outside as I pulled up in front of our little place. The two houses on either side still sat empty. I had tried to talk Dorie into buying one of them after she sold her thrift store, but she balked at the possibility of being the nosey granny next door. I'd reminded her that she wouldn't be the child's grandmother—officially, that is. But she balked at that, too, saying something like, *Who the heck else has been your mother figure for the past twenty-five years or so?*

Duncan wrapped one of his beautiful, muscular arms around my shoulders, and we kissed.

"Love you, babe," he said.

"Ah, Dun. What would I do without you?"

"You'd be fine. Just not living above Dorie's thrift store any longer."

"Speaking of Dorie, let's invite her for dinner tomorrow night."

He hesitated. "Sure, yeah. Sounds good. But it means you have to be home long before eleven p.m."

I kissed his whiskered cheek. "What did you have for supper?"

"Made myself a chicken sandwich from the leftover bird we baked earlier this week," he said, opening the front door.

"*We* baked?"

"Yes, we. If I remember correctly, you turned on the oven."

"I promise to learn how to cook while I'm on family leave," I announced.

"Uh, not a good idea."

I shoved him playfully. "Not nice."

"I'm being serious. It's really not a good idea."

∼

I woke to Duncan's soft snore. He lay on his side, his back to me, my ripe body pressed into his. I thought about the night before. There was a time, if anyone had suggested that lovemaking during pregnancy could be amazing, I would've accused them of making shit up.

Just went to show I didn't always know what the hell I was talking about. Sex while expecting was every bit as satisfying, just a little more adventurous. I rose slowly from our bed, drew a robe over my bulbous tummy, and moved quietly downstairs.

Standing before the garden doors facing the snowy Strawberry Mountain Wilderness to the southeast, I was suddenly grateful for being alive, for the good fortune of loving and being loved, for the child I now carried. I began to weep.

"Babe," Duncan whispered, standing behind me. "Are you okay?"

"I'm fine, very fine. But you could hold me. I'd really like that."

Duncan wrapped his bull rider arms around me. We stood there for a few minutes until he steered me toward my mother's rocker, which he'd collected from the attic before I returned home last evening.

He sat down and gently pulled me onto his lap.

"I don't know why I was crying," I said. "I'm very happy."

"Drake's murder investigation going okay?"

"It's going...I'm just impatient for it to be over."

"I wish...," he began, but left his thought unspoken.

I was certain I knew what he was wishing for. "So do I."

He kissed me sweetly, and we sat quietly holding one another.

"Think I'll go take my shower," I finally said and slipped from his lap.

~

Shortly before eight thirty, I phoned Charlotte Johnson. After several rings, the call went to voicemail. I cleared my throat and left a message asking her to get back to me ASAP.

I brought out my laptop and placed it on the dining room table. Hollis had agreed to write up reports on our discussions with Lowell Gregg, Burt Greely, Sandy Connor, and Maeve and Clell Robertson over the weekend. That left me with our visits with Charlotte Johnson, the community meeting, and the conversation with Hannah Barnhart that followed last night's gathering in Monument.

I logged on to our unit's OSP account and began writing my reports. Fortunately, there wasn't much to say about the discussions with Charlotte or, in the end, the community meeting. The surprise discussion with Hannah Barnhart was another matter altogether. Even so, I had jotted down some clear notes and my good memory was still intact, so it had taken me a little over an hour to finish putting all the reports together.

I was beginning to think Holly had gotten the short end of the stick on the divvying-up of report-writing chores, when my phone buzzed. Charlotte Johnson was on the line.

"Good morning, Mrs. Johnson," I said.

"I'm sorry I didn't catch your call. I'd turned off my phone."

Something was different about her voice. She sounded hoarse and nasally.

"I wanted to chat with you before you headed out to John Day. I'd appreciate it if you and I could set up a time to meet at my office."

She sighed. "Today isn't a good day for that, Sergeant Blackthorne."

"Is that so?"

"I'm afraid I was called to the nursing home last evening. But my mother passed away before I was able to get there."

"I'm very sorry for your loss," I said. "But I'm afraid it's very important we meet."

"I'm not sure I can speak coherently today."

"Mrs. Johnson. Charlotte. Someone has come forward with information about one of your daughters."

"Dear God. This can't be happening."

~

I had insisted we meet but agreed to come Charlotte Johnson's way. Duncan wouldn't like it one bit, but he was working at the feed and tack today and then meeting up with Hollis afterward for a beer. I had plenty of time, and my plan was to question the woman and promptly drive back home. Easy peasy.

I was driving the sporty Subaru Crosstrek I'd bought last year, and the day was dazzling. The swiftly moving river mirrored the high-desert sky with its showy white clouds drifting over the golden hills of bunch grass and jade alfalfa fields.

I had picked up one of the mellow channels coming in via satellite radio. My father, Tate, was on my mind. Before he'd begun to accede to his annihilation by booze, he'd loved roaming the hills, mountains, and back roads of John Day River country, tracing the forks and tributaries, and exploring the heart of its long, winding waterway.

A fiddle rendition of "What a Friend We Have in Jesus" sounded from my phone.

"Hi, Dorie," I answered. "I was set to call you today. Duncan and I would like you to join us for dinner tonight."

"Too late. I'm calling to invite you to my place tonight. Kind of a house-warming party, but just you, me, and your hubby. And I'm cooking up one of your favorite meals as we speak. Clam chowder and homemade sour-dough bread."

"How can I say no to that? What time would you like us to be there?"

"I was thinking six thirty. Does that work?"

"I think so, but let me text Duncan and make sure. I'll call you right back."

I pulled off the highway and texted him.

He responded right away. "Sounds good. See you there after I meet Hollis for a beer. How's your day going?"

"A-okay. Yours?"

"Boring."

"Slow, huh?"

"Yeah. Although Cecil Burney just drove up. See you, babe."

I pulled back onto the highway. Cecil was the cantankerous operator of the only gas station in Seneca, and I hadn't seen him for quite a while. I wondered what on earth that old turd could possibly be shopping for at McKay's Feed and Tack.

Arriving at the Johnsons' home, I parked out front. Before I could knock on the door, Charlotte opened and stepped outside.

"Can we talk in your SUV? I don't want to risk having the girls hear our conversation."

The woman sitting across from me in my Crosstrek was clearly in the throes of grief. I momentarily rethought the timing of our discussion, but my role here was to go after any possible lead in our murder case, and I wasn't leaving till I heard what she had to say.

I liked Charlotte Johnson, liked how she was with her daughters, but I didn't like the fact she had recently acquired a gun, something that was supposedly out of character. Where to start the questioning of this distraught woman, though? It turned out that she knew where to start.

"I don't have a gun to off myself," she began. "Or to off anyone else, not even the disgusting bastard who came after my Paula."

"You're talking about Mike Drake, correct?"

"Who else would I be talking about?"

"So you were doing some acting when I informed you he'd been killed this past Wednesday?"

"I lied about how nice he was, if that's what you mean. Although he had been *very* nice to me and to my husband, Troy. It's a good thing Drake's already dead, though, because Troy would've gone after that asshole after he heard the news about Paula."

"Just not with a gun, I take it."

"No, Troy's six foot seven and very strong. He would've pummeled the hell out of Mike Drake."

"And you haven't told your husband yet?"

Her eyes teared up as she indicated her husband hadn't yet been informed of his daughter's assault. "I can't comprehend it yet myself. That or my mother's death; and it doesn't matter I was expecting her to go at any moment. When that moment came…"

I waited until she'd collected herself.

"Let's go back to Mr. Drake. Did Christopher ever let on there was considerable animosity between his father and him?"

"No. I didn't have any idea about that. Christopher and I were sexually attracted to one another, and that was all. And only for a short while."

"And your diary reflects that?"

"My diary reflects all kinds of shit. Probably like my daughters' diaries."

"Who called off the relationship?"

"Christopher."

"And you weren't depressed after he broke up with you?"

"It wasn't like that, Sergeant Blackthorne. We were friends who let things go too far. We met up sporadically for about a three-month period, and then it was over. I don't think Christopher's built for a long-term relationship."

That might be news to Lydia Reed.

"Are you and he still friends?" I asked.

"I hope so. More importantly, I hope I still have a marriage after Troy comes home and I tell him about the affair."

"Let's talk about the gun Paula found."

"Several months ago, we began having incidents at our place. Little ones at first. For example, one morning while the girls were at school, and I had gone shopping, someone came into the house and stole all of the coins in our change jar. We had left the back door open, so I assumed it was some neighbor kid who came in and took whatever they could easily grab and get out."

"And you asked Paula and Laney about the missing change?"

"They're free to take what they need for lunches and whatever, but they always ask or let me know."

That wasn't completely an answer, but I let it stand for now. I wanted to hear what else might've spooked her into procuring a gun.

She paused and blew her nose before continuing.

"I'd almost forgotten about the change jar theft, when I discovered several of my husband's power tools had been taken from our shed. I reported that to the Sheriff's Office. Soon after, someone had attempted to jimmy the locks on my car, and I ended up with some damage to a couple of the doors."

"Did you also report that to the sheriff?"

"Well, in both cases, my insurance agent required me to report the incidents to law enforcement when I submitted a claim. So yes, I reported it to the sheriff."

Charlotte massaged her temples.

"Would you care for some water? I brought a fresh thermos full."

"I just want to get this over with."

"Is there more you need to tell me?"

"Yes. Last month, while Troy was again off on one of his long-haul trips, someone came onto our property in the middle of the night and shot and killed our dog. They also left a note, telling us to get out, we weren't welcome here."

That surprised me. "Is your family new to the area?"

"We've owned this place since before the girls were born."

"Any idea who left a note or why?"

"None."

"And I have to assume you didn't contact the sheriff about this incident, because my office would've also been alerted to it if you had."

"No, Troy and I are still processing the whole thing."

"Is that when you bought the gun?"

"I didn't buy it. Troy's brother helped him decide what handgun to buy."

"It was my understanding that like the Drakes, you and your husband were opposed to such weapons, handguns in particular," I put in.

She looked at me curiously. "I don't recall telling you that, but yes, we had been. But after our dog was shot and the note was left, Troy was worried about leaving his family alone without protection. He's been calling nearly every day to check on us."

Charlotte paused. "But most importantly, this is our home. Troy and I don't want to leave, and we don't understand who or why anyone would kill our dog or threaten us."

"Do you know the brand or caliber of the gun your husband purchased?"

"I have no idea, Sergeant."

"And where is the weapon right now?"

"It's in my dresser drawer."

"Are you sure? Because yesterday, Christopher Drake discovered someone's handgun in the horse stable at Poison Spring Ranch."

"Shit," the woman said and climbed out of my rig.

I did the same and followed her inside her house.

15

MIDDAY, APRIL 10

I stood near the front door while Charlotte moved through the living room, down the hallway, and presumably into her bedroom. She emerged a short time later, knocked gently on the door across the hall from her room, and let herself in.

I heard her speak softly, urgently, and then she moved back to the hall and walked toward me.

"Please take a seat, Sergeant Blackthorne."

I did, and she seated herself across from me and stared in anticipation at the hallway. One of her daughters, Paula, I believed, soon slouched toward us, the epitome of teenage anger and insouciance, and stood sulking at her mother.

"Sit down, Paula," Charlotte commanded.

The girl sat. Reluctantly.

"You remember Sergeant Blackthorne?"

"She's not in uniform, so no, I didn't recognize her at first."

"Did you remove the gun I kept in one of my dresser drawers?" her mother asked.

"Yes."

Charlotte continued. "And what have you done with it?"

"I stashed it in the horse stable at Poison Spring Ranch."

"Why?"

"I thought it might make trouble for your lover—or should I say, the ex-lover who dumped you."

"Are you trying to impress the officer here with your snotty attitude?"

"Did you know the gun wasn't loaded?" I asked as a possible means of changing the dynamics at play here, although what the fuck did I really know about those dynamics.

The girl was quiet for a beat. "No."

"Mrs. Drake and her son called us out to retrieve the gun. And among the possible sets of fingerprints our forensics expert will find on the weapon, one set will be yours."

"I watch TV, officer, and I remembered to wipe it off before dropping it behind some kind of box in the corner."

"Which means you also got rid of anyone else's prints on the weapon."

"Just my parents' and mine."

"Also problematic, but my point, Paula, is your little stunt amounts to interfering with a homicide investigation, and it's an offense punishable under Oregon criminal statutes. And it's possible you could be tried as an adult rather than go through a juvenile proceeding," I stated in rather dramatic fashion.

"So?"

"If found guilty, you could be sentenced to an adult prison rather than a youth detention center," I said, exaggerating somewhat. "But let's talk about something else. Why did you stash the gun at the Drakes' horse stable?"

"I wanted to get it out of our house and, like I told you, maybe get Christopher in trouble."

Paula Johnson didn't pull any punches.

"You don't know much about firearms, do you?" I asked.

The girl shrugged.

"Ever see anything about forensics on those TV shows you watch?"

"Yeah, so?"

"Yeah, so a forensics expert will be able to figure out if that gun was used to kill Drake senior." Not a statement that could be made with one hundred percent accuracy—as in there being some potential for human error—but it was close enough for my purposes here.

I continued. "Not only that, but forensic analysis can also determine if the weapon you left in the stable had ever been fired." Again, that wasn't necessarily a certainty.

Paula's chin quivered. "Why did you buy that stupid gun, Mom?" she sobbed.

Her dazed mother responded, "I didn't, sweetie. Daddy bought it. He was worried about us after Snuffy was killed."

I had to assume Snuffy was the dog.

"What's going on?" The youngest daughter had joined us.

"Go back to your room, Laney. Please," Charlotte said.

"Is Daddy okay?"

"He's fine, honey."

"We're talking about that other thing, Lane," Paula said.

"Okay, but I'm hungry."

"Hi, Laney," I piped up. "I'm almost done visiting with your mom and sister. Everything's going to be okay."

Laney walked back to her bedroom. She didn't even slam the door.

I turned to her older sister. "Everything's going to be okay, right, Paula?"

The girl nodded. "I'm sorry if I made your investigation harder. But I'm not sorry that man is dead."

Paula and at least one other person could say the same.

"Honey, why don't you go into the kitchen and make breakfast for yourself and Laney," Charlotte suggested to Paula.

"Mommy, I'm so, so sorry I said those mean things to you." The girl got out of her chair and embraced her mother. "How about I make breakfast for all three of us? Oh, and for you too, officer."

"Sounds good, sweetie," her mother answered.

I stood. "Thanks for the offer, Paula, but I need to be on my way. Mrs. Johnson, would you mind walking with me back to my car?"

Charlotte rose from her seat and followed me outside, closing the door behind us.

"Your daughters are terrific," I said as we walked toward my Subaru. "I hope my kid grows up to be somewhere in the vicinity of their brand of terrific."

"You're not pressing charges?" she asked.

I shook my head. "Paula's been traumatized quite enough. But I do have one more question for you."

"What's that?"

"Your gun wasn't loaded. Why not?"

"After Troy left on his most recent long haul, I unloaded the weapon, put the bullets back in the box of ammunition, and hid the full box inside our shed."

"Your husband's returning tomorrow, right?"

"He is."

"When he hears about everything that's been going on, he might be glad the ammo wasn't available to Paula, assuming you haven't told him you put it in the shed."

"No, I've not told him about that either. I don't really know where to start."

"I can't advise you on that."

"Don't think anyone can."

"I'll contact you again if we need anything more from you, Charlotte."

I got back in my Crosstrek and motored down the driveway toward the highway. In the rearview, I watched her turn and walk back to her little house.

∼

By the time I reached Dayville, I realized I was famished, so I stopped at the little café in town and ordered their famous steak sandwich and fries, with a side of horseradish for the sandwich.

Halfway through my meal, Duncan texted me. "I'm home for lunch, where are you?"

"In Dayville enjoying a steak sandwich."

"Dayville?"

You've been busted, Blackthorne.

"I'm checking out antique stores, looking for a housewarming gift for Dorie." Which wasn't a lie, exactly. I planned to hit up the little place thirty-two miles up the road in Mt. Vernon.

"Did you finish your reports?"

"Yep."

"Yay!"

"How's your day going?"

"Still slow. I'll check in with you later, babe."

I'd thought about asking Dun why Cecil Burney had stopped in at his feed and tack store this morning, but it was best to keep our text convo short. I had promised not to do anything work related today, other than catch up on report-writing and possibly stop in at the office to visit with a potential witness. I was relieved he hadn't broached that last matter; I didn't believe I could've out-and-out lied about meeting with the witness at her home near Kimberly instead of my office in John Day.

Still, I wasn't sure I'd ultimately manage to avoid the argument that no doubt would've ensued if I hadn't left out that last part. No matter what, the deed was done, and I wasn't one bit sorry about it.

I finished my steak sandwich, paid my tab, left a nice tip, and got back on the road to Mt. Vernon. Paralleling the course of the John Day River, I passed by the pastures and hayfields fed by its waters and tucked against the flaxen hills laden with sagebrush. This route was as familiar to me as any among the network of highways, back roads, and dirt tracks I'd traveled daily over the last four-plus years.

I arrived in Mt. Vernon and pulled up in front of June Bug Antiques located on the main drag. It seemed odd to name a business after an insect considered a pest, but it had attracted me because of the display of antiques on the front porch of the two-story building.

A bell chimed as I opened the door, and a tiny woman reminiscent of Dorie popped up behind the counter.

"Afternoon! Let me know if you need any help."

"Thanks. I'm not even sure what I'm looking for."

"Oh, you must be shopping for a gift, then."

"That's right. For a special friend, a woman who's known me all my life. She just moved, and I want to find something special for her new home."

She slipped from behind the counter. "How sweet of you. I'm June Turner, and you are?"

"Maggie Blackthorne."

"I used to know a gal named Zoey Blackthorne."

"My mother. She passed away a long time ago."

"Yeah, I remember. You must've been just a girl then."

I nodded. "I was fifteen."

"That's a terrible time to lose a mama."

"It was. The gift I'm shopping for is going to Dorie Phillips, my mother's best friend and the woman who's been like a mother to me ever since."

"Dorie's awful good people."

"You know her?"

"Everyone knows Dorie. And loves her because she's kindhearted and good-natured. Just the kind of person who would take a fifteen-year-old under her wing. I'd forgotten she just sold her thrift store and bought a house."

"I'll just take a look around and see if anything has Dorie written all over it," I said, eager to find just the right gift.

"If you're thinking furniture, that's all upstairs."

"Thanks, maybe I'll take a peek."

I checked out the items on the first floor, entertaining the idea of a set of matching bowls, but decided they were too froufrou for Dorie. I moved upstairs where the antique furniture was displayed in a lovely, uncrowded, and well-lit space. And there it was in the corner, a twin of my mother's rocker. I sat down and rocked back and forth a few times. I looked around for the price tag. Four hundred dollars.

"That's perfect, Maggie."

I jumped and found June, the proprietor, standing behind me.

"Apologies for sneaking up on you like that," she said.

"I love this rocker. I actually have one exactly like it. It was my mother's."

"Well, that calls for the Zoey and Dorie discount. A hundred bucks per."

"Two hundred dollars off? I couldn't ask you to do that," I protested.

"And I just figured out you're in charge of the State Police office in John Day. So that's another fifty bucks off."

"June, that's way too much."

"No, it's not. That old rocker's been sitting up here for years just waiting for you to show up. And as a special gift to Dorie from me, I'll throw in the fifty-dollar brocade pillow that's sat in it for as long as I've been trying to sell the rocker."

"I don't know how to thank you."

"Well, you don't need to name that baby after me or anything, but spread the word that June Bug's is the place to go for antiques."

"I definitely will."

"What're you driving?"

"A small black SUV. It's parked out front. To make room for the rocker, I'll probably have to adjust the back seat so it lays flat."

"Okay, you sit here in the rocker while I go get my son from across the street. He's in charge of carting furniture up and down the stairs, especially when the buyer's a pregnant lady."

While June went to retrieve her son, I sat and rocked, admiring her stock of stuffed chairs and couches. I could've done without most of the framed artwork, so-called.

She soon returned with a very tall guy who was probably around my age. "Maggie, this is my son, Wayne."

I stood and shook his hand, and his face turned scarlet. "Nice to meet you, Wayne. And thanks for loading the rocker in my vehicle."

"Nice to meet you, ma'am. And, um, you're welcome," he mumbled while staring at the floor.

"Let's get to it," June said to Wayne and picked up the brocade pillow. "Is your SUV locked?"

"Yeah." I extracted my keys from my coat pocket and handed them to her, and we all filed downstairs, Wayne toting the rocker.

Standing at the front counter, I wrote out a check to June Bug Antiques for four hundred and fifty dollars, folded it, and waited for June. I heard the bell chime, signaling she was back or another customer had entered.

"Okay, Maggie," June said, picking up the check and placing it in the drawer of her cash register. "You're all set except for a receipt."

After making the receipt out for one hundred fifty dollars, she handed it to me. "If you have a girl, don't name her June."

"June's a nice name."

"No, it's not. Other kids will call her June bug, and she'll hate it."

"I hear you. Kids always called me magpie."

"There you go, you see what I mean."

"I do. And maybe I'll own a store like this someday and call it Magpie's Antiques."

"Ha. But I'd advise you to stick with law enforcement. At least you've got a good pension in your future."

"Be sure to tell Wayne I said thank you for loading the rocker. And thank you for having such a nice piece of antique furniture to sell me."

"Give Dorie my love."

"Will do."

~

I landed back at home just before three o'clock, and after I sat with Raleigh Cat for a while, I let him outside, climbed upstairs, and went to sleep.

I was awakened when my phone once again sounded the fiddle rendition of "What a Friend We Have in Jesus."

"Dorie?" I answered.

"I'm here with your hubby, and dinner's ready."

"What time is it?"

"Time for you to get over to my house."

"Sorry, I fell asleep and..."

"Alrighty. That's a good reason. We don't mind waiting for you, gal."

I flew out of bed, ran a brush through my hair, and considered putting on some lipstick, but that wasn't the look I was going for these days. On opening the front door, Raleigh Cat dashed back inside. I had managed to disappoint three of the beings I loved the most in the world, but at least I felt rested and energized. I'd find a way to make it up to all of them. In fact, I already had Dorie covered, and Raleigh Cat would soon get over it.

Back in my Crosstrek, I drove to Dorie's new home on a hill just above town. Duncan's feed and tack truck was parked outside her place. It also seemed that a neighbor must've been having some kind of gathering, because several vehicles were parked in the vicinity. It was Saturday night and apparently time for a party.

I knocked and opened the door, expecting Dorie's hug-filled greeting, but I was met with nothing but a dark room and silence.

"Wait a minute," I said.

A chorus of voices cried out, "Surprise!" Then the lights came on.

I had heard Hank's voice in the mix, so I knew not to say anything profane, but I really wanted to ask what the fuck was going on. It wasn't my birthday...ah, it was a surprise baby shower. And I would endure it, no matter what.

Dorie and Duncan hugged me, and the rest of the partygoers crowded round. Sherry Linn saluted me with her glass of wine, Harry followed suit with his can of beer. Lil, Hank, and Holly stood together in a corner, smiling, and then Hank was allowed to run to me for a hug. Doug Vaughn was in attendance with some shy woman I'd never met. And there were folks I hadn't seen in a while, the most interesting of which were Lynn Nodine and Cecil Burney sitting together, each sober and holding a can of 7 Up.

I'd never seen Cecil cleaned up, let alone sober, but he raised his glass for the first toast of the night. "To Maggie Blackthorne, the best effing cop I've ever met. And I know I don't gotta go through the details with you all, but I've met up with a lot of cops during my time on this planet."

Hollis followed with his own toast. "To the best police partner I could have."

"Likewise, bro," I said.

"Just have to say," Duncan began. "I'm one of the luckiest guys on this earth. Thank you for being who you are and for our life together."

With that, I teared up, and everyone quieted.

Finally, I could speak. "I wouldn't have much of a life without Dorie, Duncan, and all of my colleagues and friends." I laughed suddenly. "Or one former nemesis. Talking about you, Cecil Burney, talking about you."

"You're welcome," he said, and we all laughed.

Jen and Vicky Wilson arrived with little Tori in hand and apologies for being late.

"Time to eat," Dorie said, and everyone noisily lined up next to her table, which she had set up buffet-style.

~

Later in the evening, Dorie and I drifted to the kitchen to put away leftovers and stash plates, glasses, and utensils in the dishwasher. Meanwhile, Duncan had toted all of our gifts out to my car and carried the rocking chair I'd purchased that afternoon and set it up in Dorie's living room before driving home in his delivery truck.

When we were done tidying up the kitchen, I followed Dorie back to the living room, where the rocker now sat.

"What's this?" she asked.

"It's your new rocking chair," I told her.

"You can't be giving me Zoey's rocking chair."

"It's not Zoey's. I found it at June Bug Antiques, and I couldn't resist."

"Junie Turner had this pretty thing at her antique store?"

"Yep, she said it had been there for years waiting for me to buy it for you."

She hugged me tight before trying out the new rocker. "It's perfect."

"You'll have plenty of opportunity to use it after this baby's born," I warned her.

"Come here and give me your hand, please," Dorie said.

I did as she asked, and she took it and held it over her heart. "I love you, kid."

"I love you too."

"You have my permission to give your child a hyphenated last name."

"Well, thanks. But you do know we were already going to do that."

"I know, but I prayed over it and came to the conclusion it wasn't any of my business. Or the Lord's, for that matter."

"Glad to know I'm square with you both."

"Now, go on home to your husband so I can sit in my new old rocker and read my Bible."

I kissed the top of her head. "Good night."

"Good night, honey. I'm betting the next time I see you, you'll be holding Baby Blackthorne-McKay."

16

MORNING, APRIL 11

Duncan had fixed a Sunday breakfast to beat all Sunday breakfasts—steaks, eggs, biscuits and gravy. And for a topper, he had brought home a frosted pound cake from the bakery in town.

"I didn't think I'd be able to eat that piece of pound cake, but as you can see, I managed it quite nicely," I said. "It was all delicious, Dun. Thanks."

"You're welcome, babe," he said, then paused. "I have a favor to ask."

"Let's hear it."

"Promise me, no work today."

"Can't really promise that, can I?"

"Hollis is on call, right?"

"Yeah, and Doug's out on patrol somewhere."

"So, the emergencies are covered."

"The emergencies are covered."

"How about a picnic dinner at Strawberry Lake, then?" Dun suggested.

I peered out the garden door windows. The mighty Strawberry Mountain, where the lake was located, stood to the west of us. No question about it being a beautiful place, but it was still largely covered in snow.

"A picnic at Strawberry Lake sounds cold as hell. How about the fossil beds?"

"Aren't you sick of that part of the county, babe?"

"Well, I was really thinking about going to the Painted Hills." The kid suddenly began moving in waves. "Well, hello!"

"What's up?" Dun asked.

"Little dude's going for a swim or something."

"Or dudette. Maybe she's reminding you she's almost here."

"I hardly need to be reminded," I said.

"We'll have to ask her to explain herself when she arrives."

"Or him."

He winked. "All right, you talked me into a picnic out at the Painted Hills."

"Wow, you're easy."

"And maybe we can fit in a roll in the hay before we leave."

"Now you're talking."

~

We lazed around after our bedroom foray, talking about the various folks who attended last night's surprise party.

"Did Cecil stop by the feed and tack yesterday to offer up his name for our child?" I asked.

"Nah, he wanted to know what we needed for the baby."

"God, what a turnaround in that guy."

"Yeah. I figured he'd be a goner by now."

"Me too. Like a decade or so ago."

"I thought Lil looked healthy and in good spirits last night," Duncan said, changing the subject. "And Hank. What a good kid."

"And smart."

"You chatted with Lil for quite a while," he added.

"She's excited about the birth of our baby, and I suggested we get together for coffee next week. Hollis mentioned she was feeling down."

"Wouldn't know it from her mood last night. Friendly, laughing, having a good time. She's often kind of reserved."

"My guess is she wants to get on with her life now, leave the threat of cancer behind."

"I don't blame her. But anyway, I was almost pissed when I saw the rocker you planned on giving to Dorie. Thought it was yours at first, but then I saw the price tag from some antique store. Which I removed, by the way."

"You see, that's why I keep you around. Anyway, I was a little rattled when Dorie woke me from my nap. Guess I forgot to peel off the damn price tag."

"Oh, but you were so cute when we turned on the lights and shouted, 'Surprise!'" he said.

"What are you talking about. I'm always cute."

"Well, sure. I meant cuter, of course."

"Change of subject. I want the middle name to be the same as yours if we have a boy."

"I know. James. I guess I'd be okay with that, but it's kind of boring," he said.

"Hey, I forgot to tell you Dorie gave me the thumbs-up about giving our baby a hyphenated last name. She had to pray on it first, but she decided it wasn't her business—or the Lord's."

Duncan laughed. "We dodged a bullet there. But you're still going by Blackthorne, right?"

"Just when I'm on the job. Thought you were fine with that."

"I am, babe. But I could make some crack about you always being on the job."

"Har, har."

"Okay, we have James as a middle name for a boy, but what about a first name?"

"I think I might have to see this kid before I come up with a first name. Girl or boy."

"Oh, come on, just throw a name out there," he said.

"How about Willow for a girl?"

"Willow Belle Blackthorne-McKay. Yeah, I don't think so."

I sighed. "I don't know. How about Kathryn, then? Maybe Katie for short."

"Kathryn Belle Blackthorne-McKay. I like it, except for one thing. Kathryn's my sister's name. I love her, but I don't want to name my kid after her."

"That reminds me. Why didn't Kat come to the baby shower?"

"She's in Corvallis visiting Rain."

"All right, I'll give her a pass, then. Now back to Kathryn Belle Black-thorne-McKay. It's also a mouthful."

"Well, I guess we chose to go with a mouthful last name. Makes us stand out."

Duncan Blackthorne-McKay, ever the optimist.

"I noticed Cecil didn't use it when he toasted me last night, but I didn't want to correct him. He might not even know."

"More likely, he doesn't care. You'll always be Maggie Blackthorne to Cecil."

~

Our Sunday afternoon excursion to the Painted Hills—rightfully listed as one of Oregon's scenic wonders—was liberating. It was amazing what a few hours exploring a beautiful, prehistoric marvel did for a person's general attitude. And as an added bonus, cell service was unavailable.

It had been several years since either of us had visited the place, and we both had forgotten how surreal and stunning it was. The undulating knolls, forged of volcanic pumice and ash, were infused with rust, ochre, and coal-black layers of mineral deposits, all of which created an ethereal, other-worldly effect.

"That was awesome," I said as we finished our hike of the Carroll Rim Trail.

We had hiked all five trails within the Painted Hills "unit," as some unimaginative government toady had decided was the official term for various areas within the boundaries of a national monument. Of all the trails, Painted Cove had been my favorite. There, we walked between ancient scarlet knolls so close to us we could feel the heat radiating from the surface of the collective formations.

We now sat at a picnic table shaded by a grizzled juniper, its branches rustling in a dry wind. We had packed enough food to feed a horse, but other than a dubious-tasting energy bar and a small thermos of water, I hadn't had anything to eat or drink since Duncan served up his scrumptious breakfast this morning. Plus it was past four o'clock, and I was famished.

"I'm damned hungry," Duncan said. He stood and walked to my Subaru parked nearby, fetching a large cooler from the back.

Problem solved. And I didn't even have to whine.

After placing the cooler on the picnic table, we retrieved all the sandwich fixings and the pound cake left over from breakfast. I put together our sandwiches—about the only meal I could handily muster, besides boiling ramen and seasoning it with whatever spices were captured in the foil packet that came along with the dry chunk of noodles. I was also good at microwaving frozen entrées.

"How's your sandwich, Dun?"

"Delicious. That's smart to salt the tomato slice a bit."

With that, he took a sip of his beer.

"I loved Painted Cove Trail," I said.

"I did too. And I'm happy you were able to come hike all of them, including the Carroll Rim Trail. I mean, you're essentially nine months along. Gotta say, you rock, babe."

I blushed a little. "I'm in training for birthing your kid."

"I see it now. Right after the baby's born, you'll rise from the birthing bed, put on your uniform, and head out."

"Look up the name Lola Baldwin," I suggested. "In the early 1900s, she was the first female cop in Portland, right here in Oregon. And she served as a detective in some division having to do with protecting women."

"Why are you telling me this?"

"Lola Baldwin did her job, but she also had a personal life, a family."

"Was she investigating murders while pregnant?"

"I don't believe so. But that's not my point. She and other women paved the way for Maggie Blackthorne-McKay to become a cop."

"In your case, a good cop," Dun said. "Maybe too good."

"Hopefully, I'm a good cop. And a good mother."

Duncan placed his sandwich on his paper plate, picked up his napkin, and wiped his large hands. He tossed the napkin on his plate and moved one of those hands under my off-duty smock and up my round belly to my breasts.

"You are beautiful. Ripe. Thank you for this life, this experience, this possibility."

I took his other hand. "You're welcome. Without you here to love me for who I am, this would never have happened."

～

Duncan drove on the way back home, with the Yo-Yo Ma channel playing in the background. Interestingly, the music went with the day.

When we finally met up with cell service, I picked up a message from Christopher Drake. I'd forgotten Hollis had passed along word to Lisa Drake that I wanted him to give me a call sometime this weekend.

I leaned back on the headrest, listened to the celloist play Dvořák's "Going Home," and decided my conversation with Christopher could wait until tomorrow when I was back in the office.

In short order, we passed by Poison Spring Ranch, as well as the homes of Roger and Corky Edwards and Charlotte and Troy Johnson. The lights were out at the Drakes' ranch house but were on at the Edwardses' home, which may have meant the wife was back from Bend. The Johnson household was lit up, and a heavy-duty truck and chassis was parked beside the family's station wagon, signaling the return of Charlotte's husband, Troy.

I drifted off to sleep and was awakened by Duncan shutting off the engine, and with it, Yo-Yo Ma and his cello. Outside, the night sky had settled in.

"You were snoring," Duncan said.

"What?"

"Snoring. You were snoring."

"You're full of it."

He laughed. "Maybe, but you were still snoring."

"Bullshit. I don't snore."

He opened the driver's-side door. "If that racket wasn't you snoring, you need to get your rig to a mechanic ASAP."

I ignored him, opened my door, and slid out. "Smells great out tonight."

"That's the wild yellow roses, I think."

"Mixed with the scent of sagebrush?"

"Think you nailed it."

My phone buzzed. It was Hollis. "What's up?"

"I'm at the hospital. Christopher Drake's been shot. He's alive, and he wants to talk to us. More like he wants to talk to you."

"Where'd this happen?"

"Poison Spring Ranch. Mrs. Drake is inconsolable and apparently doesn't know anything except that Lowell Gregg found him in the stable after taking his horse out for a ride."

"What are his chances for survival?"

"No one's saying. I'm not sure they know."

"Who reported it?"

"Mr. Gregg. He called for the ambulance, and the dispatcher contacted me around six o'clock after sending the ambulance on its way."

"I've been out of cell service range most of the afternoon, but Christopher left a voicemail. I haven't listened to it yet, so let me put you on hold while I do that."

I pulled up voicemail and listened to the message. "Um, good afternoon, Sergeant Blackthorne. This is Christopher Drake. Mother said you wanted me to call you sometime this weekend. Anyway, I'll be available for a conversation anytime this afternoon and evening. Oh, and one more thing, something arrived in the mail for Father yesterday. We think it may be another threatening letter like the ones sent to him years ago. There's some chance we're mistaken, of course. But we haven't opened it, and we'd like to turn it over to you for inspection."

I got back on the line with Hollis. "Christopher phoned because his mother passed along word I wanted him to call me. Anyway, the interesting part of his message is that his father may have received another of those threatening letters."

"Who would wait thirteen years to send another one of those missives?"

"Maybe someone who's been out of commission for a while?"

"Like in a care home?"

"Or maybe in prison? Wouldn't be prudent to send threatening letters from the hoosegow."

"The possible new threat letter aside, what might it have to do with the shooting of Christopher Drake?"

"Perhaps nothing."

"Just a sec, Maggie," he said.

I could hear someone speaking to him in the background. I waited anxiously. Even though his likely affair with Charlotte Johnson seemed a bit out of character—to me, at least—I had grown to appreciate Christopher's streak of kindness, even his formal mannerisms. If he didn't survive his wounds, that would go down as a real loss.

"Are you still there?" Hollis asked.

"Yeah. What's the news?"

"He's going to be fine. And he's eager to speak to you tonight."

Duncan had carried the cooler containing our picnic leftovers into the house while I was on the phone, and I assumed he was still in the kitchen putting everything away.

"I'll be there as soon as I can, Holly."

"Room one fourteen."

17

NIGHT, APRIL 11

I dreaded telling Duncan I needed to take off for a while. We had shared a wonderful day at the Painted Hills, and now I had to leave.

"That was Hollis," I began.

"Yeah, I recognized his voice. And I'm pretty certain it wasn't a social call. I'm also sure you need to meet him somewhere."

"Blue Mountain Hospital."

"Well, that's better than having to drive to Kimberly. Now come give me a smooch and go do your thing."

I kissed him, grabbed my lightweight OSP jacket out of the front closet, and raced to my cop Tahoe. After arriving at the hospital, I quickly made my way to the front counter. The receptionist, a young man I didn't recognize, looked up from his knitting.

"How can I help you?" he asked.

I lifted my ID from my pocket and placed it on the counter. "I'm Oregon State Police Sergeant Blackthorne. Can you direct me to room one fourteen?"

"Um, yeah, I've heard of you, I think. Sorry, but it's after visiting hours."

"Mr. Drake is the patient in that particular room, and he asked that I come speak with him tonight. He has some important information to share with me."

"Wait here while I go ask the night nurse."

I checked his name tag. "Sorry, William. I don't have time to wait for you to go ask the night nurse. This is an important police matter."

His face reddened. "It's just down the hall."

I turned and moved down the hall in the direction William had indicated. The hospital was relatively small, and finding room one fourteen was as simple as counting to fourteen. I knocked quietly, and Hollis opened the door.

Christopher lay in bed facing the far wall and a bank of windows. His hospital gown had been removed, and I could see by the mass of bandages he'd been shot in his upper left side. I wasn't an expert, but the shooter may have been aiming for his heart. Or maybe his head. Again, forensic science wasn't my expertise.

Lisa Drake sat quietly in a chair not far from her son's bed. She appeared frazzled and in shock, but also relieved.

"I'm glad you're here, Margaret," she said and stood. "I need to step out and make a call to Sam Damon."

Her husband's funeral was scheduled for tomorrow, and perhaps she needed Sam to postpone the proceedings.

I touched her arm lightly. "We'll find out who did this, I promise you."

She smiled impassively. I was certain she was exhausted, primarily by life itself.

After she closed the door to his room, I moved to the other side of the bed to speak with Christopher. He appeared to be asleep but opened his eyes tiredly.

"Sergeant," he said, his voice hoarse. "Thank you for coming."

"Of course. Trooper Jones is here too."

"Yes, he's been helpful. You two make a good team. Could you come closer, please?"

I did so. The combined odor of body sweat, antibiotics, topical medications, and blood was overwhelming, forcing me to sit down in the chair between the bed and the wall.

"It was a woman. She came up behind me suddenly. Told me to raise my hands. Screamed as the gun fired. It happened so fast. I heard her run out of the stable, start an automobile...drive away. Think I passed out then, because the next thing I remember is Lowell...he was working to stop the bleeding using the first aid kit we keep in the tack room. Mother got me to the emergency room around five, I think."

"How are you feeling?"

"Exhausted."

"Any thoughts on who the woman was?"

Christopher was silent, so I threw out a name. "Lydia? Was it Lydia who shot you?"

"We...I broke up with her this morning, and she was a little pissed, I guess, or maybe she was just surprised," he said and flinched. "We weren't in a committed relationship, definitely not. So, no, she didn't come after me with a gun."

Perhaps Charlotte Johnson had pegged it right when she said she didn't think Christopher was built for a long-term relationship.

"You're sure she wasn't angry enough to try and kill you?"

"I am. And I certainly would've recognized her voice."

"Sorry to keep pressing the matter, but did you recognize the voice?"

Again, he was silent as he considered the question.

"The voice was familiar, on edge," he whispered. "But I can't place it exactly."

"Was it Sandy Connor?" I asked.

"Sandy? She's my buddy."

I took that as a no.

"Was it Charlotte?"

He hesitated. "She's not the type to scream."

I wondered if that comment was some kind of confirmation they had been involved for a short time. Other than that, I was out of guesses about who the female shooter was. Then something came to me.

"Could it have been Corky Edwards?"

Christopher winced. "Why would Corky shoot me?"

"I think that's enough for now, Sergeant Blackthorne." Dr. Hilliard, the hospital director, had quietly entered the room. We'd had a few encounters in the past, all positive. And I wasn't going to argue.

I moved from the chair. "I think you're right, sir."

"Why did you want me to call you this weekend, Sergeant Blackthorne?" Christopher asked.

"That discussion can wait until you're up and around," I said.

Christopher took a shallow breath. "Did it have something to do with Charlotte Johnson?"

I paused.

"It's all true," he continued. "And it's all my fault."

~

Hollis and I stood together in the hospital parking lot under a new-moon sky saturated with stars. Nearby Canyon Creek rushed toward the John Day River, carrying the sweet scent of mountain snowmelt. Being outdoors was a relief after the hospital room.

"So what do you think about all of that, Maggie?" Hollis asked.

I had just finished telling him about the discussion I had yesterday with Charlotte Johnson and her daughter Paula.

"I think we have a shitload of unanswered questions. I also think Christopher Drake has a problem when it comes to getting a read on some people."

"All right, Nostradamus, who does he have a problem getting a read on?"

"They tend to be women. My guess is Lydia Reed has gotten tired of being just a girlfriend, and maybe she found out about his tryst with Charlotte Johnson and confronted him."

"Do you think that's why he broke up with her?"

"Possibly. Speaking of Charlotte, she's a bit of a hot mess—smart, lonely, bored, stuck out in the hinterlands, and Christopher took advantage of that."

"Do you believe it's possible she shot him?" Hollis asked.

"I don't. She's the woman who hid the ammunition for the gun her husband purchased. Besides, after our discussion yesterday, I don't think she would stroll to Poison Spring Ranch and shoot her neighbor and former lover."

"Yeah, I'd have a hard time believing that too."

"And as I've wondered before, Corky Edwards might easily have wanted him dead," I added.

"Because Mr. Edwards's stroke followed on the heels of Christopher's confirming Mrs. Edwards once had an affair with Mike Drake?"

"Yes."

"That's all very Shakespearean," Holly opined.

"First Nostradamus, and now Shakespeare? What's up?"

"I always trust your intuition, Mags, but what does all of this add up to?"

I sighed. "I was just thinking out loud, I guess."

"Maybe. But of those three women, Corky Edwards stands out to me."

"Only if she left her ill husband back in the Bend hospital to carry out the deed."

"Right. Or perhaps he passed away, and she's back home," Hollis suggested and pulled out his phone.

"Well, I think someone's there. Duncan and I drove by the place on our way back from hiking in the Painted Hills, and the lights were on."

"I'm looking through obituaries on the *Blue Mountain Eagle*'s site. There's not one for Roger Edwards. Or it's not been published yet, anyway."

I checked my watch. It was a few minutes past nine o'clock. "No matter what, we should leave all of this until tomorrow."

"Detective Bach is back then too, right?"

"Right."

"So first thing in the morning, we have a murder board to update." He reached into his pocket and pulled out a small evidence bag. "Almost forgot. I took custody of the slug they removed from Christopher's shoulder. I'll turn it over to Harry tomorrow."

"You're the best, Holly. See you in the morning."

∾

Halfway home, my phone buzzed, and seeing it was Sandy Connor, I pulled over and answered.

"Good evening, Sandy," I said.

"Hi, Sergeant Blackthorne. Um, this may be nothing, but I was wondering about something. I don't know if it's useful to you or not."

"Please, continue."

"I really like Burt Greely, and as I've already told you, he thought Mike Drake was a mean asshole to Christopher. Well...and I want to assure you, I'm an open-minded person, and I don't care who other people are attracted to. But I'm pretty sure Burt has, um, strong feelings for Christopher."

"Are you suggesting Mr. Greely might have something to do with Mike Drake's murder?"

"I guess I'm suggesting you might want to have an in-depth conversation with him about it."

"What makes you think we haven't?"

"Well, I ran into him at PSR today. I go every Sunday and ride my horse all over the ranch property. Anyway, Burt said he'd put on his slow-witted act for you and Trooper Jones."

I thought back on our encounter with Burt Greely. Grouchy and a bit obtuse was my take on the guy. And, at the time, I'd also wondered if he had romantic feelings for Christopher Drake.

"Was Christopher around while you and Mr. Greely were there?"

"Not while I was there, I don't think. His dad's convertible wasn't parked out front, so I assumed he was gone, but maybe his mother had driven it somewhere."

"Thanks for the word about Mr. Greely. I'll bear it in mind."

"Oh, you're welcome. I hope I didn't come off as a gossip."

"Not at all."

"You have a nice evening," she added and hung up.

Afterward, I wasn't sure what to think about her call, but perhaps I was beginning to be suspicious of everything and everybody.

~

Monday morning, six a.m., and I was exhausted. I hadn't expected this at the end of my pregnancy, even though I'd been told and had read over and over that it was a likely possibility. I had recently turned forty-two, and I'd suffered the illusion that my body was a great deal younger. Nature's big joke was on me.

I sat up, swung my legs out from under the covers, planted my feet on the floor, and stood.

"Are you okay, babe?" Duncan asked sleepily.

"Yeah, sorry I woke you."

"Don't be sorry. I want to make sure you're okay."

"I'm fat, my feet are swollen, and I have a murder to solve. And more."

"What's the 'and more'?"

"Someone else was shot yesterday."

"That'll be all over the local news today, so you might as well tell me who."

"You mean it will be spread throughout the gossip chain today."

"One or the other. Possibly both."

I sighed. "Somebody tried to kill Christopher Drake."

"My God. What the hell?"

"That was the reason I had to go to the hospital last night. He's going to live, but the shooting complicates our other investigation."

"May I ask why?"

"Jesus, Dun. Could you just take my word for it?"

"I'm worried," he said.

"The baby will be fine."

"Damn it. It's *you* I'm worried about."

"I'm going to go take my shower," I said and proceeded to waddle out the bedroom door and down the stairs.

Once in the bathroom, I stared at my reflection in the mirror. I saw Zoey there. My sad mother preparing to give birth to me, her only child.

"I could use your advice about now," I said.

My wild dark hair came from Tate. He had tried, I guess, to be a real father to me after Zoey's suicide. All that booze, he couldn't muster the wherewithal.

I stepped into the shower and let the hot water run until it turned cool. I got out and dried my bulbous torso, my inexplicably large breasts, my new ass. I wrapped myself in a robe and padded to the kitchen, where I knew I would find Duncan fixing my breakfast. But I was wrong. I listened for him, then trudged upstairs to apologize. He wasn't there. I peered from the bedroom window. He had already left in his feed and tack truck.

"Goddamn it," I whispered. I had looked forward to presenting him with some possible names I'd thought of for our child.

I detached my phone from the charger on my dresser and dialed Duncan's number.

"Hi, Maggie. I can't really talk right now. A couple of John Day police officers called me while you were in the shower. Someone broke into the feed and tack last night or early this morning."

"Is everything okay?"

"Well, so far, I haven't discovered any missing inventory."

"I wanted to call and apologize for being a snot earlier."

"No worries, babe."

"Call me later, Dun. I love you," I said before hanging up.

Retrieving a pad of paper from a bureau drawer, I wrote down the names I wanted to remember to suggest to Duncan. After which I dressed and fixed myself a bowl of cereal. While I sat at the dining table eating my breakfast, I thought back to last night's rambling discussion with Hollis.

"Shit." I suddenly remembered something.

I rinsed out my cereal bowl, retrieved my laptop, and sent an email to Hollis and myself at the office. "Find out what time Charlotte's husband, Troy, got home yesterday and whether or not she told him about her affair with Christopher."

~

I dropped by the feed and tack on my way to the office—not to interfere, but to get a sense of the extent of the theft. I also didn't like how the day had started off. More to the point, I didn't like how I'd begun the day.

Inside the store, Officer Bob Nolan and an officer I'd never met appeared to be checking for any damage and searching for clues.

"Hi, Bob," I said, entering the crime scene. "Is Duncan around?"

"Good morning, Maggie. He's in the storage room checking inventory. But you should probably wait right here."

I pulled a pair of nitrile gloves from my pocket. "I'll be careful."

I walked toward the storage room, and that's when I saw the message the perpetrator had left for Duncan. *TELL YOUR WIFE TO BACK OFF!*

"Hmm. This murder case gets curiouser and curiouser." I pulled out my phone and took a picture of the sign. Whoever wrote it out removed a few items—a couple of horse blankets and ropes—and stacked them neatly on the checkout counter before tacking up the message written in precise lettering on a large piece of white posterboard.

Duncan emerged from the storage room.

"Babe. You should've told me you were coming."

"So you could hide the sign?"

"No, so I could give you a heads-up."

"Well, I'm here now. I came to make sure you were doing okay."

"I'm doing fine. It appears that nothing was stolen and whoever wrote that message doesn't know you very well. Because I don't know anyone who could tell my wife to back off," he said and put his arm around me. "But be careful out there. And please don't go anywhere without Hollis."

"I hear you," I said.

"Who do you think might've written this?"

"I have no idea, but I'd bet the farm it was a woman."

"Because it's got a few flourishes?"

"Well, that and it's legible."

18

MORNING, APRIL 12

On my way out of McKay's Feed and Tack, I noticed Sheriff Cal Norton had arrived to add his two cents to the investigation of the break-in. I decided to take the opportunity to chat with him about the theft of power tools from the Johnsons' place, as well as the damage inflicted on Charlotte's car when someone tried to jimmy the locks.

"How's the Drake case going?" Cal asked before I could get to my questions.

"A lot of loose ends to tie up yet," I said. "But in talking to a neighbor of the Drakes, I learned they had some power tools stolen out of their shed a while back, followed by someone attempting to break into their car."

"You're talking about the Johnsons, right?"

"That's right. Did you ever pick up any clues about those incidents?"

"Nothing, I'm afraid. And I figured they weren't related."

"I have a feeling they could be, but only because Mrs. Johnson told me someone came onto their property in the middle of the night last month and shot and killed their dog."

"That's at least the second dog shooting in recent months. But the Johnsons didn't get in touch with me about it. That poor animal."

"And apparently whoever killed the dog also left an unfriendly note telling the Johnsons to clear out."

"What?"

"Yeah, afraid so. But I'd appreciate it if you didn't approach Mr. and Mrs. Johnson about that until we figure out whether or not any of those incidents are connected to our investigation."

"No problem, and I'd appreciate you keeping me in the loop if there are any more threats to the family."

"Will do, Cal."

That said, I didn't plan on letting the sheriff know about Mike Drake's molestation of Paula Johnson. I deemed it unnecessary given Drake's demise, and it also would've been a breach of trust.

⁓

When I arrived at the office, Hollis, Harry, and Sherry Linn were dissecting the surprise baby shower, particularly the shift in Cecil Burney's health habits—from falling-down drunk to teetotaler.

"I honestly don't know how he's lived this long," Harry said.

"He's led a pretty tough life, all right," I said and hung up my jacket.

"How are you this morning, Maggie?" Sherry Linn asked.

"Pregnant."

She laughed her Sherry Linn laugh. "I see that."

"Are you ready to hear my report?" Harry asked.

"Absolutely."

"Good morning, everyone." Detective Al Bach had arrived, with Trooper Doug Vaughn trailing right behind.

Our front office area wasn't designed for five people, let alone six, and one of them taking up more than her share of the space. The attached room containing four officer desks couldn't comfortably accommodate many extras either. And the alcove in back, near the evidence locker and bathroom, was but a tad larger, although it at least had a table to gather around and enough wall space to tack up a murder board, even two, as had been called for in the past.

"I don't know about anyone else," I began, "but I need to check my email before we get started."

I moved toward my desk, Hollis following close behind.

"Speaking of emails," he said, "what did that cryptic note about Troy Johnson mean?"

I turned on my computer. "He was supposed to return home from his long-haul trip yesterday. I don't know what time he was expected, but it's possible Charlotte told him about her affair with Christopher Drake. She might've also told her husband that Mike Drake assaulted their daughter."

"So she confirmed the affair?"

"She did. Also said it didn't go on for long."

"And all we know about Troy Johnson is that he's a long-haul truck driver?"

"That and he's six foot seven and strong."

"Really?"

"That's what his wife told me when I met with her on Saturday."

"I remember now. She was coming this way to go shopping with her daughters, and you were planning to call her and ask her to meet you at the office."

"As it turns out, her mother died on Friday night, so I drove out to Charlotte's place. I learned her hubby bought the gun after their dog was shot dead. Anyway, her oldest daughter decided to stash it in the stable at Poison Spring Ranch."

"To get Christopher in trouble?" Hollis asked.

"Yep."

"You had an interesting Saturday, Mags."

"Just all the way around."

"Anyway, didn't Christopher say it was a woman who shot him?"

"Well, for the time being, let's assume it's possible he could be wrong about that. Oh, and before I forget," I added, snared my phone out of my utility belt, opened up to the shot of the sweet little note left in Duncan's store, and passed the phone to Hollis. "Someone broke into the feed and tack and left this."

"Oh, they don't know who they're dealing with, do they," Holly remarked.

"I guess not."

"I think it looks like a woman wrote it."

"That's what I said to Duncan." I gazed at the handwritten warning for a moment. "On Saturday, Charlotte Johnson told me someone shot and killed the family's dog a while back. They also left a note, telling the Johnsons to get out, they weren't welcome there."

"Did she save the note?"

"I didn't ask, but I'm going to now."

Al Bach cleared his throat behind us. "Maggie, Hollis. I'd appreciate you filling me in on what I've missed."

∼

We invited Harry to join us in the alcove as we brought the detective up to speed and updated our murder board. In the midst of the discussion, Sherry Linn interrupted to let me know Lisa Drake was on the phone and anxious to speak to me. I followed Sherry Linn back to the front counter and picked up the call she'd placed on hold.

"Good morning, Mrs. Drake," I said. "How can I help you?"

"Christopher checked out of the hospital earlier this morning, and I have no idea where he went."

"Did he talk to anyone at the hospital?"

"He collected his prescriptions and told the nurse he had to attend his father's funeral this afternoon. Dr. Hilliard called me, but Christopher had already left the hospital. I phoned Lydia, but she said she hadn't seen him, and I got the sense that they'd had a quarrel or something."

It not being my place to inform her that Christopher broke it off with Lydia, I remained silent on that point.

"You stepped out of your son's room last evening while I spoke with him," I began. "You said you were going to call Sam Damon. Was he not able to reschedule the funeral?"

"Yes, he was, and Christopher knew that. Sam even volunteered to contact the newspaper and radio station to help get the word out."

"So why do you think Christopher left the hospital?"

"I wish I knew, Margaret."

"And he was without transportation?"

"As far as I know."

"Who would he call for a ride somewhere?" I asked.

"Other than me or Lydia, I have no idea."

It went without saying that Grant County had no taxi service, but I had a few thoughts about who might've given him a ride but decided to keep those thoughts to myself.

"I'm in a meeting right now," I continued. "But I'll call you back as soon as I can. In the meantime, if he turns up, leave a message with our office manager."

"Thank you, Margaret. And I'm going to contact all the motels in John Day. He may have checked in to one."

"That's a good idea."

"There's one more thing. He left a message with hospital staff for you."

"Oh, what was that?"

"He said to let you know you're on the right track."

Exactly what the hell did that mean?

"Well, I hope so, Mrs. Drake."

"I'm praying you are, Margaret."

I rejoined Al, Hollis, and Harry in the alcove, where I discovered the results of Harry's forensic analysis had been jotted down on the murder board. He had come up with very little regarding the snowmobile tracks, the thirteen letters, or fingerprints—other than those belonging to the Drake family.

Harry had been able to identify the larger set of boot prints near the dead bull as belonging to the murder victim. The casts of the second set of boot prints found there were unidentifiable in terms of size. And those collected on the ground by the passenger side of the dead man's truck were but a mishmash of tread marks. Similarly, any fingerprints on the passenger-side door were obliterated, likely due to a wipe-down by the killer.

Harry had also just been handed the gun found in the stable, but that didn't stop him from opining about it. "Ah, a Smith and Wesson subcompact. I'm betting it's never been loaded or shot. I'm almost one hundred percent certain of that. It's also been wiped clean. And as I've already noted, the .22 found in Mike Drake's Ram pickup had never seen a bullet either."

"Good to know the gun in the stable has probably never been used. It was stashed there by a seventeen-year-old girl who had been assaulted by

Mike Drake," I announced. "And for reasons not associated with our homicide case, the girl wanted to make trouble for Christopher Drake."

"I trust your judgment here, Maggie. We don't need to get a seventeen-year-old involved in our investigation if we don't have to," Al said.

"But we may need to get her father involved in our secondary investigation. Someone shot Christopher Drake yesterday."

"Yes, Hollis told us about that incident and turned over the slug to Harry."

"The girl's father's name is Troy Johnson. He's a long-haul truck driver, which keeps him on the road for long periods of time. The Johnson family lives up the road from Poison Spring Ranch. And Mr. Johnson's wife explained to me on Saturday that she had a brief affair with Christopher Drake, and I strongly believe she told her husband about the affair when he returned home Sunday."

"I see. But you're not certain that's the case."

"I'm certain Mr. Johnson returned yesterday, as expected, because I saw his truck and chassis parked in front of the family home as my hubby and I drove back from the Painted Hills last evening."

"There is one catch to that, right, Maggie?" Hollis put in.

"You're right. Christopher Drake told us he was shot by a woman. Said the shooter came up behind him, told him to raise his hands, and screamed when firing the shot. Hollis and I talked to him last night at the hospital, but we haven't had an opportunity to question him further."

"I see," Al said. "Perhaps we should call on him sometime today."

"Well, I'm afraid that's what the phone call was about."

"Oh, no," Hollis remarked. "Did he pass away?"

"No, he checked himself out of the hospital this morning."

"That surprises me. He seemed pretty miserable when we talked to him last night at the hospital."

"Yeah, surprised me too. His mother called to tell us, and she was distressed, and maybe a little angry with her son. She's hoping she'll find him in a motel somewhere in town. But he did leave a message for us with hospital staff."

"What's the message?" Al asked.

"He said to tell us we're on the right track."

"Regarding what?" Hollis wondered.

"Good question. Last night I asked him if he thought his attacker was one of the women he currently has regular contact with. But he said no to every woman I mentioned."

Hollis stepped to our murder board and began listing the women's names and their relationship to Christopher:

- *Lydia Reed, ex-girlfriend as of April 11*
- *Sandy Connor, horse boarder, so-called buddy*
- *Charlotte Johnson, neighbor, recent affair*
- *Corky Edwards, neighbor*

"Might as well include everything," I nudged.

He added a comment regarding the stroke Roger Edwards suffered and what the man had learned shortly before he fell ill and was hospitalized in Bend.

"You should know too, Al, that Drake's relationship with Corky Edwards was one of many such dalliances he had with other women over the years."

"And there's no reason to believe Mrs. Drake might've killed him?" Bach asked.

"I wouldn't say no reason. And until we have something more definite, we need to remain open to any possibility," I affirmed.

"Good answer, Sergeant."

"There's something else I want to add. The lights were on at the home of Mr. and Mrs. Edwards last night. I don't know if there was a vehicle parked outside, and they may always have their lights on a timer so the house is lit up at night while they're away."

"Have you tried to call them?" the detective asked me.

"No, I just now remembered, I'm afraid."

"There's a lot going on, Maggie," Al said.

"Speaking of a lot going on," Harry said and stood. "I have an appointment with Burns OSP and need to get on the road."

"What's that about, if you don't mind me asking?" Bach inquired.

"A string of robberies, and they're struggling to get to the bottom of it all." Harry put his hat on. "I'll let you know if my assessment about the gun found in the stable is correct."

"Take it easy, guy," I said as he left. He gave me a thumbs-up and kept walking.

"Maggie, show Detective Bach what was found in Duncan's store this morning."

I brought out my phone and turned to Al. "Someone broke into my husband's business last night or this morning. They didn't take anything, but they left this note."

He took my phone and read the message that had been left by whomever.

"This person doesn't know you very well, does he or she?"

"She, I think. And no, she doesn't know me very well."

"Are we assuming that the sign has something to do with the homicide investigation?" Hollis asked.

"I guess I am," I answered.

"What else would it be in reference to?" Bach asked.

I gazed at the list of women Hollis had written on the murder board. Next I thought about any negative encounters I'd had recently with any of the locals, but nothing came to mind. But for some reason, something else was quietly eating at me. I scrolled through the petite online landline listing for Prairie City until I found the number of the nursing home, pulled out my cell phone, dialed the number, and turned on the speaker.

"Good morning, Prairie City Residential Care."

"Good morning, I'd like to speak with one of your residents. Would you be able to connect me to her room?"

"The name, please."

"Gloria Harrison."

"I'm sorry. There isn't anyone by that name living in our facility."

"Perhaps she passed away recently?"

"I've worked here for seven years, and we've not had a resident by that name."

"Thank you for your time."

"You might try Prineville. We have a sister care home in Prineville, and there might be other facilities over there I don't know about."

"Thank you for the suggestion. Sorry to take up your time."

"Ah, not a problem, ma'am."

After hanging up, I was pissed. Mostly at myself. "Charlotte Johnson is quite the actress. She must have had a good laugh about putting on her little act for two hick cops."

"Fill me in on Charlotte Johnson, Maggie," the detective said.

"This might help explain it, Al. Hollis, please add *lied about her mother being in the nursing home in Prairie City* next to her name."

"Why would she lie about that?" Hollis asked.

"Better question, what else has she lied about?"

19

MID-MORNING, APRIL 12

Charlotte Johnson's mysterious lie made no sense to me. Why would she make up the fact that her mother was in the nursing home in Prairie City, let alone tell me her mother had died there on Friday night?

"We should've checked out her story in the first place. I don't know what I was thinking," I said.

"I found her completely credible too, Maggie," Hollis offered.

"You can fire us right now, Al."

The detective shrugged. "I don't think being snookered by a witness in a homicide investigation is a legitimate cause for termination."

"Here's the scary part. The woman seemed visibly shaken by the supposed death of her mother. Almost as upset as she was about what happened to her daughter."

"Her daughter was the girl assaulted by the murder victim, correct?" Bach asked.

"Yes."

"And that's not a lie too?" the detective wondered.

"No, if you recall, a very concerned school counselor informed us about that and listened to the girl's conversation when she told her mother about it."

"Right, right," Al said. "Did Mrs. Johnson fabricate the relationship with Christopher Drake?"

"Well, he's pretty much confirmed there was a relationship, Detective," Hollis put in.

Bach sighed. "Could this investigation get more convoluted and confusing?"

"Well, Al. Now that I've discovered Charlotte Johnson lied about her mother's death, I'm not sure it could."

"Yeah, I found her to be the most even-keeled of all of the folks we've talked to about Drake," Hollis said. "But we now know she's been untruthful about her mother, so she was obviously lying when she told us she and her daughters drove to Prairie City early on the morning Drake was killed."

"That's right," I said. "They were supposedly on the way to visit her *very ill mother*."

Hollis pointed to the names of the women noted on the murder board. "I guess that leaves Sandy Connor as the most even-keeled of the four women we've listed."

"That reminds me. I had a somewhat odd phone call from Sandy Connor last night. She wanted to let me know she thought Burt Greely had 'feelings' for Christopher."

"You're using air quotes?"

"Why, yes I am, Trooper Jones."

"Was Ms. Connor suggesting that Mr. Greely might've been someone to investigate further for the murder of Drake senior?" Detective Bach asked.

"I think so. Mr. Greely didn't view the man as particularly nice to his son," I said, then paused. "I might regret saying this, but he just seemed like a crank, not a killer."

"He also said he'd never had any dealings with Drake senior," Hollis added.

"All right," the detective said. "How can I best assist you at this point?"

"Excuse the interruption, everyone." Sherry Linn had joined us. "Christopher Drake is here to speak with you, Maggie."

Would hardly be prudent to invite him back to the alcove, where our murder board was tacked up on the wall.

"Thanks, Sherry Linn. Tell him I'll be out there shortly," I said.

"The guy seems like he's in quite a bit of pain," she added.

"I take it you think I should go talk to him ASAP."

"I'll stay back here while you do that, Maggie."

"All right, I'll go talk to him."

"Do you need a witness?" Hollis asked.

"Maybe. And he thinks we make a good team, remember."

"Perhaps you need another witness," Bach suggested. "Like a homicide detective."

"Excellent idea, Al."

We all rose and strolled to the front counter. Christopher Drake looked terrible, and Sherry Linn had pegged it—he was in a world of hurt.

Hollis and Detective Bach stayed behind the counter, and I moved closer to the bandaged man, picked up the metal folding chair next to his, placed it in front of him, and sat down so we were seated face-to-face.

"What's going on?" I asked.

"I made a mess of things," he answered, his voice heavy.

"We're taking you back to the hospital."

"I have all of the medications I was being given there, including the painkillers, and I'm going home. Mother is on her way, and she's quite capable of changing out the bandages. I asked her to meet me here."

Our police station was a bus station now?

"Who picked you up at the hospital?"

"No one. I walked from there to the pharmacy. And from there, I walked to the park just to think things through. That's when I decided to come see you."

"You said you made a mess of things. Were you talking about your breakup with Lydia?"

"No, that was bound to happen."

I threw out another name: "Charlotte?"

"She was a mess to begin with. Mental illness, I think. And I made it worse."

I could now see mental illness as a possibility. And I'd missed any signs of it. Thought the opposite, as a matter of fact.

"Might she be the person who shot you?" I said.

"I seriously doubt that. She's really afraid of guns."

"Could it have been her husband?"

He winced. "It was a woman, Sergeant, remember?"

"Charlotte's husband returned home sometime yesterday."

"Troy's my friend. We have a lot in common."

"Like Charlotte, for example. And she might've told him about the affair."

"Stop, please," Christopher whispered. "What time is it?"

I checked my phone. "Ten thirty."

His hands shaking, he picked up the large white pharmacy bag he'd placed on the floor beside his chair, pulled out a bottle of pills, and took one.

"Would you like some water?"

"I have a bottle in the bag." He retrieved his water and drank slowly.

"Tell me about the mess you made," I said.

"Roger Edwards. I answered honestly when he asked if Father and Corky were involved in a relationship several years ago. I caused his stroke when it would have been so easy to have lied."

"I've never met Mr. Edwards, but he must've known somehow. You only affirmed it."

"And now Roger is dead. He passed away two days ago. And I'm responsible for it."

"Who informed you of that?"

"Mother. While she was still at the hospital last night, a friend of hers phoned to let her know."

"I'm sorry to hear about Mr. Edwards's death," I said. "Why did you leave a message for us with hospital staff saying we were on the right track?"

He sighed. "Yesterday you mentioned Roger's wife, Corky. I sort of scoffed at your question about her being the one who shot me. But the more I thought about it, the more it made sense. My actions ultimately killed Roger. An eye for an eye, and all that."

"If you think it's possible she shot you, how likely is it she killed your father? Source of the problem, and all that."

"I'd have to think about that."

"Her husband's stroke occurred a few days before your father was killed. She could have returned from Bend early the morning of the murder to check on their place, as she also recently did."

I suddenly remembered the drive Hollis and I took to the end of the ranch road. "I noticed a gate between Poison Spring Ranch and another property. It was fairly close to one of the trailhead and visitor information sites in the John Day Fossil Beds."

"Yeah, up the road from the spring."

"If you remember, it snowed the day your father was killed. Someone had driven a snowmobile to Poison Spring coming from the gate and ending where the dead bull was found. Is that the Edwards place on the other side of the gate?"

Christopher sighed. "Yes."

I continued. "In fact, she could've gotten on one of the snowmobiles she and her husband own, gone through the gate to the next property over, and driven along the road, found the bull, and let your father know about the animal."

"And then she killed him afterward where he was parked further up the road?"

"All I know for sure is someone killed him later further up the road."

"Who told you Roger and Corky owned snowmobiles?"

Lisa Drake stepped into our office at that moment, interrupting my snarky retort.

"Oh, Christopher," she said. "You look to be in terrible shape. Please don't scare me like this again."

He clutched his sack full of medication and stood up shakily from the metal chair. "Let's go home, Mother."

"Yes, let's. But there is one thing I need to do before we go."

She withdrew a baggie from her purse, which contained what was likely the fourteenth threatening letter mailed to Mike Drake. Posthumously, as it were.

She handed it to me. "Please note that you will discover my fingerprints on the envelope but not on the contents."

"Thank you, Mrs. Drake."

She took Christopher's hand, and mother and son departed. Once the door was closed, I moved to the front counter.

"Let's see what that letter in your hand says," Al said.

I gloved up and carefully removed the envelope from the baggie, opened it, slid the letter out, unfolded it, and placed it on the counter.

There the message was, and as expected: *YOU FUCKED OVER THE WRONG PERSON.*

I turned to Hollis. "You're charged with performing some of your research magic. I want to find out if any eastern Oregon resident was sent to prison thirteen years ago. And whether any of those individuals were recently released."

"That'll take ten minutes, tops. You want me to do that now?"

"Please."

Hollis and I stepped to our desks. He got to work on his research while I checked emails. Al sat down at Mark Taylor's old spot and logged on to his laptop.

I'd received a short note from Doug—who apparently decided not to interrupt the murder board discussion going on in the alcove before leaving the office. He wrote to tell me he was patrolling out on Antelope Mountain, an awe-inspiring point near the southern border of Grant County.

Doug's trip would take him to a high desert plain of bitter brush and juniper where that single peak rose as a beacon above the plateau, the Strawberry and Aldrich ranges off to the northwest. Further south, the stunning Steens Mountain ascended to an elevation of nearly ten thousand feet and stood above the Alvord Desert, an eighty-four-square-mile alkali lake bed—a vast landscape the size of the better part of New England.

Perhaps my day trip to the Painted Hills yesterday had sparked more of a desire to pay closer attention to the part of the world I called home. But I let all that go for now and moved on to the next email, from Daniela Park, as it turned out. She had agreed to let me know today whether or not she was still interested in joining our team.

I opened it. "Sergeant Blackthorne, This morning I submitted my request for a transfer to the John Day unit. I look forward to working with you and the rest of your team."

I was happy that she hadn't been effusive. We would get along just fine.

But before I answered it, I remembered I hadn't asked Sherry Linn her impression of the woman. It was important to me that she be comfortable with the hire. After all, Sherry Linn was the rock, the constant in our office, and it would not do to have her be less than impressed with Trooper Daniela Park.

Sherry Linn hadn't drifted back to the front counter yet, so I went looking for her. I found her in the supply room rearranging the locations of items and reorganizing them into tidy little rows and sensible categories. She wasn't particularly subtle about wanting her office colleagues to stop creating disorder in the miniscule space. We tried, but over and over, we failed to leave the pencils, pens, reams of paper, and file folders where they belonged.

"Hey, there you are," I said. "I have a question for you."

She turned toward me, her wrist bangles clanking together. "Let's hear it."

"I received an email from Daniela Park letting me know she had thought about her possible transfer to our office over the weekend and is definitely still interested in working in our unit. However, I haven't checked in with you about whether or not you think she would be a good fit in the office."

"Are you kidding? Dani reminds me of you. Tough, driven, smart, and hopefully pretty witty. Also, the references you had me contact raved about her work ethic."

"So you think she'd be a good addition to our staff?"

"Hell, yes. Write back to her before she changes her mind."

"Okay, that's all I needed to hear."

I scooted to my desk and sent Dani a response. "Trooper Park, I'm pleased you decided to join our team. At your earliest convenience, let me know when we should expect you. We'll probably throw a little shindig in your honor. And then we'll get to work."

∽

I found Detective Bach and Hollis back in the alcove chatting about the Portland Trail Blazers' chances in the playoffs. I didn't even pretend to know the team's standing or who the coach was, or even the players, except for Damian Lillard, of course. So, I sat quietly until their speculating came to an end.

"I have an announcement," I began. "Daniela Park turned in her request for a transfer to John Day."

"Great," Hollis said. "Doug will be pleased."

"She probably doesn't know when yet, though, right?" Al asked.

"No, but I'm counting on you to nudge Major Macintyre along, if need be."

"Will do. So where are we on our homicide case?"

"I believe we have a couple of avenues to pursue," I said.

"Corky Edwards and Mrs. Johnson?" Hollis asked.

"Yes, but first I want to hear what your research turned up."

"Fifteen men from eastern Oregon were sentenced to the state prison in Salem thirteen years ago. Remarkably, no women residing on this side of the state entered the women's prison system during that year. Seven men have since been released, including one Trevor Jacob Wynn, who resided with his parents in Canyon City at the time of his arrest. Mr. Wynn was released from prison last week on Wednesday, April seventh. The day Mike Drake was murdered."

"This most recent letter, like the thirteen before it, was postmarked in John Day, a mile away from Canyon City."

"Doesn't Canyon City have its own post office?" the detective asked.

"Yes, Al. It's a matter of pride and history. In the 1860s, gold was discovered in Canyon Creek near or in Canyon City, which became a boom town for a while with a population larger than John Day's and even Portland's at the time."

"I guess I knew that."

"I've heard it a million times myself," Hollis said.

"If someone lives in Canyon City, sending mail from the John Day post office is a matter of taking a short walk or drive," I said, unnecessarily stating the obvious.

"For what crime was Mr. Wynn imprisoned?" Al asked.

"He stole a livestock truck full of beef cattle from a ranch just across the Harney County line," Hollis announced.

"Hmm. We might have to pay a visit to Mr. Wynn," I said.

"He was twenty when he was arrested," Hollis continued. "His parents' address was and is 113 Rebel Hill Road in Canyon City, and my guess is that's where we might find him."

"But is that where we want to start today?" Bach wondered. "I'd be interested in having a discussion, perhaps an official interview, with Mrs. Johnson, and perhaps her husband. And also Mrs. Edwards, even though her husband just passed away."

"Perhaps *because* her husband just passed away," I put in.

"I have a suggestion. Why don't we have Harry check the envelope and letter for prints before we approach Mr. Wynn?"

"I like that idea, Hollis. Even though the first thirteen contained only Mike Drake's prints and occasionally his wife's, perhaps the sender messed up this time and left his or her fingerprints all over the letter and envelope," I said.

"And so what if that's the case?" Holly asked.

"It gives us more of a reason to approach the guy."

"In general, there's probably no case to be made against whoever sent all of those letters. The message contained no specific threat. But since Mr. Drake died by homicide, we might want to have a word with Mr. Wynn, and certainly if his prints are on either the letter or the envelope."

"Maybe we'll get to the bottom of our homicide case first," Hollis uttered softly.

"Don't be such an optimist," I teased. "Anyway, I'll ask Sherry Linn to take it home this evening and let her know it's a priority, and that I'd like Harry to get back to me tonight, assuming he's not spending the night in Burns."

"Excuse me again, Maggie." Sherry Linn had stepped quietly into the alcove. "Harry planned on leaving Burns later this afternoon. It's only about a half hour from our place in Silvies."

"Yeah, a half hour is nothing out here."

"Except when it snows," she said.

"I'm hoping we're done with that."

She knocked on the fake wood card table for good luck. "I'm taking an early lunch, if you're okay with that."

"Sure. We'll probably be gone when you get back. But you know the drill."

"Yep. Put the key in that little hole in the door and turn to open."

That made me laugh.

"In case you're still out at quittin' time, don't forget to stash the evidence you want Harry to examine in my inbox before you leave."

"Will do. Have a nice lunch, Sherry Linn," I said.

"You all be careful out there."

20

LATE MORNING, APRIL 12

Our murder board up-to-date, and having concluded our discussion, we were preparing to drive toward Kimberly and speak with Corky Edwards and have another conversation with her neighbor across the highway, Charlotte Johnson and her husband, Troy.

"My thought is to speak with the Johnsons separately," I began. "I believe Charlotte has quite a bit of fear churning inside. Christopher said mental illness, but how could she not be lonely and needy, possible mental illness aside. Loneliness drives people to do things they wouldn't do ordinarily."

"Like murder?" Hollis asked.

"Well, and we certainly know something drove her to lie about her mother."

"My preference here," Detective Bach put in, "would be to begin our interviews with Mrs. Edwards. And I'll tell you why. In my experience, after losing a loved one, grieving family members often tend to let their guard down when speaking with law enforcement. If there's a guard to let down, that is."

"All right, Al. You're the expert, we'll follow your lead."

"I could be wrong, though, Maggie. It happens, I promise you."

"Depending on what we learn in our discussions with Mrs. Edwards and the Johnsons, it might be a good idea to drop in on Christopher Drake and his mother to ask if they have any information for us regarding Trevor Wynn. Or I can call them from the road, assuming they drove straight home."

"Why don't you do that, Maggie. I have to head back to Bend after we're done today. I need to be there for an all-detectives meeting in the morning."

"You can't participate via videoconferencing?"

"Definitely not. Lots of politicking at these things, and I want to protect our unit and head off any shenanigans by some of the others."

"Well, Detective Alan Bach," I began. "I had no idea you had a political vein in your body."

"That's how I got you Trooper Dani Park."

"I'll remember that."

"I apologize for having to take off after just one day. But I'm pleased it's not another homicide case I'm traveling to. Anyway, let's take a fifteen-minute break and then head out."

We beat feet to our computers, me to check out emails and any blog updates from the Oregon State Police Officers Association. I found little of interest, although I had received another message from Dani Park.

"Thank you for confirming receipt of my email. I look forward to joining you and your team soon, but what does one wear to a shindig?" she had written.

I wrote back, saying, "In answer to your question, I'd recommend you wear your uniform. We look forward to welcoming you to our team."

I visited the lavatory, retrieved my lunch cooler from the refrigerator, and choked down my pre-natal vitamins. Back at our pod of desks, I asked Hollis to drive today.

"Are you feeling okay?" he asked.

"Yeah. Let's solve these crimes. Then I'm going on family leave."

"Are you sure you shouldn't do that sooner, Mags?"

"Partner, I promise I'll let you know if I need to."

He raised his little finger. "Pinky swear?"

I locked my little finger in his. "Pinky swear."

Al rejoined us. "Are we ready to go?"

"I'll get my lunch, and then let's take off," Hollis said.

~

We had passed through this part of the county several times in the last many days. It was largely overcast today with the sun occasionally breaking through the clouds and illuminating the river and rimrock canyons. Further along, we met up with our old friend, Cathedral Rock. As we passed by, the spires of the ancient volcanic outcropping were abruptly bathed in a dramatic slant of light.

"Wow," Hollis said. "I wish I was a good photographer. But alas, I'm not."

"I hear you. It's interesting how the appearance of these formations can change, depending on the angle of the sun and cloud cover."

"Yeah, it's borderline surreal."

On the ride, Hollis had tuned in Rodrigo y Gabriela. Not my favorite choice in music, but they were both damn good acoustic guitarists, no doubt about it. We hadn't said a word about our current murder case or Christopher Drake's shooting, but I had been thinking about those incidents, and then Trevor Wynn popped into my head.

"How does someone get put away for *thirteen years* for stealing a truck full of beef cattle?" I asked.

"You start out with a long record of theft, and not the petty kind either. Then you steal a very expensive cattle truck and fill it with about thirty stolen yearlings and drive them to a livestock auction in Reno, Nevada, where, guess what, law enforcement is waiting for you to arrive, along with the actual owner of the animals. And finally you get your sentence added to by pilfering drugs from the pharmacy in the medical services unit of the Oregon State Correctional Institution in Salem."

"So the guy's not very bright. Is that what you're saying?"

"Well, he might've grown up by now. Or got counseling. Or both, I suppose."

"Wynn. The last name is familiar. Do you remember the parents' first names, by any chance?"

He thought for a moment. "I believe the father's name is Roy."

"Is his wife's name Delia?"

"Yeah, that's right, I think."

"I bet they're actually his grandparents. I remember them from when I was a kid, and they've gotta be in their mid- to late eighties now. And Trevor is what, thirty-three?"

Hollis shrugged. "I might've made an assumption about Roy and Delia being Trevor's parents, I guess."

"They had a daughter. Jessie, I think was her name," I added. "Maybe ten or twelve years older than me."

Rodrigo y Gabriela's music filled the cab. They might've been growing on me.

"This morning, I read back over the discussion we had with Mrs. Edwards last Thursday," I said. "She didn't realize Christopher and Lisa Drake were aware of her affair with Mike Drake. And she said she was going to call on them the next morning with condolences. I wonder if that actually happened."

"What difference does it make?" Hollis asked.

"It might speak to her character."

"Or she might've just forgotten."

"Which also may speak to her character."

"Well, we know the two women haven't spoken in several years. And Mrs. Edwards needed to get back to her husband in the hospital in Bend. Condolences weren't top of mind for her."

"Maybe." I pulled out my phone and called Lisa Drake.

"Margaret?" she said as she answered.

"How's Christopher feeling?"

"He's in the guest room on the first floor sleeping. Neither of us thought it was a good idea for him to climb the stairs to his own room."

"I'm calling to ask if you know anyone named Trevor Wynn?"

"I don't believe so. I used to know Roy and Delia Wynn before we left our church community in John Day."

"They're his grandparents, I believe."

"Could be. They had a daughter. Oh dear, I can't recall her name."

"Jessie, if I remember correctly," I said.

"That's right. I believe she passed away several years ago. I remember something about her being homeless and living in Denver."

"That is just sad."

"The loss of a child you've raised and nurtured, that must be an unbearable grief."

"I'd say so. I do have another question for you. Has Mrs. Edwards expressed her condolences to you?"

"No, but she's had plenty of her own worries lately."

That was true, no two ways about it.

"I sent her a card after learning of Roger's death. Those two were very close."

That last bit gave me pause for some reason. "Thanks for your time, Mrs. Drake."

"You're welcome, Margaret."

After ending the call, I listened to Rodrigo y Gabriela and gazed at the scenery.

"Well, what did you learn from Mrs. Drake?" Hollis asked, faking his impatience.

"She knows the Wynn couple. Their daughter, Jessie, died homeless on the streets of Denver—or as they say these days, houseless—but Lisa apparently doesn't know Trevor. And Corky Edwards hasn't yet spoken to her about Mike Drake's death."

"Living on the streets, and in Denver, with its cold winters. Yikes."

He slowed his vehicle and turned on the blinker, signaling to Al following behind us that we were about to turn into the Edwardses' property. Once we had, there was barely room for the Tahoe and the detective's Interceptor to park beside her small sport utility vehicle. I hadn't noticed the license plate on her car during our last visit: BIRDER.

If the woman had watched us suddenly pull up in front of her home, she might very well have freaked out, whether or not she'd committed a crime. As it was, she didn't appear to be there. I knocked twice, and we were about to get back in our rigs and leave, when she walked up the dirt lane that ran to the right of the house and which I assumed led to the gate adjoining Poison Spring Ranch.

Indeed, Corky Edwards was taken aback when she saw us standing beside our police vehicles.

"Sergeant Blackthorne?" she said once she came closer to us.

"Good day, Mrs. Edwards. You remember Trooper Jones, and this is Detective Bach."

"Nice to meet you, Mrs. Edwards." Al handed her his card.

She glanced at it and fiddled with the spotting scope that hung from her neck. "Homicide?"

"That's correct," Bach answered. "My condolences for your loss."

"Thank you," she answered hoarsely and stared at the three of us. "Would you like to step inside the house?"

"Yes, if you don't mind," Al said.

"It's a bit disorderly right now."

"We're fine with that, Mrs. Edwards."

She led the way inside. The living room was virtually spotless and quite orderly except for the suitcase placed against one wall. A plastic hospital bag sat next to it and likely held whatever paraphernalia someone had gathered from the cabinet next to her dead husband's hospital bed.

Corky Edwards placed the spotting scope atop her credenza. "I apologize for the mess. I arrived back home yesterday. I haven't...I'm not ready to go through Roger's things."

"We understand, Mrs. Edwards," I assured her.

She indicated the couch and chairs in the living room. "Please, have a seat."

The three of us followed Corky's lead and sat down.

We had agreed earlier that Al would begin the questioning. "Mrs. Edwards, what time did you return from Bend yesterday?" he asked.

"Oh, late morning, I guess."

"I know what a long drive it is from Bend. My office is there, as is my home."

"Yes, I've made the trip there and back three times since this past Monday. I won't miss that drive anytime soon." She stared at her lap. "What do you want from me, Sergeant Blackthorne?"

I took note of the number of trips. "We're not looking to take up much of your time, but we'd like to know when you last took one of your snowmobiles out for a ride?"

She eyed me as if I'd rummaged through her drawer of unmentionables. "You know we have snowmobiles?"

192 LAVONNE GRIFFIN-VALADE

"Yes, in the outbuilding next to the road."

"You looked inside?"

"We did," I answered. "When was the last time you rode one of them?"

"I really don't recall."

"This past winter? Last year? Five years ago? Longer ago than that?"

"Roger and I went out sometime this past winter. To spot birds. I just don't remember when exactly."

"I'm a birder myself," Hollis announced.

Holly was many things, but a birder wasn't one of them.

"Oh?" She suddenly became slightly animated.

"Yeah, I've started teaching my son." He indicated the spotting scope on the credenza. "What make and model do you use?"

"We each have a Vortex Razor HD."

Hollis smiled, expressing his approval. "Excellent choice."

"Mrs. Edwards," Al put in. "Let's go back to Sergeant Blackthorne's question. When was the last time you rode one of your snowmobiles?"

"I'm sorry. I honestly don't remember exactly, Detective."

Bach turned to us. "Do we have more questions for Mrs. Edwards?"

"I do," I said. "I recall when Trooper Jones and I dropped by last Thursday, you assured us you hadn't returned to your home on Wednesday, the day before we last spoke to you. Which was also the day Mike Drake was killed. But you indicated just now you had made the trip to Bend and back three times this week."

"I don't understand," the woman said.

"Correct me if I'm wrong, but didn't you take your husband to the emergency room in Bend on Monday?"

"Yes, as I said, it was Monday, a week ago today. And I returned on Thursday to check on our property. I drove back to Bend on Friday."

I continued. "Your husband passed away on Saturday, and you drove back home yesterday. So far, that makes up two trips to Bend and back, not three."

She looked ill, and I couldn't help feeling a bit sorry for her. Not if she was our killer, though.

"You're right, Sergeant Blackthorne. I got confused. I drove to Bend and back two times this past week, not three."

"I have one more question," I said. "Do you own a gun?"

"No, and neither did Roger. We never would have hunted any animal."

"How about handguns?"

"Never."

Al stood. "Thank you for your patience, Mrs. Edwards."

Hollis and I rose as well.

"Will there be some kind of remembrance for Mr. Edwards?" I asked.

"Of course. He had requested cremation and to have his ashes buried on our property." She took a ragged breath. "We have a small bird sanctuary just over the hill behind the house. Friends and family will gather—probably in early summer—and after a brief service, scatter his ashes there."

The three of us took our leave, and when I was back in Holly's Tahoe, I called Al, who was going to follow us to the Johnsons' home, basically just across the highway.

"Did you notice Mrs. Edwards didn't question *why* we were asking her about the last time she rode one of their snowmobiles?"

"That's a good point, Maggie. My guess is, she will eventually remember when it was she and her husband went out on their snowmobiles last winter."

"Or fabricate a date."

"Always a possibility."

We hung up, and I turned to Hollis. "What was up with the *I'm a birder myself* story?"

"I've never gone birding in my life," he said.

"Ah, so you were going for the old good-cop-bad-cop routine."

"No, I wanted to know what kind of scope she used. I'll check it out online, but I bet it's top-notch."

"So?"

"If you remember, the snowmobiler had to ride down and then back up an incline to get to the gate."

"Perhaps the hill behind their house Corky mentioned just now."

"Likely. Which means there might be a point on the Edwards property that would allow someone with a good pair of binoculars or a top-notch spotting scope to get a birds-eye view of some of the goings-on at Poison Spring Ranch."

"Hmm. Aren't you the clever sleuth."

"Grabbing at straws. I'll look up the Vortex Razor HD later today."

"Well, given where we're at in this case, grab away."

"We've been here before, Mags."

"Yes, too many damn times."

~

I hadn't noticed whether or not the heavy-duty truck and chassis were still parked in front of the Johnsons' home as we had driven past it on our way to speak with Corky Edwards, but I saw now that it wasn't. Neither was the family station wagon.

I suggested that one of the girls might be out with the station wagon, so we pulled onto their property and parked.

The three of us walked to the front door, and I knocked. We heard movement, a door being closed, and Charlotte Johnson opened the door. She was dressed in a robe and appeared to be nursing a massive hangover. She had also obviously been crying.

"What is it, Sergeant Blackthorne?"

"Is your husband available?"

"He had a short run to Pendleton today to pick up a load of something. Why?"

"May we come in?"

"Do I have a choice?" she asked sarcastically and opened the door, walked to her kitchen, and returned with a cup of coffee.

The three of us stood in her front room, waiting for an invitation to take a seat.

"Please sit down," she said.

We did so, and she took a chair herself.

"I haven't met you before, have I?" she remarked to Al.

"Homicide Detective Bach." He handed her his card.

Charlotte sighed. "So I see."

"Mrs. Johnson," I began. "Are your daughters at school?"

"Yes, they drove today. Some sort of something is happening after school, so they took the car."

"I'd like to begin with your mother. Why have you lied about her illness and death?"

"So, you finally called the nursing home."

"You must have expected we would at some point."

She shrugged tiredly.

"What else have you lied about?"

"I lie every day about being happy in this place, being happy with my life, my marriage. If it weren't for the girls..."

"Speaking of your husband, he arrived home yesterday?"

"Yes."

"What time?"

"Around four in the afternoon, I guess."

"And when did you tell him about Mike Drake assaulting your daughter?"

"I haven't told him about that."

"When did you tell him about your affair with Christopher Drake and the aftermath?"

"The aftermath?"

"Paula stashing the handgun in the stable at Poison Spring Ranch to make trouble for Christopher," I said.

"How do you know I didn't lie about the affair too?"

"He's confirmed it."

She kneaded her temples. "I haven't told Troy about the affair either, Sergeant. We haven't had time to talk about anything."

"Is it possible he found out about your relationship with Christopher Drake another way, like from Paula herself?"

"I know she's angry with me about that, but it's not possible that she would tell her father. It's just not possible."

Charlotte broke into tears and cried for several minutes. Hollis fetched a few tissues from somewhere, and she finally calmed herself.

"Why are you asking all of these questions about Troy?"

"Because Christopher Drake was shot yesterday."

"Oh my God." She stood. "Tell me he's alive."

21

AFTERNOON, APRIL 12

We had assured Charlotte that Christopher was alive and recovering at home, but it was clear the news of his injury was but one more bit of anguish she had to bury and then get on with life.

I was better at grilling people than talking to them sympathetically, but I knew I was the one to comfort her.

We all waited for her to collect herself, and once she had, I began. "Charlotte, it seems like you're carrying around a good deal of grief and anxiety."

She half laughed at that, as if I would have no idea of what grief and anxiety did to a person.

"My mother died a horrible death. She was in a great deal of pain, and she was afraid and helpless. And I was the only person there with her at the end. That...those terrible weeks did something to me."

"How long ago was that?"

She paused. "A little over a year ago. Troy's mom stayed with the girls while I went to be with my mother in Roseburg. It was a terrible time for everyone, but Troy had to keep working, so what else could we do."

Charlotte turned to Al. "I have not killed anyone, Detective. Please believe me."

She shifted her gaze back to me. "I'm sorry I lied about my mother being in the nursing home in Prairie City. I'm sorry I made up a story of traveling there with my girls to visit her the morning Mike Drake was shot. I don't think I can make amends for any of that, but earlier today, I remembered something about that day which might be helpful."

My interest had been piqued. "Then I think we need to interview you formally."

"What does that mean?"

"We read you your rights, and if you agree to waive your rights, you sign a waiver. And then we record the interview."

"All right, Sergeant Blackthorne. I guess I'm fine with that. I haven't done anything worse than lie to you, my husband, and myself. But may I go wash up and put on some clothes first?"

I glanced at the detective, and he responded with a nod.

"Absolutely," I said to the woman.

After she left the room, Bach turned to me. "Your intuition is quite suited to questioning a witness, Maggie."

"Oh, I don't know, Al. Hollis has had to rescue me a few times."

"That's because he's quite suited to questioning a witness himself."

"Is this another pitch to join the homicide unit in Bend?" I asked.

"I'm close to retirement, and there's a need for good investigators."

"How close?" Hollis inquired.

"Two, maybe three years."

"Who'll take over after you leave?" I asked.

"That's what I'm worried about."

"But you'll be outta there. Traveling the world, hanging out with your wife and daughters. And maybe playing with your grandkids."

"That's what my wife keeps saying."

"I'm not sure I'm supposed to ask you this, but what's your wife's first name?"

"You're free to ask me about my family, Maggie. Diana is my wife. And the girls are Susan, Rebecca, Kathleen, and Lulu."

"Gosh, you went hog-wild with that last daughter's name, didn't you?"

"She's actually named Louise. Lulu's her nickname."

"All right, Sergeant Blackthorne, Trooper Jones, Detective Bach." Charlotte had returned. "Let's get this over with."

I turned on the recorder, read out her Miranda rights, and she signed the waiver form.

"State your full name and address, please."

"Charlotte Anne Harrison Johnson, 35374 Highway 19, Kimberly, Oregon."

"What was your relationship with Mike Drake, fatally shot on his property at Poison Spring Ranch?"

"He was my neighbor for the past decade, and I learned recently he had sexually assaulted—not raped, but assaulted nonetheless—my seventeen-year-old daughter. He continued to harass her until someone killed him. I thought he was a nice man until I learned what he did to my daughter."

"Did you murder Mr. Drake as retribution?"

"No, I trusted that law enforcement would come after him. My daughter had reported the sexual assault to her school counselor, who was required by Oregon law to alert the appropriate authorities."

"When did you learn about the incident with your daughter?"

She mulled that over. "Last Monday. That's when she sat in the counselor's office and told me about it over the phone."

That matched what we had learned from Hannah Barnhart, the school counselor.

Al cleared his throat. "How did you feel when you learned about the assault?"

She teared up slightly. "Do you have daughters, Detective?"

"Four of them. And I'm very protective."

"I would assume so," Charlotte said. "But you would rely on Child Welfare and law enforcement to deal with a matter like that, right?"

"Absolutely."

"And that's what I did."

"Mrs. Johnson," I said. "You indicated you had remembered something else about the morning of the day Mr. Drake was killed."

"Yes. I'm not sure why I remembered it, or why I forgot it in the first place. But Corky Edwards called me the morning of the snowstorm. Last Wednesday. She asked if Troy was home, and if so, might he be willing to put her tire chains on her SUV. She needed to get back to Bend, where her husband was hospitalized."

I glanced at my colleagues. If true, they knew what that meant. Corky Edwards had lied to us. Or as may have been the case, she had gotten confused.

"What did you say to her?"

"I let her know that Troy wasn't home. I volunteered to put the chains on for her, but she poo-pooed that idea. I also suggested she call Christopher, but she was not at all interested in asking him for help."

"There were snowmobile tracks present in the area that morning. They stopped at Poison Spring where one of Mr. Drake's bulls had been slain, and it appears that Mr. Drake was alerted to the fact by an unknown party, who may have been the snowmobiler. Was that possibly you?"

"Absolutely not. Several folks in the area own snowmobiles. It could have been any one of them." She paused. "Including Corky and Roger. Well, just Corky, I guess."

"And it's your assertion that you absolutely did not drive to Poison Spring Ranch—by either automobile or snowmobile—on the morning of Wednesday, April seventh."

"That is more than my assertion. It's a fact."

"Are there any further questions?" I asked of my colleagues.

"Not at this time," Hollis said.

"It's possible we may have other questions in the coming days," Al added. "Thank you for your time, Mrs. Johnson."

I clicked the recorder off.

~

As we walked back to our police rigs, I suggested we drive to a picnic spot in the Fossil Beds National Monument, located about ten minutes from the Johnsons' place. We could eat our lunch there at a table and make use of the visitor facilities. But more importantly, it would give us an opportunity to have a discussion about our conversation with Corky Edwards and our interview with Charlotte Johnson before the detective left for Bend.

We parked at a spot near the entrance to the Flood of Fire Trail, so named for the molten basalt that had once breached the Earth's crust in a blazing deluge.

After retrieving our lunches, we gathered at a shaded picnic table.

Al scanned the area. "Interesting name for a hiking trail."

"I think it's fitting, given the geologic history going back eons," I responded.

"Volcanic activity?"

"Yep."

"Guess I'm not as familiar with this part of the state as I should be," he said. "Especially since I've driven through it often enough."

"Don't get her started, Detective. Or Trooper Doug Vaughn either. He's a complete geology nerd. And he has some actual facts he likes to go on and on about," Hollis put in.

"Thanks for the heads-up. Speaking of a heads-up, I received an email from Dr. Lewis."

"The medical examiner in the Drake case, right?" I asked.

"Yes. Don't let this get out, but I found her to be not very respectful of the two of you. And I don't want to work with someone like that again if I can avoid it. Anyway, I probably shouldn't have characterized her that way."

"Yes, you should've, Al," I countered. "Anyway, what did she say?"

"I'll forward the email to you both, but the most important thing she reported had to do with the bullet slug removed from Drake senior's body. It came from a Glock 43 nine millimeter."

"Harry identified the gun Christopher found in the stable as a Smith and Wesson. That means Mike Drake wasn't killed with the weapon the Johnson girl stashed there," I said.

"Doesn't quite get Charlotte Johnson off the hook, though," Hollis said.

"Meaning?"

"It might seem unlikely, Maggie, but Mrs. Johnson could've separately acquired a gun on her own and without telling anyone."

"I suppose that's a possibility," I answered.

"A slim one, I think," the detective remarked. "At least from what I've read and heard about the woman as well as witnessed. Her mother's death likely inflicted quite a bit of trauma. People often do things that are out of character in those circumstances."

I knew that all too well. "Are you heading back to Bend after this, Al?"

"Probably. Was there someone else out here you specifically wanted me to meet with?"

"Well, it's unfortunate Troy Johnson wasn't available to speak with us. Although, and I'm reluctant to say this, but I believed Charlotte when she said she hadn't told him about the affair. And I guess I also believed her when she said that Mr. Johnson arrived back at home around four in the afternoon."

"I found all that believable as well," Bach said.

"So did I, Maggie, especially since she told us what time her husband arrived back home before she learned Christopher had been shot."

"That's right."

"And I believed her when she told us she also hadn't talked to her husband about what happened to Paula," Hollis added.

I sipped from my water bottle. "There's still the niggling issue of Charlotte lying about her mother."

"I understand why that continues to give you pause, Maggie. And so that means the two of you need to be wary of something like that happening again."

"You're right, Al. For instance, should we believe Charlotte's story about Corky Edwards calling her on Wednesday to ask if her husband Troy was around to put tire chains on her vehicle?" I asked.

"Well, Wednesday was the day of the snowstorm, we know that for sure." Hollis stated the obvious.

"Would there be a reason for her to lie about that?" Bach asked.

"Not unless she's attempting to implicate Mrs. Edwards in Mike Drake's murder."

That comment from me cast a bit of a pall over the conversation, and the three of us finished up our lunches in quiet.

The day had remained cloudy and cool, and now the wind had picked up. I mulled over the dark prospect of not being able to identify the killer and/or whoever shot Christopher anytime soon. I thought about possible suspects in one or both of those incidents, and that brought to mind Lydia Reed. She hadn't been a fan of Mike Drake, and now she was also the woman Christopher had broken up with yesterday morning. We hadn't had

202 LAVONNE GRIFFIN-VALADE

a conversation with her since last week, so I decided to suggest we have another.

"You know what, Al. Before you take off for Bend, I'd like to drop by and check in with Christopher Drake's now former girlfriend."

"Oh?"

"She lives with her aging father on a small ranch not too far from here."

Hollis decided to weigh in. "I think that's a great idea, Maggie. She also might be a little more talkative with a homicide detective present."

"If you remember, Christopher ended his relationship with her yesterday, before the shooting, obviously," I recounted.

"On the other hand, when we talked with her initially, she had declared they were just friends...," Hollis added.

"She actually said *friends with benefits*. And I'm sure Al knows what that means."

Bach smiled. "I'm not particularly worldly, but I am the father of grown and nearly grown daughters, and they keep me up-to-date. So I do know a thing or two, including what *friends with benefits* means."

I thought of my medical examiner pal, Ray Gattis. Until recently, she had been Al's friend with benefits for several years.

"Let's pack up," the detective said. "I'll follow you to Ms. Reed's place."

∾

The first time Hollis and I spoke with Lydia Reed, I viewed her as tough, her life affected, maybe even thrown off course, by her father's condition and inability to get around or speak. But she also came off as pretty damned committed to his care.

It was also interesting she had shown up at the meeting with community members regarding the recent spate of homicides in the county. She didn't make a comment or ask a question, and she seemed aloof and unfriendly, which didn't bother me one bit. Sometimes that's what a person had to do to get through a rough patch. But one thing seemed clear during our initial conversation with her: she took shit from no one.

We found her parking a large tractor beside other ranching equipment, all of it stored under a large metal canopy. Lydia climbed down from the tractor seat just as we met up with her.

I introduced her to Detective Bach. She asked for his card and glanced at it once he passed it to her.

"What's up?" she asked.

Speaking in a direct manner and cutting to the chase was the best way to converse with this woman. Didn't take a rocket scientist to figure that out. And it may have been what had gotten to Christopher Drake in the end. If so, in my view, that was Christopher's problem, not Lydia's. Unless she shot the dude, of course.

"Have you heard the news about Christopher?" I asked her.

She shrugged. "The news that he's not going to fuck me anymore?"

"No, the news that someone shot him yesterday."

"What! My God, what happened?"

"You didn't know?"

"No. That must be why his mother called me. I haven't listened to her message." She teared up and removed a handkerchief from the back pocket of her jeans and dabbed her eyes. "How bad off is he?"

"He's going to be fine, Lydia. He actually left the hospital this morning. His mother has taken him home and is caring for him."

"Well, Chris and I *are* still friends, that was always part of the deal. I'll get in touch with Lisa about paying him a visit."

"Ms. Reed," Al began. "Please give us an idea of your whereabouts yesterday?"

"Chris was here with me until about ten in the morning. Then it was time for my father's bath—he's a paraplegic. After that, I took him through the exercises he has to do every day to keep his muscles from atrophying. Then I fixed his lunch and fed him. He's usually very tired after all that, so I moved him to his bed and waited in his room to make sure he fell asleep. At about one o'clock, my neighbor Eunice Ford arrived to spell me for a while so I could drive to Chester's Market in John Day and get our groceries for the month. I still have the receipt in the house if you want to see it. I also picked up his medications from the pharmacy—I have that receipt, too— and I sneaked in a late lunch-early dinner at the Blue Mountain Lounge."

"They make a mean chocolate and peanut butter shake," I said.

"They do?"

"Yep."

"I'll have to try one when I drop by next month. So anyway, I returned home about five o'clock, and Eunice went back to her place. And then the nightly care ritual for my father began. After that, I was exhausted, so I took the most recent John Grisham mystery upstairs and fell asleep reading."

"Thank you, Ms. Reed," Bach said.

"I'll go get those receipts."

"That won't be necessary."

"I insist. I need to go check on Dad, anyway. I'll be right back," she replied and hot-footed it to the house.

I noted the ramp that had been added to the porch of the old farm-house. "I'd like to suggest that we wait for her outside the house."

Hearing no objection, I walked in that direction, Hollis and Al following. I could see the house, and really the entire place, was in need of a few repairs, but it was also obvious Lydia had her hands full. And my guess was, there also existed a lack of funds.

Lydia appeared on the porch with her father in his wheelchair and introduced him to the three of us. I liked that she spoke to him as if he was cognizant of his surroundings and our presence.

She handed us the receipts from Chester's Market and the pharmacy. Both were dated for the previous day.

The detective returned the receipts to Lydia. "Nice to meet you, sir. Thank you for speaking with us, Ms. Reed. Your information has been very helpful."

I wasn't sure of that last statement, other than it fairly well exonerated her in the matter of Christopher Drake's shooting. And I realized I was glad it did.

"Don't forget about the chocolate and peanut butter shake at the Blue Mountain Lounge," I reminded her.

"I won't. Thanks for the recommendation."

"You're welcome. I'd also suggest trying out Angie Dennis's burgers at Prairie Maid."

Lydia gave me a wee smile and moved her father back inside the house.

22

LATE AFTERNOON, APRIL 12

Standing next to our rigs still parked outside of the Reeds' home, the three of us strategized about our next move.

"I say we pay Corky Edwards our second visit of the day and ask her if she contacted Charlotte Johnson last Wednesday during the snowstorm. If she says no, we know one of them is lying," I reasoned.

"Or mistaken," Al said.

"Just think of it this way, we all have to drive back by her house to get to where we're going."

"I suppose."

"And Hollis here can buffer the visit by chatting her up about birding," I said.

"That reminds me." Hollis opened the door of his police vehicle and fetched his laptop.

"Are you looking up Mrs. Edwards's spotting scope?" I asked.

"Yep. The Vortex Razor HD."

I let him do his thing and turned to the detective. "Hollis is curious about the ability to spy on Poison Spring Ranch with the spotting scope."

"What's that about?"

"I think the theory is, if she was interested in finding Mike Drake out there alone on his neighboring property, having a good spotting scope might come in handy."

"The scope is said to be top-notch," Hollis said. "Its features are pretty highly rated by users, and it supposedly has an amazing range of vision."

"Better than my new binoculars?" I asked.

"I'm not sure, but a person can apparently see a fair distance, and quite clearly."

"So are you saying Mrs. Edwards could easily spy on her neighbors from somewhere on her property?" Bach asked.

Hollis shrugged. "If she were so inclined and depending on the viewpoint, I think she could."

"Spying on a neighbor is different than killing a neighbor, I'd say."

"It is indeed, Maggie. But it doesn't mean that a neighbor couldn't do both," Hollis replied.

"Here's what I'd like to do next," Al said. "Let's try to determine which days Mrs. Edwards was in Bend. We already know she was absent for at least part of Thursday, April eighth, because the two of you met with her at her home."

"We had also stopped at her place the day before—the day of the murder—but other than finding a mishmash of tire tracks in the snow, no one was around," Hollis reminded the detective.

"But we could contact the place she was staying in Bend. Something ubiquitous, like the Mountain Motel, I think," I said. "It's close to the hospital, she told us."

"Was it the Mountain High Motel?" the detective asked.

"That's it. Right, Hollis?"

"I believe so."

"Well, after the all-detectives meeting tomorrow, I'll go to Mountain High Motel and request to go through recent guest registries. If I'm granted permission, I'll let you know right away which nights she stayed there and which she didn't." He checked the time. "It's a little past four thirty. I think I'll make my way back to Bend. There's a bit of prepping I need to do before that meeting in the morning."

"And by the time we get back to John Day, it'll be time to call it a day."

"Yes, and Maggie," Bach began. "I want you to actually call it a day. Trust me, you'll need your strength soon enough."

All the condescending bullshit was starting to get to me. But I chose not to say so.

"Be careful, Detective," Hollis said. "She's pretty much had it with folks giving her that kind of advice."

"Menfolk in particular," I whispered loudly.

"Ah, thanks for the warning, Hollis," Bach said. "No offense intended, Maggie."

"Yes, I know, Al. The need to constantly warn pregnant women to take care of themselves is pretty universal."

"But I should try harder not to do that," he said.

I turned to my buddy Hollis. "We all should."

~

On the way back to John Day, Hollis invited me to choose some traveling music. I scrolled through the trove of albums I'd downloaded to my phone and tuned into the Tracy Chapman channel.

We listened to "Talking About a Revolution" from her debut album.

"Good choice," he said afterward.

"I make them on occasion." My phone suddenly buzzed, and I answered the call. "Harry, how was your trip to Burns?"

"Boring as hell."

"So did you check the letter and envelope for prints?"

"Yep. Only found Lisa Drake's on the envelope, and none on the letter."

"Kind of what I expected. Thanks for getting back to me."

"It's quittin' time, Sergeant," he responded.

"Hollis and I are on our way to John Day right now."

"Talk to you later. Say howdy to Hollis."

"Harry says to tell you howdy," I said after ending the call.

"We're fortunate to have Harry close by."

"Not to mention Sherry Linn."

"Yeah, for all kinds of reasons."

I sat quietly, listening to Tracy's next tune. "Let's go have a chat with Trevor Wynn."

"Were his prints on the envelope and/or letter?"

"His prints weren't on either."

"Then why the need for a chat? He was released from the prison in Salem on the same day Mike Drake was murdered but *after* someone else shot him."

"Let's start with the thirteen, now fourteen letters. I want to know if he's the person who sent them and why they were sent. The impetus for doing that may be connected to something from the past, and that something might lead us to Drake's killer," I reasoned.

"Where is this coming from?"

"I don't know, maybe it's the Tracy Chapman songs. The angst and sadness she expresses about poverty made me think about the guy. The Wynn couple are very poor, as I recall. Now I'll admit, I'm basing that on blurry memory, but if I'm right, raising their grandson Trevor must have been a financial burden."

"Do you have something to go on besides a blurry memory?"

"They went to the same church as Lisa Drake, and the same church I attended for a while when I was a kid. What I remember about them is probably similar to what they might remember about me. Patched clothing, dime-store shoes, hoping for a better life."

Hollis was quiet for a good minute. "That description might've fit me when I was younger, too. But I do have a question. You went to church as a kid?"

"Got baptized and everything."

"Maggie Blackthorne. I learn something new about you every day."

"Not *every* day, Holly."

"Anyway, it can't hurt to go talk to Trevor Wynn."

"Do you remember the address?"

"Uh, Rebel Hill Road in Canyon City...The house number is 113, I'm pretty sure."

"I'll look it up." I brought out my phone. "You're right, 113 Rebel Hill Road."

"Sometimes the old noggin clicks in," he said.

"And sometimes not."

"I'll assume you're talking about *your* noggin."

"I am indeed," I responded.

"On another note, the more I think about it, the more I view your notion to visit with Mr. Wynn as a pretty good idea."

"If we learn anything significant from our conversation with him, I'll send Tracy Chapman a thank-you card."

~

We found our way to Rebel Hill Road, which was supposedly named after some local incident during the Civil War. I didn't recall what that was or if it was really just another Wild West fiction.

The Wynns' property reminded me of where I'd lived as a young girl— out front, an old snowball bush struggled to survive in the midst of several dog kennels. The small house hadn't been painted in an age, and an old, rusty Jeep pickup sat in the yard.

We parked in front of the chain-link fence, opened the gate, and went to the front door. I knocked and waited. The television was on inside. It sounded like some guy was watching a wrestling match and rooting for somebody called Dolph.

"Let me try," Hollis offered and banged his large fist on the door.

A youngish guy, who I assumed to be Trevor Wynn, pulled back a curtain and peeked outside. Then the volume on the wrestling match was lowered and he opened the door.

For some reason, I hadn't expected him to be ruggedly handsome. He stared at the two of us with his fierce aquamarine eyes, and I sensed he was both scared shitless and angry.

"I already checked in with my parole officer."

I moved a step forward. "Is your name Trevor Jacob Wynn?" I asked.

"Yeah, so what?"

"I'm Oregon State Police Sergeant Blackthorne, and this is Senior Trooper Hollis Jones. We need to question you about an incident that occurred thirteen years ago."

"What the hell?" he said.

"May we come inside?"

"My grandparents ain't home."

"We didn't come by to talk to your grandparents," I said. "Or we can question you out here in the yard."

"Fuck no."

"All right, let's all get in our cop vehicle and drive to the police station."

"This is bullshit," he complained and opened the door wider.

Hollis and I followed him into the living room, which was singularly lit by a large television featuring a tangled mass of two men wrestling. Trevor led us into the dining room, where he slid a few dirty dishes into a corner of the Formica-topped table.

"Is here all right?"

"Here is fine," I answered.

We each sat in one of the three ladder chairs tucked next to the table.

"Are your grandparents away?" Hollis asked and placed his card on the table in front of Trevor.

"They went to see some doctor in Baker City. What's the thirteen-years-ago thing you wanted to talk about?"

"You were sent to the Oregon State Correctional Institution in Salem thirteen years ago," Hollis said.

"I remember, dude."

Hollis continued. "The same year you were sent to prison, a local rancher named Mike Drake received thirteen anonymous letters with the exact same message."

The guy's face reddened. "What's that got to do with me?"

"Mr. Drake received another such letter shortly after you were released last Wednesday."

Trevor shrugged.

I placed my card beside Hollis's. "The whole thing is a bit of an odd mystery. The exact same short message was contained in every one of those letters. What it said wasn't explicitly threatening, but it was off-putting, nonetheless. In all caps, it read, 'You fucked over the wrong person.'"

Again, he shrugged.

"Mr. Wynn, have you read the local newspaper or watched or listened to any news since you returned home?" Hollis asked.

"I don't watch or listen to the news, and I'd never follow anything or anyone on Twitter or Facebook or any other crap like that. This world is already fucked up enough."

"That may be, but if you had been following the news, you would've learned that Mike Drake, owner of Poison Spring Ranch, was murdered last week," Hollis said.

"I'd like to cut right to the chase here," I said. "Your fingerprints were discovered on several of the letters sent to Mr. Drake thirteen years ago and on the fourteenth letter sent to him last week."

"That's not fucking possible. I wore cop gloves, even when I was cutting the letters out of magazines. And I didn't know dickhead Drake was dead."

"But what we really came to ask you about is this. What did Mr. Drake do to prompt your trips to the post office and send him that message?" I clarified.

He sighed and raked his hands through his thick hair. "He cheated me, and I wanted to get under his skin."

"How did he cheat you?" Hollis asked.

"You two know why I was sent to the pen, right?"

"We do," I said.

"Dickhead and I were going to split the profits on that load of beef I nabbed and drove to Reno, but he called the cops and claimed his livestock truck was stolen. And I guess the cops put two and two together since they spotted the truck traveling south on Highway 95 into Nevada with a bunch of cattle packed in the trailer."

Hollis leaned toward Wynn. "So, let me understand you. What you're claiming is that Mr. Drake backed out of the deal, and you were hung out to dry?"

It was my turn to lean closer to the man. "Did you explain that to the Nevada police?"

"You think they believed me? The owner of the truck was a respected Oregon rancher and a Grant County Commissioner, no less."

"And then you were extradited back to Oregon for the trial," I said. "But you must have been out on bail in order to be able to send the first thirteen letters to Drake."

"I was, yeah. But I had a shitty attorney who did a piss-poor job of poking holes in the prosecution's arguments."

"You still would've gone to prison," I told him.

"That's right. And that asshole would've landed there too."

There was no guarantee of that last, of course, but what was the point of saying so.

"All right, I think we're done here. Unless you have more questions, Trooper Jones."

"I don't. I think Mr. Wynn has been pretty direct with us." Hollis turned to the younger man. "I hope you can put all that behind you and put your life on a better path."

"Don't take this the wrong way, but you sound like the prison preacher. Anyway, I'm hoping I can do that too."

"Good to know," I noted and stood to leave.

Hollis followed suit. "I hear the hardware store is looking to hire."

"Thanks. My parole officer mentioned that."

"Good luck."

~

My patrol partner was quiet on the short drive to our cop shop. In the silence, I felt a small twinge—the baby turning or just saying hello, I wasn't sure.

"Long day, huh?" he said as he idled his Tahoe in the parking lot next to our police station.

I opened the door. "Sure was."

"Hey, there's something I keep forgetting to tell you. I talked to Duncan when we went out for beers the other night, and he didn't have much to say about Mike Drake, except that he was a good customer."

"I think I'll try questioning a witness over beers sometime." I got out slowly. "See you tomorrow, Holly."

"Don't go inside the office, Mags."

"I didn't plan to, Dad."

He laughed, and I retrieved my pack, shut the passenger-side door, and climbed in my look-alike police rig.

On the way home, I received another call from Sandy Connor, but I let it go to voicemail. I decided to listen to it in the morning. I was too exhausted to hear about her suspicions regarding Burt Greely at the moment.

Once I arrived at our little house, I noticed the patch of red tulips in the bed at the front of the house were beginning to bloom, and I teared up.

"What the hell is wrong with you, Blackthorne?" I took a breath, opened the door, and found Duncan reading. "Hi, Dun. What are you reading?"

"Hi, babe," he said and moved from his chair toward me. "This is a book."

"Har, har."

We kissed, and he put his arm around me. He then showed me the cover of the book. The author, Claire Vaye Watkins, was one of my favorite writers, and he was reading her latest novel, *I Love You but I've Chosen Darkness*.

"I really like her writing," I said.

"I know. That's why I got this for you."

He handed it to me, and we shared one of those long kisses that, even very pregnant and tired, made me want to take off my clothes and make love.

"We're going out to dinner. I made seven-thirty reservations at the Anchor Club."

"What time is it now?" I asked.

He checked his watch. "About six fifteen."

"Come with me." I took his hand and led him to our bedroom upstairs.

23

MORNING, APRIL 13

Proud of myself for waiting until I got to the office and was sitting at my desk before playing the voicemail Sandy Connor had left for me last evening, I brought out my cell phone and finally listened to what the woman had to tell me.

"Hi, Sergeant Blackthorne. This is Sandy Connor. I was riding my horse around Poison Spring Ranch this evening, and I came upon a target tacked up on a pine tree. It looked like someone had been practicing with some kind of gun. And the target looked like a silhouette of a person. I tried to get in touch with the Drakes, but I couldn't raise either one at the house, so I left a voicemail. I know they wouldn't be very happy somebody had brought a gun onto their property. Anyway, I thought you might want to know, too."

I turned to Hollis. "You want to hear something interesting?"

He moved away from his computer. "Sure, I'm getting bored writing up the report you assigned to me."

I handed him my phone, and he listened to the message. "What the heck? And a human silhouette, no less."

"Yeah, weird. We can inquire about that when we drive to the ranch to talk about the information Trevor Wynn shared with us last night. Mrs. Drake had previously told me she didn't know him. And maybe she just doesn't remember the name, but I'm assuming her husband had to testify at Trevor's trial."

"One would think so."

"Let's catch up on our reports and then head out to Poison Spring Ranch."

"Sounds like a plan."

I noticed Doug was still working to get through the pile of paperwork on his desk and had brought in a small chunk of petrified wood to hold the stack in place.

"Nice paperweight," I said. "Have you always had that at your desk?"

"Yeah. I keep a small collection of other rocks I've picked up along the way, too." He pointed to a little wooden dish elsewhere on his desk.

"No arrowheads, though, right?"

"I'd have to arrest myself if that was the case."

"Where do you plan on patrolling today?" I asked.

"Think I'll try Logan Valley again."

"Probably won't get stuck in any snow today."

He closed down his computer in preparation for the drive out to Logan Valley. "Sounds like the two of you are heading back to Poison Spring Ranch."

"Afraid so."

"Be careful out there, you guys," Doug cautioned and gathered his pack and thermos.

I sighed. "We will be. I'm hoping this is our last trip to PSR."

"PSR. That stands for the ranch right?"

"Well, beginning now, I guess."

"See you later, Doug," Hollis managed to say as he rat-a-tatted away on his keyboard.

Shortly after Doug took off, Sherry Linn showed up at my desk. "Whitey Kern is here to see you."

"Thanks, send him on back."

Sherry Linn must have tried to engage in a conversation with Whitey, because when he arrived at our little huddle of desks, his face was flushed, and he avoided looking me in the eye.

"Good morning, Whitey."

He nodded shyly and sat in the empty chair next to my desk. "Maggie, I was wondering if I could call Mrs. Drake or her son and let 'em know they can come get that pickup."

"Let me talk to Harry Bratton. I'm pretty sure he's done with his forensic work on the truck."

I dialed his number, and he answered right away.

"Maggie?"

"Morning, Harry. Whitey Kern's here, and he'd like to know if he can call the Drakes and let them know they can come get Mike's pickup truck?"

"Yeah. Apologize to him for me, will you? It takes up a lot of room in his shop, but it slipped my mind to get in touch with him and let him know I was done, I guess."

"All right, I'll let him know."

"Thanks."

I hung up. "Harry sends his apologies. He meant to call you before this and let you know he was finished searching the truck for additional evidence."

"Well, thank you for your time, Maggie."

"Tell you what. Hollis and I are driving out to Poison Spring Ranch here in a short while. I'd be happy to pass along the message to the Drakes."

"Oh, thank you. I don't wanna be no bother while the grieving's going on."

I wasn't sure how much grieving was going on at this point, but Whitey didn't need to hear that.

"Hollis and I are happy to do it, aren't we, Hollis?"

"You bet."

He rose from the chair and tipped his hat. "Thanks. I'll be on my way now."

"Have a good day, Whitey."

～

Around eleven o'clock, we heard from Al Bach regarding his trip to check out the guest registry at Mountain High Motel. It turned out Corky

Edwards had registered and paid for every night beginning Sunday, April fourth, through Friday, April tenth.

"So it's possible she stayed every night at the motel," I said. "We met with her at her home in the late afternoon on Thursday the eighth. I don't know if she returned to Bend after our discussion, but perhaps it's neither here nor there in terms of our investigation."

"The drive is only two hours and thirty minutes," the detective said. "I've driven it a few times now."

"Which leaves open the possibility that she drove back and forth a few times."

"Is there anything to suggest she drove home on the day of Mr. Drake's murder?"

"Only the possibility that she drove one of their snowmobiles onto Poison Spring Ranch until she met up with the dead bull."

"For the time being, it might be more fruitful to pursue other avenues, Maggie."

"Good advice, Al."

After the call ended, Hollis and I made our way toward Poison Spring Ranch, our lunches packed into a small cooler as per usual. I decided to do the driving this time but couldn't help but sneak the occasional peek at the few lingering white clouds in the cornflower blue sky.

Hollis took a turn at picking out music for the ride. He chose blues-rock guitarist Stevie Ray Vaughan, a musician I had listened to a great deal when I was younger.

"Good choice. It'll block out any road noise."

"You're not a fan?"

"Just the opposite, Holly."

"I always thought he was great."

"He died in a helicopter crash, right?"

"Afraid so."

We listened to Stevie and Double Trouble all the way to Dayville, mostly without our usual chitchat back and forth.

Finally, Hollis decided to weigh in on the countryside. "I suppose if we have to drive around sixty miles somewhere and back every day, we couldn't travel through much nicer terrain."

"True dat," I answered.

"Dat said, I'll be glad when we catch a break in this case."

"Couldn't agree more."

The John Day River, now flowing fuller and faster, had also begun to carry the muddy runoff from the mountain watercourses, down past the lush fields and the usually dry and wheat-colored—but now temporarily spring green—hillocks on which grew a few straggly juniper and a plethora of sagebrush.

"Maybe that human silhouette target will tell us something," I said.

"If it's still there."

"Well, that's the problem with waiting until this morning to listen to Sandy Connor's message. If I'd answered her call last night or at least listened to the message, I could've called her and asked her where on the ranch she'd seen it. But by the time I bothered to listen to it, she was already at her teaching job in Monument."

"Poison Spring Ranch seems—"

I interrupted him. "You mean PSR, don't you?"

"Whatever. PSR seems like it's easily accessed from surrounding properties, including from one of the Fossil Beds trailheads and visitor facilities."

"Is that your way of saying just about anyone with a gun could've tacked the target up on one of their pine trees?"

"Well, kind of. Until we know more, anyway."

～

When we arrived at the Drake ranch, only the older Ram truck was parked out front. The place appeared to be abandoned except for a couple of Black Angus bulls in the field and the horses in their paddock.

"Since the convertible's missing, I'm assuming Christopher is feeling better and took a drive somewhere," I said as I parked the Tahoe.

We stepped to the porch, and I knocked. A light breeze stirred the Lombardy poplars as we waited. I knocked again. Then we heard someone inside call out, seemingly with difficulty.

"Is that Christopher?" Hollis asked.

"I believe so."

"Shall I check the back door?"

"Well, let's see if the front door is open first. Lots of folks out in the country don't see any reason to lock up their homes." I turned the handle, and we stepped into the foyer. "His mother said he was recuperating in the guest bedroom on the first floor."

Christopher again called for help, his voice distorted, wild.

"He's down that hall to the left," I said.

We headed toward his voice, but the bedroom door was locked.

"Maggie, please step back. I'm going to try to break it down."

"It's an oak door. You'll injure yourself."

"I'm going to try."

"Hollis, I carry a crowbar in the back of my Tahoe," I explained and handed him the keys.

He moved quickly to retrieve the crowbar. I stood at the bedroom door and tried to calm Christopher, who was now howling.

"We're breaking you out of there," I kept saying until Hollis returned with the crowbar and wrenched the door open.

"What in God's name happened here?" I whispered to Hollis.

The man was clearly drugged and unable to articulate how he came to be in this condition. His bandage was bloodstained and desperately needed to be changed. The same could be said of his bedsheets and covers. And by the odor in the room, he may not have been able to find his way to a toilet.

"We should get him to the hospital. Maybe in the back seat of my Tahoe?"

"He may need medical attention sooner than we can get him to John Day. There's a volunteer ambulance organization in Monument with fully trained medics, and it's only about twenty minutes away." Hollis fetched the phone from his pocket and looked up the number.

As Hollis punched in the number, I tried to coax Christopher into drinking the rest of the water in his glass on the bedside table. He sipped slowly, and I checked the nearby containers of medication. One of them was made out to Lisa Drake, not her son.

"One moment, please. I'll ask," Hollis said to the dispatcher on the phone. "They're asking for the mailbox address."

"I've seen mail piled in a basket on the small table in the foyer."

Hollis dashed out of the room, and I tried to get Christopher to drink more water.

"Yes, here it is. House number 35377 on Highway 19, Kimberly, Oregon," Hollis told the dispatcher as he walked back into the guest room.

"Mother...," Christopher whispered.

"I'll call her right now," I said.

"No," he pleaded and managed to shake his head.

"You don't want me to tell her you're being transported to the Blue Mountain Hospital in John Day?"

He shook his head again, slightly more vigorously this time. "No...please."

I picked up the medication that had been prescribed to his mother and handed it to Hollis. "Will you please try to figure out what this is? It was prescribed to Lisa Drake."

"Xyrem, or however it's pronounced," he said and began searching for the medication on his phone. Hollis always took on a serious, sometimes studious, pose when he was online trying to get to the nub of a subject. But today he was also nervous.

"Well," he said after diving into his phone for a while. "It's a regulated drug for people with narcolepsy."

"Narcolepsy? Isn't that when people fall asleep all the time?"

"The chemical GHB, which is short for something I can't pronounce. And it apparently works on your brain in a lot of ways, and I don't understand exactly how, but it's used illegally as a date-rape drug and a party drug."

I checked Christopher's reaction, but he had fallen back asleep.

"So, basically, his mother has been drugging him since yesterday," I said.

"Seems so."

"Why, though?"

He exhaled. "Maybe she thought it would ease the pain, or allow him to sleep longer or more deeply?"

"It just doesn't make any sense to me. And why was he locked in his room?"

"Given that he doesn't want his mother to know he is being taken to the hospital, maybe he locked himself in here."

"Maybe. But it all seems out of whack."

～

The ambulance arrived less than twenty minutes after the call out. Hollis had intelligently written down the names and dosage of all of the medications lined up on the bedside table, including the Xyrem prescribed to Lisa Drake.

"I had a thought," I said, sitting in the Drakes' foyer and watching the ambulance pull away.

I nabbed my phone and called the office. "Afternoon, Sherry Linn."

"How are things going?"

"Christopher Drake was just taken by ambulance back to the hospital. We'll fill you in on the details later, but I'd like you to put together a search warrant for the home and outbuildings belonging to Lisa and Christopher Drake. Their residence is 35377 Highway 19, Kimberly, Oregon. And mention they are the wife and son of Mike Drake when you see the judge."

"That was 35377 Highway 19, Kimberly, Oregon, correct?"

"Yep. And after the judge signs it, please take a photo and text it to us."

"Is the rationale for the search warrant related to the homicide investigation of—is it Michael or Mike Drake—at the Kimberly address?"

"I believe it's Michael. That's actually Christopher's first name, so it makes sense he was named after his father, and yes, it's related to the homicide investigation."

"Okay. I'm on it."

"Thank you. For everything, by the way."

"Well, don't let this get around, but you're the best boss I've ever had."

"Thanks for that too."

After clicking off, I complained to Hollis that I was hungry.

"I'll go get the cooler out of the truck."

"Let's have lunch in the sunroom again," I suggested.

"Great idea."

I walked up the stairs slowly. At the top of the stairs, I felt a twinge in my lower back, similar to the one I'd felt yesterday.

"What did you expect, Blackthorne, you're about to have a baby," I mumbled.

Zoey Grace or Lucas James—not both, I hoped—and I found a place at the table in the sunroom and waited for Hollis.

I heard him close the front door and bound up the stairs. Soon enough, I'd be able to bound up a set of stairs as well.

"Here you go," Holly said and handed my sack lunch and thermos to me.

"Thanks, dude."

I unwrapped my sandwich and bit into it just as my cell phone rang. I saw that it was another call from Sandy Connor, so I scarfed down what I'd bitten off, activated the speaker on my phone, and answered the call.

"Hi, Sandy. Sorry I missed you last night, but I listened to your message this morning. I planned to get in touch with you when your workday was over."

"This is my prep period, so I decided to try and reach you again. I've been thinking about that target I mentioned in my message to you about last night. I believe something weird is going on at Poison Spring Ranch."

And she would be right about that.

"I can't go into detail with you, but I'd like to know where you spotted the target."

"It's actually relatively north of Poison Spring if it's still there. The Drakes fence off the larger section of the ranch north of the spring to keep the cows and heifers separated from the bulls until late April or early May. There's a gate, of course, and when it's opened, the entire herd can move back and forth from one section of the ranch to the other. Horseback riders too. Anyway, the target was attached to a nearby lone pine tree on the other side of the gate."

I vaguely remembered something about bulls and the rest of a herd being separated for a period of time, although I also knew not all cattle ranchers did that.

"Did you remove the target or leave it on the tree?"

"No, I left it there. I didn't think it was my place to remove it."

"I'm glad you left it there. That way we can go take a look. Is the gate locked?"

"It is, but if your colleague is with you, he could climb over it."

"Can we drive to it?"

"Yes. You'll see a dirt track before you get to the spring. It takes you to the gate."

"We'll check it out. And thanks for calling a second time. I really do appreciate it."

"Of course. I still haven't been able to touch base with Mrs. Drake or Christopher."

I considered telling her that Christopher was on the way to Blue Mountain Hospital but decided that wasn't news to be broadcast. At least not yet.

"Again, I appreciate the information," I told her. "I'll let you get back to your prep period now."

"Goodbye, Sergeant Blackthorne. I hope you get to the bottom of things really soon."

"Me too, Sandy."

I clicked off and looked over at Hollis.

"Remind me," he said. "Heifers are young female cattle?"

"Yep, a heifer is referred to as a cow after it gives birth to its first calf. Now let's eat our lunch and go see if that target is still on the lone pine tree."

24

AFTERNOON, APRIL 13

Sitting in my police vehicle, I checked in with Detective Bach before we took off to look for the target. I let him know about Sandy spotting it tacked to a tree, as well as the condition we'd found Christopher to be in when we arrived at Poison Spring Ranch this morning.

"So you're theorizing his mother gave him the medication that had been prescribed to her?" Al asked.

"Yeah, but we don't have a theory about why. But we do know he didn't want us to contact his mother to let her know he'd been taken by ambulance to the hospital. Mrs. Drake is out somewhere, so we're waiting for her to return. We're also waiting for Sherry Linn to text us a copy of the judge's signed search warrant. And I think another formal interview is in order."

"I concur," Bach said. "Sounds to me like things are under control."

"Well, as under control as things can be in a murder investigation."

"Keep me posted. And take care."

"Will do."

We took off after the call and had driven about a quarter mile up the ranch road when we came to the dirt track Sandy had mentioned and which supposedly led to the gate that opened to the larger section of the ranch. I turned onto it and reached the gate in fairly short order. I parked, and Hollis and I got out.

About twenty-five feet beyond the fence line stood a solitary lodgepole pine tree.

"I don't see a human silhouette target, do you?" I asked.

"Nope," Holly responded and climbed over the gate.

Once he got to the tree, he looked back toward me and shook his head, meaning he'd found no target. I watched him put on gloves and use his pocketknife to dig something out of the tree and put it in an evidence baggie. On the way back to the gate, he pulled out a separate baggie, squatted, and began to collect items from the ground.

He returned to the gate, climbed back over the fence, and showed me the bags. "A couple of bullet slugs and spent brass bullet casings."

"Well, someone was out here shooting a gun."

"I thought we might end up needing these. There were a few more bullets lodged in the trunk. I have to say, it's pretty idiotic to use a tree to hang a target on. Even though pine trees have softer wood, and a lodgepole's bark is thin, bullets can still ricochet off of them."

"Or otherwise harm the tree. And when did you become a lodgepole pine expert?"

"I studied forestry science for a semester in college, even considered becoming a forester. Anyway, you have thoughts about who might be responsible for shooting up the tree?" Hollis asked.

"Jesus, there might be several, including some stranger looking for a place out in the country to go target shooting."

"Well, whoever it was, they were out here at least twice."

"Because Sandy saw the target yesterday evening, and now it's gone?"

"Yeah, so for the sake of discussion, let's narrow the possibilities down to the Drakes and those six horse boarders. For now, anyway."

"Everyone but Sandy, I would think."

"I agree," Holly said.

"So where the other boarders are concerned, Sandy and I both suspect that Burt Greely has strong, possibly romantic feelings for Christopher—well, *romantic* was my take on it."

"If the two of you are right about that, he probably didn't go target shooting on the ranch or shoot Christopher. On the other hand, Mr. Greely might've spoken to Christopher about his feelings and was reproached."

"Reproached. I like that word, but I'm still not buying that Greely shot Christopher. But do you think he might be a suspect in Mike Drake's murder, given how the father treated the son?" I asked Hollis.

"He did say he thought the ranch's gun ban was asinine, but he also wanted to board his horse here, so I guess he was willing to put up with something he found asinine. Anyway, I'd put Mr. Greely pretty low on the list of suspects. At this point, anyway."

"Yeah, I agree."

"How about Lowell Gregg?" Hollis suggested.

"I would have a hard time believing that. Even if he confessed to doing it."

"And Clell and Maeve Robertson were very fond of Mike Drake, it seemed."

"Even organized that community meeting," I reminded Holly and myself.

"So that's the list of the horse boarders. Anyone else we might want to consider? Besides Christopher and Lisa Drake?"

"Well," I began, "Charlotte Johnson springs to mind, of course, but I still don't see it. But Corky Edwards? I know she booked and paid for a room at that motel in Bend from April fourth through the tenth, and she'd supposedly only come back home on Thursday the eighth, the day after Mike Drake was killed, but I still wonder. In theory, she had reason to be angry with both of the Drake men."

"I'm not there with you on Mrs. Edwards, Maggie. But I do think Mrs. Johnson is close to being the lead suspect right now."

"Well, I trust your judgment. However, I think there's still some possibility Greely might've pegged it right when he suggested Lisa Drake. At least in regards to the first shooting."

"You think we should put Mrs. Drake on the list of suspects in the murder of her husband?"

I thought about his question for several seconds. "Well, Greely suggested she probably had the most reason to kill the guy."

"How would he know, really? But if it's true, then she's a dang good actress. I'd call it an award-winning performance."

"Perhaps she is quite the actress after all, especially considering the condition we found Christopher in today."

We both mulled that idea over.

"I think it's strange he didn't want us to call his mother," I noted.

"Yeah, I agree."

"And if she was feeding him that date-rape drug. That's bizarre."

Each of our phones pinged. The search warrant had arrived.

"Let's go see if Mrs. Drake is home," I said.

～

Lisa Drake still hadn't returned when we got back to the ranch house, but Lydia Reed sat waiting on the front porch. We parked and joined her.

"Good afternoon," she said.

"How are you today?" I asked.

"I was hoping to visit Christopher. Do you know where he and Mrs. Drake are?"

"We don't know where Mrs. Drake is." I peeked at my watch. "Christopher is probably in the Blue Mountain Hospital by now. He was taken there by ambulance earlier."

"What happened?"

"We arrived and found him in worse condition than he was in yesterday. So we called the Monument volunteer ambulance."

"How long ago?"

"Over an hour."

"Do you think I can go see him?"

"I don't know." I handed her one of my cards. "But if necessary, tell them you're his girlfriend and you spoke to Trooper Jones and me, and we sent you to the hospital to be with him."

"I'll need to see if Eunice Ford can stay with my dad again."

She dialed and walked out of earshot while she spoke to her neighbor. Hollis and I waited on the porch for her to return.

"Eunice wasn't very happy about watching Dad so soon after she had spent most of a day with him, but I told her Christopher was in the hospital," Lydia explained after making the call.

"I'm glad you were able to talk her into it," I said.

"I have to pay her double this time, but it's worth it. And I might try out that burger place you mentioned while I'm in John Day. Prairie Maid, right?"

"And the chocolate and peanut butter shake at Blue Mountain Lounge for dessert," I reminded her before she stepped into her rig. "It's to die for."

"Christopher's a fool," Hollis said after Lydia pulled away from the ranch house and onto the highway.

"You mean to dump someone like Lydia?"

"Yep. It's hard to figure out what makes that guy tick."

"It could be money," I suggested. "After all, he has his CPA, and he's the ranch's accountant, right?"

"Right."

"Christopher could be of the opinion he has more to gain by selling the place."

"What are you getting at, Maggie?"

"If I remember correctly from when I was a kid, Drake had inherited the place after his mother passed away and when he was relatively young. He later married Lisa."

"So you're saying he could've been the sole owner prior to his death?"

"I believe it's definitely possible, and maybe he left the ranch to Christopher."

"You think his father would leave the ranch to Christopher alone?"

"You've got to admit, the marriage was considered a bust by all of the Drakes."

"Legally, could Mike Drake have left the ranch to Christopher only?"

"I'm not completely sure, Holly. But it still might be interesting to see Mike Drake's will, assuming there is one."

"I'll bet there's a will, because if not, everything is automatically Mrs. Drake's."

"And their son the accountant would know that," I clarified, punctuating this discussion.

Someone pulled onto the ranch road and parked next to the stable. Burt Greely got out, opened the paddock gate, and walked toward the stable.

"Let's go talk to the man," I said.

By the time we caught up with Greely, he had retrieved a bit and reins, along with a rubber curry comb. He was walking toward the only palomino in the paddock.

"What's your horse's name, Mr. Greely?"

He hadn't noticed us and jumped when he heard my voice.

Greely turned toward us. "Oh, it's you two again. Uh, her name is Angel. This mare is always calm and easy. That's how she got her name."

He patted the horse and slipped on the bit and reins and began grooming Angel with the curry comb.

"You two need something?" Greely asked.

"We have a couple of questions for you," I began. "First, do you know about Christopher?"

"I know he's been very upset about your investigation."

"Is he upset about the investigation, or is he upset about his father's death?" I asked. "And the investigation is what it is, Mr. Greely, until we identify the killer."

"You cops don't get it, do you? Being questioned all the time, thought of as a possible homicidal maniac, messes with a person's head."

"Why do you think Christopher believes we're questioning him all the time?" Hollis asked.

Greely took a breath. "I just got that feeling from him the last time I talked to him."

"When was that?" I inquired.

"I was here Sunday, and Christopher and me had a long conversation about lots of things. He even told me he plans on selling the ranch as soon as he can."

Well, that was interesting, if true. And maybe I had been on to something.

"What time of day were you here on Sunday?"

"Why do you want to know that, Sergeant?"

"Because someone shot Christopher on Sunday."

"What!"

"He's alive and in the hospital in John Day," Hollis assured him. "But I think you should answer Sergeant Blackthorne's question. What time of day were you here on Sunday?"

"Late morning. You can see that on the clock-in and clock-out sheet in the stable. Then I drove to John Day to visit with my folks. Ended up spending the night."

"All right, Mr. Greely. We'll check the clock-in and clock-out sheet in the stable to verify the time of day."

He nodded. "Do you think I can visit Christopher in the hospital, Sergeant McKay?"

"I'm not sure. But I'm Sergeant Blackthorne, remember?"

"Aren't you Duncan McKay's wife?"

"I am. How did you know?"

"Lowell Gregg said something about it."

"I see. Professionally, my last name is still Blackthorne." At the urging of a sudden but slightly painful twinge in my back, I avoided going into the whole hyphenation blah-blah. "We'll let you get back to grooming Angel now."

Hollis and I retreated to the stable and checked the clock-in and clock-out sheet tacked up on the wall beside the door. Sure enough, Burt Greely had checked in at ten thirty and checked out at eleven thirty.

"The guy has nice handwriting," I said.

"Especially compared to the other men who've signed in and out."

"Wait a minute..." I pulled out my phone and scrolled to the photo of the sign left at the feed and tack between Sunday night and Monday morning. "I'm not a handwriting expert, but his signature might match that lovely message left inside Duncan's business."

Hollis looked at the photograph. "It sure looks like it might be."

"I was so damn sure a woman had written it." I snapped a shot of Greely's printed name and the time he clocked in and clocked out. "And he stayed with his parents in John Day on Sunday night, remember?"

"That's right, Mags, making it even more possible he somehow got inside Duncan's store."

"What did you think about what Greely said about Christopher?" I asked Hollis.

"Which tidbit?"

"That he planned to sell Poison Spring Ranch as soon as possible."

"I guess I didn't have a reaction. Or a thought about it. How about you?"

"How would Christopher have the authority to do that? Unless, of course, Lisa Drake supports the idea."

"Or maybe it's what you hinted at earlier. Mr. Drake left a will, and Christopher somehow has a greater say in what happens to the ranch."

We stepped back outside to question Greely about the break-in at McKay's Feed and Tack, but my phone rang. It was Harry Bratton.

"Afternoon, Harry."

"I called my forensic buddies at Regional about the slug removed from Christopher Drake and the one that killed his father. Turns out both are from the same weapon. A Glock 43 nine millimeter. It's a small handgun, but deadly."

"That was fast. Thanks for getting us that info pronto."

"You're welcome. But I want you to be careful out there."

"Will do," I said and hung up. "Everyone wants us to be careful out here."

At that moment, we noticed Lisa Drake had finally arrived. Timing was everything.

"Let's go talk to her and search the house. Right now that's more of a priority than Greely's love note."

She saw us walking toward the house and quickly placed the packages she had been holding back in the BMW, shut the door, and waited for us.

"We can help you carry those packages inside," I offered when we met up with her.

"They're fine in the car for now."

"Mrs. Drake, we need to have a conversation," I told her. "Let's go inside."

"I need to check on Christopher first."

"Christopher was taken by ambulance to the hospital earlier today."

"Then I need to go be with him. Why didn't you call me, Margaret?"

"Your son did not want you to be contacted."

"That can't be true."

"It's true. Now let's go inside."

I collected my pack from the Tahoe and followed Hollis and Mrs. Drake into the house and into the kitchen. She laid her handbag on the counter and sat at the small kitchen table.

Hollis and I sat across from her, and I opened my phone and showed Lisa Drake the copy of the search warrant signed by Judge Campbell that Sherry Linn had texted to us.

"You and I are going to sit here while Trooper Jones searches the house."

"Why don't you just tell me what you're looking for."

"That's not how this works."

"Then I need to get the groceries out of my car and store some of them in the refrigerator."

"I'll fetch those," Hollis said and rose from his chair.

"This isn't right," the older woman said after a long minute.

"I'm doing my job, Mrs. Drake."

"Margaret, I've told you a few times now I'm fine with you calling me by my first name."

"Well, I guess I'm not."

Hollis returned with two bags of groceries. He placed the groceries on the counter—eggs, milk, ice cream, a few packages of meat, four bottles of red wine—and put away everything but the wine in the refrigerator or freezer.

"Trooper Jones is going to search the house now."

After Hollis began his search, Mrs. Drake and I sat quietly until she asked for permission to make a cup of tea.

"I'll make it for you," I said.

She glanced at the counter. "Never mind. I have a special way of making it."

"You could tell me what that is."

She shook her head.

"I have a question for you, Mrs. Drake. Yesterday when I called you and asked if you knew of a man named Trevor Wynn, you said you didn't. But since that call, we spoke with Mr. Wynn, who is living with his grand-parents."

"Roy and Delia?"

"Yes."

"I still don't know him, Margaret."

"He went to prison thirteen years ago and was released last Wednesday."

"The day Michael was killed?"

"Yes."

"Is it possible he's the killer, for whatever reason?"

"While Mr. Wynn felt he had a reason to mess with your husband, he was released from the penitentiary in Salem that day, but after Trooper Jones and I found Mike's body."

"Then why bring up Trevor Wynn?"

"Because he's the author of the thirteen letters, now fourteen, sent to Mr. Drake."

"Did you arrest him?"

"No, Mrs. Drake. Your husband chose not to get the police involved regarding the first thirteen letters, and he was deceased when the fourteenth letter arrived."

"The law is so irrational sometimes."

It is, I nearly said. For example, sending a stupid twenty-year-old kid to prison for a long stretch, only to have him get into further trouble while there and end up having more time attached to his sentence. I was a member of law enforcement, and I found that pattern and practice irrational.

"Again, why did you bring up Mr. Wynn, Margaret?"

"Trevor Wynn went to prison for cattle theft. He claims your husband was in on the crime but ended up double-crossing Mr. Wynn and turning him in to the authorities."

"I wouldn't doubt that in the least."

25

LATE AFTERNOON, APRIL 13

Hollis spent close to an hour searching the inside of the ranch house. Earlier we hadn't a clue about what he might turn up, if anything, but he now stood in the entrance to the kitchen holding a legal-size manila folder.

He signaled for me to join him where he stood. I did so, and he handed me the folder and indicated the label; it read *Father's Will*. Hollis removed the document from inside the folder and pointed to Article Three on the first page. Christopher Drake alone was to inherit Poison Spring Ranch.

I placed the folder label-down on the table and fetched the recorder from my pack. I also brought out a pen and waiver form, which I slid across the table in front of Lisa Drake.

The woman glanced at the folder. "Do I need an attorney?"

"You tell me, Mrs. Drake."

She didn't respond, so I cited her Miranda rights for a second time this week.

Mrs. Drake passed me a dark look, then signed and dated the form.

"Where did this come from?" I asked Hollis, referring to the manila folder.

"It was in a file cabinet upstairs in what I assume is Christopher's room."

I turned to Mrs. Drake. "Speaking of Christopher, when we found him this morning, he was in terrible shape."

"Perhaps it was the medication, Margaret."

"Perhaps it was one medication in particular. The one prescribed to you."

"What are you talking about?"

"Trooper Jones?"

"It's called Xyrem, or sodium oxybate," Hollis began. "Which is a form of the chemical called GHB. GHB is short for the scientific name of the chemical. It's more familiarly known as a date-rape drug. And it was likely prescribed to you because of narcolepsy."

"I know what it is and what it's for. But what's that got to do with anything?"

"It was among the medications on the bedside table in the first-floor guest room where Christopher was staying temporarily," I said.

"Are you trying to say I've been giving my son that medication? I'm telling you I left the bottle of my pills there inadvertently. Furthermore, I love my son, and I've done nothing but care for him all of his life."

"And so you would expect him to care for you in return," I prodded.

"He has been the kindest, sweetest boy to his mother," she said.

"But he hasn't been a boy for some time, has he? He's a man who makes his own decisions. And I suspect you don't always agree with those decisions."

"Well, of course I don't always agree with his decisions."

"Give me an example," I nudged some more, not really sure where I was going with this line of questioning.

"I was very upset when he told me he broke up with Lydia."

"He broke up with Lydia the same day some woman shot him, is that correct?"

"I don't know if it was a woman, but yes, that was the same day he ended his relationship with Lydia," she said. "And if your next question is do I think Lydia shot him, I do not."

"That was also the same day Christopher told one of the horse boarders he planned to sell Poison Spring Ranch as soon as he could."

Lisa Drake's face reddened. "I think I might have something to say about selling the ranch."

"Not unless you're prepared to contest your husband's will."

The woman eyed the folder.

"Now, back to the GHB. We have yet to learn whether or not it was found in your son's bloodstream, but we will eventually."

"He could've taken it without realizing it wasn't meant for him," she answered.

"We could hear him calling for help when we knocked at the front door. And when we found it unlocked, we raced to the guest bedroom, but that door *was* locked. Your son was howling by that point, but thankfully Trooper Jones here was able to pry it open. When we found Christopher, he was fading in and out of consciousness and needed medical attention, so we called the ambulance."

"Is that when he told you not to let me know he was being transported to the hospital?"

"Yes."

"He couldn't have meant that, Margaret."

"He stated it twice, Mrs. Drake."

Quite suddenly, I felt a painful but familiar ache. One that reminded me of sitting in some high school class during the first few days of my monthly period, trying in vain to concentrate on what the teacher was rattling on about.

I took a breath. "Excuse me, I need some water."

Hollis stood. "I'll take care of that."

He returned quickly with three full glasses of water.

"Thank you," I said and sipped. I found it refreshing, calming, and I decided to cut to the chase. "Talk about what you found in the folder, Trooper Jones."

"It's Mr. Drake's will, signed and dated on April first of this year."

"Six days before he was killed. And what's the gist of what is said in the will?" I asked.

Hollis directed his answer to Mrs. Drake. "In the event of his death, his son alone would inherit the property and any other assets connected with Poison Spring Ranch."

I looked at the woman. She suddenly appeared terribly vulnerable.

"Mike was going to divorce me and upend my life, force me to leave. He inherited the ranch from his mother before we were married, but this is the only home I've known for almost forty years."

"When did he tell you this?" I asked.

"The night before he found the dead bull."

"Do you know who called him to let him know about the bull?"

"He said it was Corky Edwards, but I believe he fabricated that. As you know, she was in Bend, where her husband, Roger, was hospitalized after having a severe stroke."

Well, the whereabouts of Corky Edwards the day Drake was murdered was one of the lingering questions still out there. But for the moment, Lisa Drake had opened a new chapter in the investigation of her husband's homicide.

"Mrs. Drake, as I mentioned earlier, Christopher intends to sell the ranch as soon as possible."

"Yes, he said he was in possession of his father's will and that he alone had inherited Poison Spring Ranch and planned to sell it," she explained numbly.

"So, in the last week, both your husband and then your son told you the ranch would be put up for sale."

She held up her glass. "Could I have some ice and a bit of gin in my water? In fact, Trooper Jones, would you mind changing this out for the gin in the cupboard and the tonic in the refrigerator?"

"We can't allow that," I said. "Did you shoot and kill your husband last week on Wednesday, April seventh?"

"Please, may I retrieve the aspirin in my handbag?"

"I'll get it for you, Mrs. Drake," Hollis said.

"No, never mind. I'll be fine," she stated, her voice raised.

But Hollis had already picked up her handbag and opened it. He gave me a look vaguely akin to that of a kid in a candy store and passed the handbag to me. Stashed amid the makeup, wallet, change purse, pens, and sundry items was a small handgun. I was betting it was the Glock 43 nine-millimeter pistol we were looking for.

"You shot and killed your husband with the weapon now in your handbag?" I asked her.

"Yes."

"And you were planning to shoot and kill us, am I right?"

"No. Just myself."

～

I suspected Lisa Drake knew where we were going next in our interview, but the details of how she managed to get to where her husband was parked on the ranch road that snowy morning he was killed needed clarification.

"How long have you owned the gun?" Hollis inquired.

"I bought it years ago."

"Why did you purchase it?" he continued.

She shrugged. "Safety, I guess. I'm a woman living next to a lonely country road. It's funny, though, I'd never even shot it until recently."

"But you've been practicing," I said. "One of the horse boarders found a human silhouette target in the section of the ranch where you keep the cows and heifers."

"Calves, too," she said, ignoring the news regarding the human silhouette target.

"On the morning of your husband's death, how did you get to where he was parked waiting for us?"

"It's simple, Margaret. I put on my snow boots, down jacket, and mittens and walked through the bull field, several yards from the fence line. I thought I'd find him waiting for you at Poison Spring, but no. And then I remembered he really enjoyed visiting an interesting red fossil formation located on our property."

I remembered also being struck by that single outcropping.

Mrs. Drake continued. "Getting near enough to it to look for his pickup truck required a bit of a walk, especially in the snow. But I was determined to get there and tell him I knew he was having an affair with Charlotte Johnson, and I planned to tell her husband, Troy, if he went forward with his plan to divorce me."

Of all the possible ways to misinterpret Mike Drake's exceedingly bad behaviors, this was perhaps one of the saddest.

I continued. "And what did he have to say, Mrs. Drake?"

"I'd ripped my new jacket climbing through the barbed wire fence, so I was already in a mood."

"Go on."

"I gave him an ultimatum about ending the affair with Charlotte Johnson. He just looked at me and laughed. And then he said, 'What's it to you, bitch?' I think he was pretty surprised when I pulled out my handgun at that moment."

She smiled to herself and hesitated before continuing on. "I almost wish I'd made him beg for his life or my forgiveness. But his life was worthless, and the capacity to forgive him had disappeared long ago. And anyway, I still would've killed him."

I was almost ready to make myself one of the gin and tonics she had brought up earlier, but this interview needed to wrap up soon. My back was killing me.

"Lisa Drake, you're under arrest for the murder of your husband, Michael Drake."

∾

Hollis refilled our water glasses. After that, he took over the interview.

"Mrs. Drake," he began. "Let's talk about the wounding of Christopher. We know he was shot by the same weapon that killed your husband."

By the look on her face, she hadn't considered the possibility we knew that fact. Or that we would've learned about it in the future.

"Why would you shoot and presumably poison your son, whom you have today professed to love?" Hollis asked.

"The two of you don't mince words, do you?"

"Please, just answer the question."

"Well, at least you say please." She inhaled deeply. "I believe I've made it clear. I didn't want to lose my home of nearly forty years. And as you already know, Christopher plans to sell Poison Spring Ranch."

Lisa pulled a lace handkerchief from her pocket and dabbed her eyes.

"We had a terrible fight about it. He told me yesterday as we were driving home from your office."

"He hadn't realized it was you who shot him?"

"No. He still doesn't know. But he will soon enough. Isn't that correct, Trooper Jones?"

"Yes. And did you also add Xyrem into the mix of medications your son was already taking?"

"I did. I believed it would buy me some time to legally challenge the directives of Mike's will. Unfortunately, I couldn't get in to see my attorney about it until next week. But once you book me into jail, or however you say it, I bet he'll come running."

She sighed deeply, and then silence drifted over the room. And in the quiet, I listened to my body. I was in labor.

"My imprisonment will get rid of one of Christopher's burdens," Mrs. Drake began. "You see, he planned to give me a generous monthly allowance. And he was quite happy to tell me he was also going to purchase an acre of land and a double-wide mobile home for me, as he didn't think I was quite ready for an assisted-living facility."

With that, she had nothing more to say, not even when Hollis arrested her for the attempted murder of her son. He also threw in a separate charge of purposely administering a controlled substance to Christopher without his knowledge or permission. But that didn't rattle her either.

~

Lisa Drake, handcuffed and seat-belted in the back seat, said not a word as we drove toward Canyon City, the county seat where the jail was located.

I had asked Hollis to drive and turn her over to Sheriff Cal Norton's deputies when we got there. He had looked at me suspiciously, but the first person I wanted to learn our child was coming a little earlier than expected was Duncan.

The feed and tack had closed down an hour ago, so I was certain he was home. I brought out my phone and called him.

"Hey, babe. Are you ready for spaghetti and meatballs?" he asked.

"Well, I have a question for you. Are you ready to become a daddy tonight?"

"You're in labor?"

"It began a few hours ago, I think. Contractions are coming a bit faster now. But I'm waiting for Hollis outside the county jail. Keep this under your hat for now, but we arrested Lisa Drake for the murder of Mike Drake and the attempted murder of her son."

"Holy cow, that's big."

"It is. Oh, Hollis has finished handing her off to sheriff deputies, and he's walking toward my rig. I'm going to have him drive me to the hospital, and I'll meet you there."

"Your suitcase is all packed, right?"

"Yeah."

"All right, babe. I love you. And I'm on my way."

"I love you, too."

Hollis climbed into the driver's side of the SUV. He was tired; I could read it in his eyes.

"Hey, pal. I have one more favor to ask," I said.

"What's that?"

"Would you drive me to the hospital? I'm having contractions."

He reached across the seat and hugged me. "Does Duncan know?"

"Yep, he's on his way to the hospital right now."

"All right, here we go." He started the engine, pulled out of the parking lot and onto Highway 395, and drove toward the Blue Mountain Hospital, arriving shortly before Duncan.

～

Our child was born at four twenty a.m. on April fourteenth. I had won out on the name, but Zoey Grace was a brunette. In my dreams before her birth, the baby had had Duncan's red hair. But I didn't care. She was beautiful, and perfect, and she was ours.

I looked over at Duncan holding her in the rocker supplied by the hospital. "I love you."

He smiled. "Next to the very first time we made love, the birth of Zoey is the most beautiful experience in my life."

"You're such a good guy. Has anyone ever told you that?"

I checked the time. Six forty. Dorie had been up for at least a half an hour. I had to let her know.

"Maggie?" she answered on the second ring.

"What's going on with you this morning?"

"The usual. Not much."

"Well, visiting hours at the hospital begin at eight o'clock, and you need to get down here and meet Zoey Grace Blackthorne-McKay."

"Oh, sweetie. That's so wonderful. I love the name. Your mama should be remembered with grace, and now she will be."